Teeria

By

Claire Webber

www.newgeneration-publishing.com

 New Generation **Publishing**

Acknowledgement

I have written this book and personal acknowledgement for my husband A Webber.

I thank you for your support and encouragement of this book.
I have immensely valued your input, opinions and editing eye.

I also would like to take this chance to acknowledge all that you have done for me and us as a family in the last year. You can hold your head up high with honour as you have been our rock.

Love you always,

Claire

Prologue

There will never be silence in the wilderness here on this bright warm day. Back home the silence is almost deafening with the lack of singing birds, calling mammals and busy insects. There are a handful of pockets for the wild to roam freely across our tired home world.

A strong and vibrant male is alone, deep in one of the forests, a good walk away from his own tribe on this new world. The male is hunched over working tirelessly wearing only minimal clothing with his back, covered in thick dark hair, open to the elements. To the naked eye he blends into his surroundings, unseen and unheard by animal or any intelligent life form. He has just caught a small deer-like creature. He is a skilled hunter and with the constant song of different sounds the creature did not hear his silent approach. The deer-like creature was taken down swiftly by a carved spear with one quick and painless move. The male is very practiced in the art of dissembling his catch and makes swift work of it. Almost all, of the animal carcass is used from its hide to its meat and only a minor amount is buried by the hunter out of respect for the animal.

His tribe welcome the good weather and it is a way they give thanks for prosperity to their spirits. A fire is lit with collected fallen branches from the surrounding forests. The male hunter, who could easily be mistaken for a warrior by his attire of highly decorated animal skin and dressed hair from beads and quills, dances with his tribe late into the evening. The weather is still warm into the evening and the smell of his sun kissed skin lingers on. He the huntsman who is of great value and standing to his tribe hunts only what is needed for his father and friends.

Chapter 1

Over seventeen thousand years have gone by on the Gregorian calendar. It *is* an inconceivable length of time. The year is 17,023. A considerable amount of events have happened in our past, including difficult decisions to act upon, devastation, illness and evolution.

After thousands of years had past on Earth, Mother Nature put us to the test. During the year 6,693 the Earth and its inhabitants took a disastrous and everlasting turn of events, and man was not prepared for what was to come. The Earth did not run its natural course and it was cut short when a glacial period hit the Northern Hemisphere. An individual ice age may normally last for ten thousand to twenty thousand years and is split into two periods, glacial and interglacial. A glacial period is an extremely thick covering of ice engulfing a lot of land. An interglacial period is due to warmer temperatures melting the ice and leaving caps on top of the mountains and the North and South Poles. This occurs between the glacial periods. Usually the Earth's natural glacial ice age occurs every forty thousand to one hundred years, but not this time. Due to the unforeseen ice age, the Northern Hemisphere was no longer able to provide man a *home* as it was not left with any stability or suitably safe places to live. There was mass extinction of all fauna and flora. All the northern countries including the United Kingdom, Europe, Asia and Canada were all lost under around three kilometres of ice! These lost countries no longer existed, except as a memory within the living and breathing people who had survived from them. The total number of survivors was few, because the warnings of the Earth's climate changes were not acted upon quickly and not taken seriously. Many had believed that the climate changes were down to man's destructive nature and not the Earth's natural cycle. Alas they had been very, very wrong on all counts of predictability and reasoning.

Once the ice had started to retreat slowly during the interglacial period after nine thousand years, the cities that had been lost were never habited again for fear of the losses of the last historic glacial period. Evidence points to on average one to two ice ages eminent in each one hundred thousand years! It would have been foolish to move back to the interglacial lands, as a precaution.

Those who had survived the glacial period ice age had to start again in countries completely alien to themselves. Countries were forced to merge and live alongside each other on Earth's remaining land masses including Africa, Australia and South America. The countries on the untouched land masses were very welcoming to the devastated people, who had lost near enough everything, apart from the clothes they wore. The welcoming countries took them under their wings and helped in every way possible, from building new homes to teaching about local food sources. Humans got used to co-habiting on the largest land masses and the why's and where-fore's of their own origins become a faint memory of the past.

NASA (National Aeronautics and Space Administration) however, did have forewarning of the onslaught of the approaching glacial period and acted very quickly. They relocated from the famous Florida's Cape Canaveral to Queensland's, Cape York's Peninsula in Northern Australia. They found a remote site; South of the Archer River, North West of Holroyd River, and West of Coen; not wishing to cause any intrusion or interference with the local residents. The relocation was done with military precision and their new headquarters was a home from home but with a consequence. The consequence was that the move was eventually leaked to the media years later after the glacial period had struck. When the people had learnt of what had happened they were understandably angry and upset because *they* had had no forewarning. They wanted justice for their loved ones. High profile groups of protesters set about getting the justice and after several years of anger, resentment and violence, the newly setup governments who only wanted peace for their people, accepted and the allegation against NASA went to a court trial. The outcome was a turning point for the governments who led their people. NASA's personnel and scientists, who were responsible for the secretive selfish behaviour, were all found to have died during the glacial period incident or from old age. The court ruled the judgement of guilty for the fact they had wronged and were recognised criminals.

The lost cities were treated like archaeological sites with many of the valuable and treasured artefacts taken and stored or shown in museums in the Southern Hemisphere. As the ice retreated slowly, as much as possible was salvaged from all of the educational facilities north of the equator. All major universities including the famous Harvard from Massachusetts, Cambridge and Oxford from the United Kingdom were relocated. Today they still have their popularity and successful standing. All the sacral grounds including the cathedrals, churches and mosques, had all debris removed out of respect. There were many sacral sites which were left to stand as memorials to the residing occupants and the lost. Each inhabitant left behind, buried or later laid to rest, knew nothing of what had become of their homeland during the year of 6,693. Going off our recorded history there was two very, very severe ice ages that occurred causing the whole of the Earth to be covered in ice, known as a "Snowball Earth" effect. This would certainly have wiped us out. Digging deep and hoarding would have been the only answer.

The most absolute and terrorising of all possible disasters was not at all over. We had to come to terms with a new disaster which was detrimental to all life on Earth and made the previous ice age look like a picnic. During the year, early 13,774, an average sized asteroid left the asteroid belt that orbits the sun between Mars and Jupiter. The asteroid slung shot out of the belt, and hurtled through space, after what was thought was due to a collision within the belt. It followed a course and skimmed the path of Jupiter and curved back and re-entered the asteroid belt like a powerful cue ball on a snooker table thus propelling out an even larger asteroid. Venus was thought to be the planet in the direct path of the giant asteroid but it narrowly missed and smashed into Mercury. Mercury was completely obliterated. It was first thought that Earth was safely out of harm's way but further extensive research showed that by the year 31,035, Earth would be perilously closer to the sun. Earth's surface would be bombarded by radiation emitted by the sun long before then which would, without any doubt, kill us. It was already known that the Sun is expanding and getting closer to Earth but not in any way that close. As a result in this present day, Earth's new orbiting alignment gradually set forth a change in the climate conditions. The atmosphere chemistry has started to change with a lower H_2O and oxygen content thus leading to hot and arid conditions, making living for all animal and plant life very uncomfortable.

* * *

The weather of the quiet suburb is overcast with an unclean hue in the air. Despite the air not being crystal clear, from thousands of years of human emissions the streets are immaculately clean, with wide empty roads, patch working their way through the outskirts of the large city, Cape Town. The well known Table Top Mountain shadows the town below. It is a constant reminder that not only is Mother Nature in charge on the Earth's surface but down in the depths too, and responsible for such a wondrous creation.

A square boxed house stands detached, like all the rest of its identical neighbours. The whole house is covered in a synthetic wood that has been white washed. The windows are all neat and square, painted in a jade green. The roof is tiled, in a man-made hard weather proof plastic. The roof is a dusky deep grey that compliments the colour of the painted windows. The house looks lifeless from the outside.

'Mail alert,' sounds the intercom. The intercom is fitted flush to the wall in the kitchen. In appearance the intercom looks like a small stainless steel disc, the size of a single grape. It is under the streamline monitor that is the thickness of a sheet of paper. It has all the facilities of a computer with Touch Screen Technology (TST).

'Gee, are you there? Would you get that love? I can't leave this dish; it's at a critical point,' says Ameel. Ameel is Gee's mother, who is pretty and slim.

'Yeah, ok,' says Gee appearing from the other room; who is nearly five foot eight and perfectly proportioned and slender with long black hair, that is hanging loosely against her pale olive skin, nearly down to her waist.

As she walks barefoot across the kitchen floor her hair gently bellows out like a glossy black cap caught in a breeze. Gee looks slightly disgruntled about the interruption. She goes over to the screen and opens the mail that is curiously addressed to the whole family,

```
* For Immediate Attention of:- Mr Posall
Goshle, Mrs Ameel Goshle, Mr Cam Goshle and
Miss Gee Goshle. This is of great
importance from the United States National
Government in association with NASA *
```

'Shit...' says Gee.

'Gee, I do wish you could try and be more articulate. What's the matter?' says Ameel.

'Come and have a look for yourself, *I'm* not opening it!' Gee is rooted to the spot.

Ameel comes over to see what the fuss is about and is immediately hesitant when she reads the screen. She opens the mail with Gee beside her and it reads,

```
* Confirm these are the members of your
family and that the basic given information
is correct. To confirm, each person needs
to enter their own fingerprint pin. Further
information will not appear until all four
pins have been entered by:-

Mr Posall Goshle = 45 years old. Teacher in
higher education. Qualifications are PhD in
Earth and Planetary Sciences and a PhD in
Geography and Environmental Science. Father
of two.

Mrs Ameel Goshle = 42 years old. Teacher of
Primary School children. Qualification in
Social Skills. Mother of two.

Mr Cam Goshle = 25 years old. Student in
Electronic Engineering Technology and
Oceans Science. Son and sibling of one
other.

Miss Gee Goshle = 23 years old. Student in
Cultural and Ancestry Science. Daughter and
```

Ameel gingerly presses her index fingerprint by her name and touches the confirm button followed by Gee.

'Get your Brother and Father back home, this is urgent love,' says Ameel.

Ameel goes and sits down at the kitchen table as if to steady herself; wondering what on earth could be so important for the government to send mail to them. Ameel is part of a good solid family that do not cause trouble for the authorities and all have an interest of some sort in work or education. She remains level headed for her daughter's sake. Gee doesn't know quite what to do after contacting her brother and father. Gee stands in the middle of the kitchen deep in thought. She is unaware that she is fiddling with a strand of her hair. She feels impatient waiting for the other two pins to be entered, and aswell as her mother, wants to know what is so urgent.

'Gee honey, stop fiddling with your hair – if you want hair like silk; treat it as such. Come over here and sit with me, they won't be long.'

'I know, but...' Gee tries to find the words. 'I just... don't understand the government sending us mail like that. Do you think we have done something wrong?' Her delicate features and green eyes show her understandable concern and she sits next to her mother.

'Well we haven't done anything wrong, I know that much, so it can't be that, we will just have to wait and see – a little patience sweetie.'

* * *

Cam Goshle is in the local bar not far from home enjoying a drink after a fruitful day as a student. He is easily distracted from his studies even though he has high promise to go far. Not only does he have stacks of potential he has good looks, dark hair, brown eyes and a strong jaw line. He does not pretend to know everything and soon admits to his own mistakes, which is an endearing quality and part of his charm. Women swoon around him because of his cool and calm persona. He generally has a keen interest from a line of females but each never last for very long. Cam is very outgoing and it will take a special female to keep his interest alive in their relationship.

Cam is very much in league of today's modern man. Over many thousands of years we had evolved. Our appearance and mind changed so subtly that they went unnoticed for a long, long time. Humans as far back as the twenty first century could almost be classed as Neanderthal like, compared to what we have become and achieved. During the early twenty first century there were still traces of our ancestors in our appearances, from the Homo- Sapiens to the even earlier, pre-historic man, the Homo Neanderthalensis. Some had a prominent brow, high foreheads, enlarged facial features and excessive thick body hair, unlike now the body hair is soft and fine. The man of today, such as Cam, is slim but toned with a slight skeletal frame. His facial features are delicate and none intrusive with an even olive complexion like his sister Gee.

Cam is about to order another drink from the skimpily dressed waitress when he is interrupted and receives a message on his caller, 'Urgent, come home now. G x'. He is in the throes of getting acquainted with a lady who has liked him for some time. The lady in question could not resist his well received offer of a drink. Cam groans not wanting to leave yet, but knows he is never summoned unless there is a really good reason. He reluctantly says his goodbyes and leaves by giving the lady a smooth kiss on the back of her hand, purposely not rushing to kiss her lips knowing this will tease her into seeing him again soon.

* * *

Posall and Cam arrive home simultaneously puzzled at what the urgency is. Posall had been working late and Cam, well as we know, Cam was being Cam.

'This better be good, I was *in* there. I was just about...' before Cam can continue, Gee explodes.

'Oh shut up Cam,' Gee marches across the kitchen. 'We don't want to here about your quests. Let Mum speak.' She joins her mother at the table.

'We have got urgent mail, go and read it for yourselves. We...' Ameel points to herself and Gee, '...can't read anyfurther till you two have entered your pins.' Cam and his father know the mail is serious by the way she is acting and her spoken words sound almost strained.

Without another word Posall and Cam read it and then enter their pins, by this time they are all standing in front of the screen wanting to know more,

```
*  Please  remain  calm  when  you  read  the
following.
It  is  of  the  most  importance  that  the
following  is  kept  to  yourselves  for
security reasons and your safety.

Your family have been selected because of
your beneficial criteria.

A future has been found for our on-going
success as a species, on a planet named
Teeria (Teer-i-a).

Along with a number of chosen others from
Earth    and    Teeria's    pre-existing
```

inhabitants, we wish you to join, them both, in the research of the planet. Six years ago individual scientist units, from each country, were sent out to live and research Teeria. The results have been a success so far and look very promising for the next two years. As it has been a success we deem Teeria suitable for relocation of Earth's mankind and thus need your further help. You will join us during the final two years of analysis – thus completing a pre-planned programme of eight years. We will then be in the very early stages of evacuating Earth years before its untimely end approaches.

Teeria was found in our searching path for a reason and with our and the combined knowledge from the natives, our future will be more certain and we will make more definitive and decisive decisions when we have to maybe move on again to yet another planet.

We would hint that your evacuation is mandatory with good reason. Should you decide that you wish to return after your work is done you can. Everyone will have a choice whether to stay on Earth or start a new life on Teeria.

Your leave will be in a month's time at 0800hrs on the 13th July, 17,023.

Further information will follow thank you.*

* * *

From the late twenty first century it was known that the Sun would burn for a further five billion years and the Earth had half a billion years left to comfortably sustain life which then changed to only thirty thousand years due to Mercury no longer existing. Luckily perceptive but oblivious in the twenty first century to the close demise of Earth, astronomers had received promising images by the historically famous Hubble Space Telescope. The images showed astronomers and scientists that outside our solar system in the arm of Orion's Spur were planets, hundreds upon hundreds of them. The exoplanets were all in their own solar systems, with a promising possibility of life. They are strewn across Orion's Spur, in our galaxy, the Milky Way. NASA then sent the Kepler Satellite to search for more exoplanets. Kepler could monitor up to six thousand light years away along Orion's Spur and the very first seed was unknowingly sown.

We still clung onto saving our existence on Earth even after the undeniable facts that exoplanets *could* support our needs and protect us from the very imminent end of life on Earth. An example of this was when scientists came up with a theory to create a huge elaborate sun shade to protect us from the rising temperatures. The sun shade would be sent up in the form of trillions of two foot-wide, very thin discs, made out of silicon nitride weighing less than a gram each. By sending those into the atmosphere to shade the Earth from the Sun, cooling of the planet would be instant by two percent. Alas it didn't get a foot hold as it would have been a very costly experiment and the disks would need replacing year after year. It was also missing the valid point that the Earth would most definitely not last forever. Were we to live out our lives and then die after a short life in comparison, like that of a field mouse? Many thought no; because even though our lives are relatively short in the grand time of things we have moved forward by evolving mentally and physically.

The old questions kept arising, now with some urgency that we eventually would be without a permanent home because of Earth's demise, so NASA got to work and looked at the larger picture they were faced with. It is true that another planet, once found, could eventually have the same problems but hopefully a younger one than ours would be found, or we could move forward again. Due to a combination of thousands of years of evolution; exceptional academic achievement; and the fear of human extinction, NASA along with the famous Dr Haffnel got to work on making space travel a reality. In the mid fifty second century, during the years of 5,157 – 69, this was achieved. This was done by Dr Haffnel thinking 'outside of the box'. He used his own theories; implemented the Hubble telescopic technology; and the heavily researched accrued known data that was gained from the Kepler satellite. Easily within his own timeline, Dr Haffnel invented the Haffnel Core, giving way to travelling beyond the speed of light. It is now possible on a large scale to travel by the speed of light. Telescopes and satellites were no longer the only source of information about our solar system, galaxy or even the universe. The Haffnel Core can be placed into a space ship or even a space station! When it is rigged up, it enables light speed travel, of any vessel, now named 'Light Travel' with NASA's authorisation.

* * *

Ameel and Gee stand in front of the screen looking dumbstruck, re-reading the words in front of them like "we wish you to join them in the research of the planet" and "your evacuation is mandatory" to a planet called "Teeria" out in the big expanse of space. After the fifth time of reading and digesting the news Ameel goes back to the table and sits down. Cam just stands there not really believing what he has read and Posall is

Posall with a calm, serene response.

'Can they do that Mum, Dad?' says Gee with more fiddling of hair.

'I don't know… well I suppose "Yes" they're the government they can do what they want,' Ameel spits out, looking shell shocked.

Gee makes her mother a camomile tea as it is supposed to have a calming quality but Ameel just stares at it hopelessly almost looking straight through the white china cup, thinking, *'after that bombshell I really don't think a herbal cup of tea is the solution'*.

The last time Gee saw her mum look so shocked was when Cam announced he wanted to take a year out of education, several years ago, and instead, go to the Northern Hemisphere to explore. This went down like a lead balloon. It then led to *all* of the family taking a vacation there instead – much to his fathers delight. During the vacation while they were on their travels they bumped into a young man called Aidy Campion. He was a couple of years older than Gee. He had a gawky, gangly appearance but overall came across as being very friendly. Aidy really liked Gee more than he let on and loved her as soon as he had been in her presence for a short while. He did all he could to get to know her better when she was in his company. Gee saw him as a friend from a completely different and cold part of the world. He didn't tell her of his feelings but made it clear he wanted to stay in contact. He needed to firstly concentrate on the matter at hand and find the EMMA (Earth's Man-Made Anchor) movement. He was determined in his own mind that he would see her again and tell her of his true feelings. Gee honestly thought they were worlds apart in every way but stayed in touch because he was very persistent with the emails. She was too polite and maintained the contact against her better judgement. He was vague in what he had said about his work when they had met each other. "Research" he had said but she wasn't convinced and took it with a pinch of salt. She was right, in the long run, because eventually he admitted he had been in search of the EMMA movement. Once he had found them and had been accepted he had told her. She let her guard down a bit because she wanted to know more about the increasing following and their cause. Gee had learned from Aidy that EMMA *is* a man-made sphere in space in orbit just outside our solar system with Earth in its sights. It was created by the Russian, Wardelf Shooper and it was completely built by 17,020.

Looking thoughtful Posall joins Ameel along with Cam and Gee. Ameel's expression brightens slightly after being joined by the rest of her family and isn't such a worrying shade of white, much to Gee's relief.

Posall takes charge knowing the full extent of the mail. Posall is a tidy looking man, tall, slender with dark hair and a kind face, young for his years. He works at a nearby university as a lecturer and achieved his PhD's from Harvard. He is level headed in any given situation. He takes the hand of his wife and daughter, with Cam sitting opposite. Then he looks at them all, one by one, taking in their reactions to the news. He is faced with anguish from his wife, boredom from his son and curiosity from his beloved daughter, Gee.

'We have known this may have been on the cards for a while now because of my work and our overall status. I had only heard nothing but rumours last month, and nothing was concrete so I didn't mention it. It seems that it is our turn to help. I will be honest and say initially I am quite excited about the move as it is my field... plus we get to meet another intelligent race. Exciting times ahead of us.'

'Aliens! They want us to live side by side with aliens Dad,' interjects Cam.

'Yes I did hear something about intelligent life and that they are very similar in many ways to us. Almost human I believe. It is a good thing they did not think as you do Son or we wouldn't have a future to run to.' They know that Posall is right and it *is* a lot to digest never the less.

Cam quietly mulls over what his father has said, 'They can't just make us move can they? I don't want to leave.' Cam doesn't notice Gee rolling her eyes.

'Sorry Son but you read it too – it's mandatory. We don't have a choice. Even if you could stay behind we wouldn't leave you, so we are all in it together.'

'But we might be attacked by the aliens or explode when we land because we can't breathe properly.'

'Don't be ridiculous, I know we do not know much at all about Teeria's own race but we would not be put in harm's way. Teeria's inhabitants are kept secret for this reason; so we wouldn't over react. The scientists have been quarantined for over six years and it's proven to be safe now. There certainly won't be anyone exploding or any hostility.' Posall smirks at his wife, trying desperately to make light of the situation, but gets no reaction.

Posall takes in the mood of his family. Ameel looks unimpressed at his attempt to lighten the mood, Cam doesn't have a realistic hold of the situation and Gee is one for taking it all in and saying nothing. He tries to rectify the anguish.

'We have all known ever since we were born, that the Earth can't be a realistically permanent home for our future families. We have to make an important choice once my work has been done for the government. I see…Teer..i..a,' Posall sounds it slowly, 'as a second chance and a very good outcome. It will open up many gates for our future as a race, once we have taken the first steps.' He hasn't done field work for many years because of the lack of opportunities.

The thought of stepping foot on a different planet; getting acquainted with what he guesses will be another intelligent race; and getting back to what he actually loves to do is overwhelming. It deserves his time to convince his family, somehow.

'But it's so alien, pardon the pun, not even in our own solar system,' Ameel points out then sips her tea.

'I know my darling. Shouldn't we be thinking long term though, for our children,' He gestures at Cam and Gee, '…and our children's, children?'

'I ain't having kids! No need to worry about that,' Cam retorts.

'Please Cam, be serious for once. You can't know what you want in the future, at the moment.'

'Ok then. What about EMMA? Closer to home, not so bloody far.'

'He has a point, of sorts,' Ameel sides, making Cam relax a little.

Posall sighs feeling a little exasperated but not willing to give up just yet, he continues, 'Ok then. We're getting off the point here but we may aswell talk about it now. You two are saying you would rather live in an enclosed oversized metal sphere that is not guaranteed in many ways, particularly in its future and safety. Once we have done the mandatory term on Teeria, we will get a chance to live on *a* planet for the rest of our lives. Teeria is firstly proven to be safe; secondly we will have soil under our feet, unlike here or on EMMA which is either concrete or metal; and thirdly there is the abundance of fresh air to breathe, so much fresher than here, and in EMMA's case they get air from an air con unit. Finally, there is a safe sun that will warm our skins…' He pauses briefly as if to take in air after his rant then continues simply by saying, 'Teeria sounds like heaven.'

They are all sat digesting what the husband and father has just said and all the faces seem eased.

'You have made some very good points,' says Ameel. She takes Posall's hand and kisses the back of it, as if to say a warm thank you for laying out the facts. She then adds, 'It seems we best start thinking about packing more than anything else, they haven't given us much time.' She looks saddened at the thought of leaving and takes in their home longingly and then her eyes rest tentatively on her offspring knowing this is where they have grown up and known nothing else.

Not letting the previous topic slip away so easily Posall says, 'Do we really want to come back here when we are done? We may get settled.' He squeezes her hand.

'A few years… settled… EMMA… a different race, aliens… oh my, let's just see how things work out. I will say that we will either come back home or stay on Teeria. I don't like the thought of all of us living in a tin – just not natural. I just want us to at least be, all on one planet – agreed?' A wry smile hides her true feelings, trying to be positive for Cam, Gee and a supportive wife.

They all agree to discuss it in more detail together after they have had time to mull it all over and set to work with the packing up of their personal effects. After acouple of weeks Cam has packed as if he is just going on a holiday, Gee packs like there will be no return and her room is left bare. Ameel and Posall put most of the larger furniture along with a large amount of Cam's remaining belongings, into storage and pack most of their personal effects too. During the month while the packing was commencing, further information came from the government, instructing that they would be picked up on the departure day and to just carry hand luggage as the rest of their chosen belongings and luggage will follow in a second transporter.

The month flies by with discretion being top priority. Posall and Ameel resigned from their jobs and, Cam and Gee informed their tutors that they were taking time out of education to travel with their parents.

Posall and Gee are both very excited about their adventure so they researched as much as possible. Gee is definitely her father's daughter with the same interests and enthusiasm for the new and unknown. They are incredibly close and Cam can get jealous especially as Gee seems particularly gifted academically like their father. Everything is set in place and the thirteenth arrives with no room for worrying about any ifs, buts or maybes.

At 0800 hrs, as stated, a small hover transporter, along with a larger one arrives out the front of their three bedroom house in Cape Town of the day in question.

A government operative leaves the small vehicle and knocks on their door. Ameel and Posall open the door together.

'Hello. Are you Mr and Mrs Goshle?' speaks the dry sounding agent.

'Yes. We are ready.' They say in unison trying to sound happy and friendly to the man before them, who is expressionless.

'I will be your escort to the docking station.'

'Oh ok. Can you tell us where the docking station is?' asks Posall, hiding his frustration with the tight lipped man.

'You will find out in due course. Now if you could please get into the transporter, time is of the essence. Your personal belongings will be loaded into the other transporter and will then follow us.' He gestures towards the larger vehicle.

Posall and Ameel do as asked and gather Cam, Gee and their hand luggage, and join the agent in the transporter. The journey is tense; nobody really speaks because of the atmosphere caused by the uptight, secretive agent. They instead take in their surroundings. The transporter is a sleek looking vehicle, with shiny black bodywork and tinted viewers. The transporters do not need a driver as they are programmed before a journey by the TST. Due to no driver the vehicle is roomy inside with the console in the center and seating around the sides. The seats have belts for safety which automatically strap the person in once they sit down.

The journey takes them cross country through the deserts of Botswana, Southern Africa then across the Indian Ocean to Australia. The transporter engages at high velocity over the oceans and the journey only takes one hour and forty five minutes. They enter an area nobody recognises but notice NASA has control of it because of some large signs. It is tucked away at the center of no mans land – NASA's head quarters. The transporter stops at the drop off point in the middle of a levelled fenced off area, which seems to go on for miles in every direction. The agent hops out of the transporter and gives Posall an electronic device. The device is a very high tech thin wrist band. It looks enormous to start with until it contracts to fit perfectly on Posall's wrist three quarters of the way round. It is immaculately smooth in appearance and to the untrained eye looks just like a highly polished black bangle, which is a snug fit. It surprisingly contains all the docking information such as their passes; a tracker, for them and their luggage, so neither can get lost or stray from the permitted areas without NASA's security being informed. They are then told by the agent to follow their luggage that has been unloaded off the larger transporter that followed them to their destination. The agent takes a seat in the small transporter and leaves to go and fetch some more important personnel.

'Well I'm glad that bits over. He was as much fun as an empty beer glass,' announces Cam.

'You're not wrong there,' agrees Gee.

'Come on kids let go.'

'Mother we are not kids anymore!' moans Gee.

'You are to me and your Father sweetheart.' Ameel ruffles her husband's hair and Cam just pulls a face stuck for words for once.

Posall is rooted to the spot taking in the view. Before him is an overwhelming sight of NASA's great expanse of a nerve centre that is responsible for his family being here. Aswell as the endless sight of man-made flat plains; in the far distance the structures are so immense that the people at the foot of the buildings look like ants scurrying about. All around them are strangers, all in the same position as the Goshles, all scattered randomly as far as the eye can see. Aswell as the Goshles looking slightly put out at being dropped off with no idea of what was to follow, the atmosphere was also tense as if they were under arrest and being held at gun point. This is because there are guards dotted about with weapons in order to help, or keep trespassers out, but Gee and several others notice a convergence of people along the entrance perimeter.

Over six years ago, humans were forced to think about the reality of Earth's demise because of the newly found habitable planet of Teeria. Many did not believe in or want the possibility of life beyond our solar system despite the given facts and some even frowned upon such a find and believed in going down with the ship. Others quite rightly pointed out that

Teeria would not last forever like Earth, but Teeria is a younger planet. Some thought it best not to have all their eggs in one basket. There were quite a few who did not accept the find and took action to stay within the solar system we all know. Those who did not support and want to accept Teeria were EMMA's key supporters, who now have quite a big following much to the surprise of the U.S. government and NASA.

It was up to the individual and their own right to live where they wanted, with the given means. Polling in the beginning showed it was a seventy to thirty percent split for Teeria. This enraged the EMMA movement further leading to more protesting and campaigning, in the end leaving fifteen percent undecided of where their future will be, in hundreds of years to come. This result pleased EMMA's head agents and made them even more confident. Due to thousands, upon thousands of years needing to pass before anyone ever really contemplating such a difficult decision, many just went along with the polls like a fashion faze out of control and carried on with their lives.

The huge percentage of earthlings who are keen to move to Teeria for a brighter and stable future have signed a legal document, so when the time is right after satisfactory research has been completed they will get their long awaited call. NASA promises that all that have signed up will see Teeria in their own lifetime and to be rest assured that those will know that their future generations will have a long, safe and successful future ahead.

The people around the perimeter, where the Goshles have just been dropped off, are protesters chanting, 'Stay here as Earthling's or be a traitor!' which is certainly not helping by the look of panic on the faces of some of the new visitors, as they have been dropped off in the middle of nowhere and are under scrutiny.

'That's not a very good start to our journey,' says Gee pointing over her shoulder at the protestors.

'Ignore them, we are under orders so we don't have much choice whether we agree with them or not,' Posall points out.

He is stood with his hands in his pockets while taking in their surroundings and continues absent-mindedly, 'as you have probably worked out they are here because of the Russians who snuck back to their homeland years ago to the depths of the ice. The very risky Russian movement, headed by Wardelf Shooper, who we have heard of, had formed and worked towards and completed the space station; EMMA. It is far bigger than Stepping where I think we are heading to. EMMA has been built with the saying 'a home from home' in mind and indeed they have done a marvellous job. These revolutionaries are the protestors against any Earthling who want to live on any other planet. As you know they constantly campaign and anyone who disagrees is classed in their eyes as a "traitor".' He nods in the protesters direction and then looks back at Gee.

'It's a first for me to see it first-hand, certainly different than seeing it on the news. They *are* peaceful and low key,' Gee observes.

'Yes I've seen worse – thought they'd be a bit more enthusiastic, unlike their dull chant,' he notes.

'Erm – perhaps they don't want to get shot,' says Gee pointing to the guards who are very notably in front of the protesters using the fence as protection.

'Come on Posall, Gee! We have to keep up with our luggage or who knows what will happen,' snaps Ameel who is getting stressed out, while her husband is giving a history lesson and is in awe of everything.

'Coming love.' He smiles widely, loving the whole experience.

'Get a grip man. I can't watch you, the kids and the luggage all by myself. Don't want us getting lost. You can take it all in once we have found our resting quarters.'

They hurry along and catch up with their luggage. It is like having their very own personal chaperone leading them to one of two ships hidden away in the massive building. Each ship can hold up to one hundred thousand people, all from different reaches of the Earth's globe, including personnel. The ships are docked in single file, one behind the other. The Goshles are escorted onto the ship furthest away. They are on level three. Posall realises once onboard that they are in fact on the front ship and will be first to take off. The ship is a large space shuttle with nine levels and is around the size of an ocean aircraft carrier. Each level has passenger's quarters, each with hygiene facilities, a bedroom with a none descript décor in light grey, with the bed wear giving a splash of vibrant colour. On each level of the ship are two large dining areas and two large lounging spaces with soft furnishings for comfort.

Chapter 2

Space Station Stepping 01 (Stepping) is a space station that had been built and completed in the year 16,678. Stepping was built just outside our solar system. The name was derived from the idea that it was the first stepping stone closer, hopefully, to man's most outstanding achievement. It was built for several factors, and for various reasons, it was kept a secret from the world's nations. One of the main factors of Stepping was to harbour Earth's civilisations if catastrophic events occurred. By working around the clock for amity with the highest spec of engineering and many dedicated personnel, evolution of our technology really moved on and grew with thanks to the late Dr Haffnel. Stepping is now primarily the home to NASA; scientists in every single field imaginable, engineers, U.S. army including the DOD; and general utility personnel.

The Stepping space station is a spectacular looking vessel. It is double the size of New Zealand and three miles in depth. NASA's head quarter's is at the center of the station like the capital of a great city. All the other specialised personnel are appointed designated areas that spiral off NASA's central centre. All living quarters are situated on the edges of the space station, looking out over space, as a reminder why they are all there. The homes are roomy flats, in multi storey curved buildings, that rise above and below, the top and underneath of the station. Attached to the buildings are large domed pods, creating the feel of outdoor space. All of the domes have gardens with a network of rivers connecting all the neighbouring pods in order to generate hydropower with advanced technology to power the station and its needs.

* * *

On level five two work colleagues from the geographic team get settled in. Ven has already unpacked and is in Tiarla's room at a loose end much to Tiarla's annoyance. Tiarla appreciates some alone time but doesn't look a gift horse in the mouth and tries to see the positive in having Ven under her feet as he is the only familiar face onboard the ship of thousands. Ven gets the hint from the silent Tiarla and goes to make sure that all their equipment is safely loaded. They make a good team, work wise, but their personalities can clash. Tiarla is a very self assured person whereas Ven whittles a lot. Tiarla is convinced that Ven has been born in the wrong year, a few thousand years wrong but she respects the way he works and they are close friends.

By the time Ven returns from checking their equipment and scouting the ship Tiarla is more hospitable and unpacked. They settle down to a relaxing journey. They are both in deep conversation about Stepping when they hear a knock at their open door. It's Posall and Cam.

'We couldn't help but overhear you talking about Stepping. Is that where we are initially going?' asks Posall.

'Sure no problem. Please do come in. All the information is in the handbook in your room.' Ven stands with a friendly invitation. They all shake hands and introduce themselves.

'Oh, we didn't hang about. We left the girls to it, my Wife and Daughter; unpacking and well you know the rest.'

'Not to worry. We will be on this shuttle overnight and docking at Stepping tomorrow evening, to refuel. The take-off uses a lot of fuel you see,' says Tiarla, aware that Cam is staring at her.

She has an athletic appearance, shoulder length brown wavy hair that looks almost scruffy but not distracting from her intelligent aura.

'So what happens on and after Stepping?'

'Well unfortunately we won't have much time to investigate Stepping, as we take leave the following morning. We then leave on this same shuttle, so you may aswell unpack for a week…' Ven points at Tiarla's personal belongings around the room.

'That's a shame,' moans Posall.

'It is, but hey, better things to come. Anyway, so once we have refuelled and re-coordinated we are ready for the last leg of the journey. Teeria here we come. I can't wait mate! What's your profession?' says Ven clearly excited about going to Teeria.

Posall tells them that he has a PhD in the field of Geography and Planetary Science. After chatting it turns out that they may all be working together. Ven has a PhD in Organic and Evolutionary Science and Tiarla has a PhD in History of Science. They have far more experience out in the field than Posall and had been lucky enough to have found the work. Cam and Posall make their way back with only fifteen minutes to spare before they depart. Ameel and Gee have settled in and unpacked what is needed.

In the room where they are staying there is another smaller lounge room. The room is next to the window looking out. There are four chairs all equipped with seat belts, all identical in white leather and comfortable in appearance. The chairs are fixed to the floor and separated into pairs each side of the window opposite each other with a coffee table in the middle with indented drink holders. They all get seated and try to relax.

As Posall had worked out, they *are* the first to take-off. During the departure sequence they are strapped in. Ameel and Gee look like a bag of nerves. Whereas Cam, has a wide grin plastered across his face after meeting Tiarla. Posall looks content by knowing what their travel schedule will be and meeting two friendly people who could soon be work colleagues.

They are all surprised at how smooth a ride it is to get up out of Earth's atmosphere. Once they are in space, the shuttles' thrusters are cut off. After what seems like seconds from leaving Earth; they float along in space on a set path towards the distant space station – Stepping.

When they are advised it is safe to leave their seats, they all go to the window to take in the view. In front of them is an overwhelming darkness never seen by any of them before and they are heading straight into it. Behind them is the view of their beloved home – Earth, looking like a shiny pearl marble.

Their attention turns to the second shuttle that is just about to leave Earth's atmosphere. Instead of it following behind their shuttle and making it into space, the second vessel is fired upon by a small fighter jet that appears from nowhere.

The hit vessel lights up and sparks to its rear right side. The sparks grow and expand quickly through the body of the second vessel from each hit as the fighter jet repeatedly fires upon it with each pass.

As the targeted ship starts to break up, the fighter jet leaves because the DOD (Department of Defence) turn up in two of their own fighter jets; arriving a fraction too late to ward off the rebel attack.

The Earth's sky is littered with chunks of the shuttles debris. It is clear to the Goshles that nobody could have survived such an attack.

Ameel automatically pulls Gee away from the window while the men watch open mouthed in disbelief. Ameel sits down with Gee and they hold each others hands tight. The intercom sounds,

'Please fasten your belts. We are on red alert.'

Posall has turned the shade of white in contrast to his usual pink rosy complexion. He goes through the motions and buckles himself in. Cam's hands are shaking so much he can't get a good hold of the buckle. He tries to shake away the feeling; flexing and rubbing his hands and gives it another go, but to no avail. Posall realises that his son is panicking and helps. He pats his son on the shoulder for comfort.

The shuttle is motionless as if it isn't moving. The Goshles are all quiet and wait for news to come through on the intercom with their eyes wide as if it will help their ears to listen. It seems like an hour has gone by but only twenty minutes have past and the intercom sounds,

'We are now on green alert so it is safe to leave your seats. We have an escort of two DOD fighter jets as a precautionary measure. It has also been confirmed that there were sadly no survivors on the shuttle craft that was attacked. It was rebels from EMMA's group.'

Gee stands up and starts pacing and angrily shouts, 'Well I hope Aidy can live with himself.' Aidy being the young man, who stayed in touch with Gee, and who was in search and found the EMMA movement. 'Those activists are murderers. If I saw him I would spit on the ground he walked on!'

'Come here honey.' Ameel gives her a much needed hug and secretly, she needed it to.

'I think we all need a stiff drink, to settle our nerves,' suggests Cam.

'I couldn't agree with you more Son.' Posall then takes charge and they all head off to the lounge area.

After being joined by Tiarla and Ven, who too, look shaken, the Goshles relax a little. They are all so thankful that it wasn't their shuttle that got hit, which in turn makes them feel guilty. News soon spreads that the second shuttle was full of supplies and just had skeleton staff. The number of skeleton staff usually means half a dozen, but still, lives were lost wrongly and unfairly.

The Goshles are relieved when they arrive at Stepping and get shown to their quarters. In contrast to the shuttle their lodgings are very roomy and spacious. Posall and Gee are both keen to go and investigate, so along with Ameel and Cam, they go and make the most of the short visit and look around. Gee had already worked out that there was a visitor's area on Stepping because she'd done what the others hadn't and read the handbook back on the shuttle.

The visitor centre is huge. It is a large open plan room. There doesn't appear to be a ceiling until on closer inspection, a glass dome can be seen in place. It is quite a sight looking into space as far as the eye can see, under the safety of the glass.

Gee and her father are completely mesmerized by Stepping. They read every bit of information on show in the visitors centre and appreciate the work that was involved in completing the marvellous and outstanding accomplishment. Cam and his mother have a look but make it around the large expanse of the room in a quarter of the time compared to their sister and husband, because they are out of their depth of interest.

After exhausting every bit of accessible information, and seeing the visitor's showroom which shows off a mock up residential suite and a domed garden, they wearily go back to their overnight quarters and settle down for the night.

Chapter 3

Stepping played a very large part in finding a habitable planet. When Stepping was fully operational it was then fully utilised and ready to take the next step to implement a Haffnel Core. Authorisation was given for an exploration ship named the Exploration Light 259 (EL) to go and search for possible habitable planets. The EL was built and docked at Stepping. The EL had an assigned crew the Mission Star Finder who had permanently left Earth, and *home* was on the space station.

On the 16th February 17,014, nine years ago, the Mission Star Finder crew of EL had a big event. They embarked on their very first expedition and search, of a possible new habitable planet. The EL is a large vessel and is still in existence today. It had living quarters for each member of the crew, technical support, all equipment for the technicians and scientist personnel. The vessel was also fitted out with provisions for six years so the exploration was not interrupted needlessly.

Initially EL stayed close to our own solar system, within the first 6,000 light years in distance terms. Mission Star Finder crew searched in great detail, recording every bit of information. They chose a likely looking planet from within a targeted solar system after each had been scanned by a very high tech telescope. Data was then collected via a probe which would be sent down to the planet. The probes that were sent out were small, the size of a handset phone making them agile. When the probe was in flight it had a delicate pair of wings that appeared, almost insect like but built out of a material that made them extremely tolerant of fluctuating temperatures. Even though the probes were very robust, many were lost during the start of the analysis procedure because many of the probed planets were very hazardous. As soon as the probe started analysing, a constant feed of visual information and stats were sent back to the EL and if the transmission was broken all was literally not lost. When the probe was successful after the first critical minutes, it then looked at the initial terrain of a planet and if it looked promising by the EL crew it would then carry on, gathering other data, such as soil type, oxygen levels, flora specimens, the water's chemistry and atmospheric make up – if available! The data would be entered into a database and collaborated together. If the results returned red then the chosen planet was of no use. A staggering ninety nine percent of the searches were void but the Mission Star Finder crew soldiered on becoming more and more experienced. It became tedious as it seemed that if one key factor was correct then another important factor was not.

There *were* possibilities found but no certainties because some of the key factors weren't correct. The Mission Star Finder crew had hoped for more promising and absolute results otherwise they would have to backtrack to the possibilities. After many, many dead ends the crew of EL became disheartened and worried that our home in thousands of years to come would be in space. They began to assume that there was no liveable planet for Earth's human species and came to realise just how complex a new find was. The crew had to think differently to gain momentum again. Finally it was realised and very apparent after all the testing that had been done and newly found experiences, that only a few important initial key factors was all that was needed to determine if a probe was to be planet bound to make further analysis. Time was greatly saved and more distance was covered. This gave the crew a fresh boost to start them on their way to find a planet that could sustain human life. As the searches sped up considerably they ended up many thousands of light years away.

Three and a half years went by. Their time was not wasted because the searches gave accurate maps and data of space. The EL was 165,000 light years away when a routine check of a planet returned back positive. The Mission Star Finder crew were elated and couldn't believe their find. Before they could really believe what they had found they went down to the planet to investigate further by doing extensive tests after determining that the oxygen, nitrogen and gravitational levels were all within the safety margins for humans. The initial results were indeed correct and it was true they had in fact found another habitable planet on the 3rd June 17,017.

One exciting and important find from the extensive and repeated investigations by the Mission Star Finder crew on the newly found planet was that there was intelligent fauna. The crew could not believe their luck in finding other humanoid life out in space after so many negative results and inhospitable planets. All of a sudden this new find had more than they could ever have imagined. The idea of finding life in one form or another had crossed the minds of all but to actually find intelligent equivalents of us was a real beauty of a find. The intelligent humanoids are called Spognoffs and are very hospitable. They called their home Teeria.

Teeria *is* 165,000 light years away from Earth. It is situated in our closest neighbouring galaxy, next to our Milky Way, in the Large Magellanic Cloud. In the galaxy of the Large Magellanic Cloud is the commonly known Tarantula Nebula or formally known the 30 Doradus. At the heart of the Tarantula Nebula there is a huge star cluster named by us, the R136. R136a is the habitable planet in question, named Teeria. Teeria has two sister planets R136b and c named Zuuron and Plylouse.

To some, Teeria was a fantasy not a reality, and the making of fantastic fictional dreams, all because of its position in the Tarantula Nebula. The home of Teeria is slap bang in the middle of a sky of that found in a fairy-tale. The night sky is a fusion of pastel colours consisting of light refraction given off from dust and gases, which is continuously embellished by star bursts from the Tarantula Nebula and the star cluster of R136. The stars are so bright they alone light the night sky and the surface of the planet below is illuminated with a dull hue.

Teeria has two moons named Ni and Caar; Ni is small similar to Pluto and Caar, is staggeringly the same size of Earth. The two moons help to stabilise Teeria on its tilted axis. When it rotates they act like stabilisers on a child's bicycle. Teeria's Sun, still to date, qualifies as one of the largest stars to exist compared to others, across our ever changing universe. The main important difference with Teeria along with her sun, against other nebulae and great stars, is that its distance from each other is perfectly like Earth's position in our decaying solar system. Everything, literally everything, was just right – like Earth, "The Goldilocks planet", from the children's book, Goldilocks and the Three Bears.

Teeria has North and South poles on a smaller scale to what we are used too, but they are still covered with ice land masses. She is a lot younger than Earth and has mainly one land mass running around the equator, generally covering two thirds due North and South of the equator. Teeria is a third bigger than our Earth measuring nine thousand three hundred kilometres around its equator. The coastlines are very jagged from volcanic events that run along most of it, leading to some fracturing of the land and giving rise to broken off islands. The sea is split into two, the Shallows and the Deep. The Shallows are between the islands and the mainland. The Deep is beyond the broken off islands and not much is known at present and is in need of further investigation and mapping by our own field researchers, who have quite a task ahead of them and a lifetime of work.

The terrain of the mainland isn't unlike ours, just different. There are miles upon miles of flat plain land, covered in grass from the coast. The further one travels inland the more one will come across acres of scattered forests and many mountainous regions consumed by Teeria's array of flora.

The Spognoffs were very happy to help the plight of the Earthlings after obviously long and extensive negotiations. They welcomed our integration onto Teeria because it would benefit both races. The Spognoffs and human race made a treaty. Within the treaty, under NASA's authorisation, the Mission Star Finder crew promised the Spognoffs that Teeria would be firstly recognised as their home and planet, and respected diligently.

Once the treaty had been signed NASA's work was done. They passed on the new responsibility and all involved, to a governing body under the same umbrella, named the Terrestrial Research Federation, TRF for short. TRF is run and duly scrutinized by General Carter whom is highly decorated. General Carter is a mature and well respected man with a no nonsense policy. He could not resist the invitation to run TRF head quarters and is the perfect man for the job with no family ties back on Earth to speak of. His position is long term and his goal is to lead and guide TRF in conjunction with the Spognoff's input and knowledge using his superior negotiating skills. The first set up human settlement on Teeria was under quarantine conditions run by TRF and in close proximity to a powerful and strong Spognoff tribe called the Gladestines. The Gladestine tribe helped with the adjustments the humans needed to face.

In our past during the year of 3,284, the Medical Council issued and enforced that on a yearly basis; every person had a full blood screening, a body scan, and the flu vaccination. The screening was more cost effective long term instead of an unknown sinister health problem going unnoticed. Every year the flu vaccine was developed to keep up with the new strain of the killer virus but it wasn't enough in the grand scheme of things.

Disaster struck us on Earth, many years after the great Ice Age – Influenza. On the 23rd February, 13,882 the flu virus took a strangle hold of human lives across the Southern Hemisphere. The ever changing strong virus took many lives. It didn't specifically hit certain age brackets but instead anyone of any age was at risk of contracting the virus. It was hoped the outbreak was a one off and the virus wouldn't raise its ugly head again after so many had been lost. But it did and the influenza hit harder, much harder than before and the Medical Council wanted to know why. A thorough investigation took place. After countless tests on willing volunteers and much analytical research, the results were staggering. The results showed that the immune system of mankind had been lowered to a very worrying fifteen percent of its once-strong and hardy predecessors at ninety nine percent. Cleanliness to the extreme was to blame. Changes were made; otherwise the future outcome for mankind's failing, was ridiculous and couldn't be blamed on Earth's demise, but because of us being too clean!

Everything to do with personal hygiene; in-house

cleaning – work and at home, was readdressed. All cleaning products were evaluated and made to a weaker potency, but strong enough for a safer hygiene. Safe hygiene was then recognised as the 'Safe Hygiene Act 30158'; it was a new beginning and a huge boost for our immune systems. Aswell as 'Safe Hygiene' being implemented in every workplace across the Southern Hemisphere, so was a mandatory Screening Booth. Each company; across all work industries from warehouse personnel to government leaders, had a Screening Booth placed in the entrances and all employers and employees had to pass through it.

The Screening Booth took on the responsibility of scanning the person to detect any cold or flu signatures by using invisible safe Viral Waves – that was a new discovery during the year 13,883. The scanned computerized image of the person was displayed on a life size, sheer black screen. The person was shown the image in a colour of blue or red depending on what matched the viral scan.

When red was displayed the person had the first stages of a strong germ taking hold and thus the Screening Booth nipped the virus in the bud. The germ carrier was refused entry into the companies' workplace and was advised to go home, regardless if they felt well or not. A simple stat report was then sent to the companies' personnel to show who was or wasn't in. Until that person showed up blue in the Booth they were not allowed clearance to enter the building. Mild germ carriers were allowed access into their work place. This helped to create the right balance which in turn helped fellow colleagues who come into contact with mild cases boost their own immune systems.

The Screening Booth was a wonderful breakthrough and it is still in effect today, probably with a few minor adjustments, and so is the 'Safe Hygiene Act 30158'.

With the combination of the Screening Booth and the Act 30158 mankind's immunity improved immensely to a healthier fifty eight percent.

Back on Teeria in our beginning as mentioned, the scientists were firstly quarantined and had set up home on some uninhabited islands, out of harm's way by three dormant volcanoes. The quarantine was for both parties; humans and Spognoffs, for their own safety until all was satisfactory between the two civilizations. In addition to helping the humans settle in, the Spognoffs helped them adapt to the natural Teerian germ levels under the quarantined conditions. The Spognoffs agreed to help because they were startled at how low the human immune system had become. Even though the humans had managed to get a grasp and get their immune system to reach an acceptable level the Spognoffs made it very clear that in order for human existence to survive on Teeria there was more they could do and help them with by working even closer and alongside TRF to make new vaccinations by adapting their own. TRF soon found out from the shared data, that a Spognoff's immune system was superior to the humans and they could easily fight off a killer virus which would only be a fifty fifty possibility for us. With the Spognoffs help and after some time humans had an immune system that worked at one hundred percent; another major stepping stone had been achieved and the quarantine conditions were relaxed. In effect the Spognoffs mended a weak and probably bleak outcome and then gave us a future. On Teeria there was no need for viral booths and the viruses that were once deadly were now easily fought. The Gladestines and TRF had worked together and paved the way for a human and Spognoff coexistence.

The islands are situated on five consecutive broken off chunks of land, a short distance from each other, and from a birds eye view, they appear in a crescent shape. The five islands all vary in size with the smallest one being double that of Earth's Madagascar. An island is large enough to initially hold two or more countries from Earth. Each island has a mountainous side, backing against the sea of the Deep. The human populations live amongst the rocky terrain and low lands, in turn facing the mainland to have the protection from the sea tides of Teeria's great oceans. Earth has seventy percent ocean coverage whereas Teeria's oceans only cover fifty seven percent.

The Spognoffs are strewn across Teeria and it is unknown what the exact total population is. The reason why their exact numbers are unknown is because the landmass on Teeria is clearly far greater than Earth. The leaders of each main tribe have a great gathering twice a year to access such things as numbers amongst other important diplomacy matters. The numbers do not account for the nomads of their kind. Despite Spognoffs choosing to live with the land and not against it, their knowledge, technology and foresight is more advanced than ours. The human resident scientists on Teeria are keen to learn and adapt to Spognoffian ways in order to preserve and look after the beautiful fauna and flora they have been kindly invited to live amongst.

When a research convoy goes out to the mainland they meet with a chosen Spognoff, delegated by the leader of the Gladestines, Mogue. The Gladestines have a settlement at a place called Roudruom which is the nearest coastal Spognoff group to where the humans have settled. The research convoy trips are for them both to learn each other's ways and each then reports back their findings and knowledge. Mogue, the Gladestine Spognoff leader, is very open minded and eager to improve their own living and has only one goal

– to look after where they live, eat, sleep and give back if taken, this is why he was made a powerful leader.

* * *

Their approaching shuttle has been travelling nearly a week and had travelled into the Large Magellanic Cloud (LMC) galaxy. The Goshles and everyone else onboard could not help but notice and marvel at the many colours given off from all of the dust and gases that are harboured in the magnificent wondrous cloud. Another stunning sight not far within the LMC is the Tarantula Nebula also a wash of colours and pricked with bright stars. It doesn't take long for their vessel to take them into the Tarantula Nebula. The whole family were mesmerized at the sights and had taken plenty of photographs with a top notch, high tech zoom lens camera, of the happy, mind blowing experience. They still had a long distance to go before they could see Teeria, but because of the excitingly new and unknown that was still in front of them through the window, it passed very quickly. On waking after each night a surprising view lay in wait in their windows. Posall had his maps and books to hand, and was star spotting. Ameel and Cam couldn't help but get enthralled into the excitement. Gee as always was beside her father in the thick of the excitement and learning alongside him.

Finally they see Teeria approaching slowly, after passing by her sister planets Zuuron and Plylouse. Zuuron is a mass of cold rock covered by ice. It is the smallest of the three planets, no larger than Teeria's largest moon - Caar. Plylouse is brown and also an unliveable planet but like and once thought of as Mars, has habitable promise for future Spognoff and humans by technological intervention. Plylouse is double the size of Teeria with a dormancy that can be tapped and researched. Gee smiles brightly at the sight of the new planet, Teeria that has only been seen by a certain human few. She traces Teeria with her finger on the window taking in everything she sees. The planet initially looks very green and blue, with the colours running parallel to each other, going across the planet horizontally. She is amazed at how bright and clear it looks compared to Earth. Posall correctly informs her it is because the planet is immaculately clean and only had a miniscule amount of pollutants leaked into the atmosphere when the Spognoffs hadn't quite got to grips with low emissions on anything mechanical, but they still had solved and improved the problem very quickly. Due to their quick thinking and corrective work they managed to preserve the crisp, shiny button before them.

Gee is impressed to hear about the Spognoffs compassion and takes more photographs eagerly, not wanting to miss a thing. As the distance between them and Teeria decreases she notices brown areas amongst the green and realises that they are the mountains her and her father had read about.

Teeria is now a real living image in front of them all with every detail to be seen. They are informed by the intercom on the shuttle that they are approaching Teeria's atmosphere and would be required to buckle up in one hour's time. Gee jumps up and down clapping her hands together like an over excited child, absolutely full of enthusiasm. Posall can't help but smile at his daughter who is still beaming.

He pulls them all close and whispers, 'This is it. I'm so happy for all of you, to see and breathe this.' He gives them all a big squeeze in their group hug.

'Cut it out Dad, you're not gonna start blubbering,' says Cam.

'Leave him be, he may be a little choked but with

good reason. Just take a good look at what you see,' interjects Ameel.

She does not want anything to spoil her husband's moment.

The hour has passed quickly and the Goshles are waiting with anticipation all buckled up and not taking their eyes off the view through the window. The entry into, and descent through the atmosphere are turbulent because it is dense. The shuttle bumps about as if it is running over huge boulders in a road. Ameel and Gee, who are sat by each other again, are gripping the arm rests so tight it is making their knuckles turn white. Gee isn't smiling anymore and Posall notices the look of worry on her face. He reassures them all that it is normal and the shuttle is made to endure the strong turbulence and that he was actually expecting this on leaving Earth's atmosphere. With his reasoning the knuckles return to pink again with relief and a smile from all.

Once they are through the atmosphere the ride is so smooth they all breathe a sigh of relief and are *all* beaming this time. Ameel can't wait to stand on solid ground again and Cam wants to know what all the fuss is about? Posall and Gee feel like they are on a very long holiday and can't wait to start their adventure.

The shuttle circles above the landing dock on the mainland. The intercom sounds and the Captain speaks for the first time. He points out the crescent shaped islands and introduces his precious cargo to their new homeland. He circles the shuttle clockwise and anti-clockwise so the passengers on each side of the vessel can see the islands below. There is a happy note to the Captains voice as if he is himself relieved they made it this far after past events. He signs off by wishing them all 'Good Luck'.

Chapter 4

The shuttle does not take long to dock on the mainland next to the coast. It comes to rest in a fenced off and levelled field. All passengers take their time and head out in an orderly fashion. The Goshles are in the middle of the group heading out of the shuttle. Everyone is overpowered by the brightness of the real light coming from Teeria's Sun. They automatically put glasses on, a hat with a brim or use a hand to shade their eyes until they have re-adjusted from the dull lighting of the shuttle.

Directly ahead is a check point, all very civilised and relaxed. A large building stands to the right of the check point on the converted site which is the headquarters for TRF and the hub of everything that has and will take place. Posall notices a General present and naturally straightens his posture out of respect. He knows the man to be General Carter who is watching over the new incomers. Posall cannot wait to formally meet him. Everyone is in such a good mood the air is filled with a low hum of chat and laughter. To the left overshadowed by the shuttle is a large racking system holding the entire luggage load awaiting collection by the owners.

The Goshles make it to the check point. The man at the barrier is wearing a belted uniform that is smartly tailored and black in colour. Every member of staff who represent and work for TRF wear the new, fresh uniform, so it is easier for newcomers to gain help and support if needed.

The man scans Posall's wrist band, which he had forgotten he was wearing because it is so comfortable and durable. The uniformed man then points the scanner in the direction of the luggage racks. The luggage suddenly materializes from the left in the fifth row up, then hovers to ground level and heads towards them. The Goshles all stand open mouthed fascinated at such technology. The man instructs them to follow the luggage as it is programmed with the location of their new home. So with that they follow through the checkpoint and under the raised barrier and walk quite close together at a steady pace.

While walking along they notice that the only unnatural material is the metal work of the barrier at the check point, the shuttle they had arrived on, and personal effects. There are no apparent roads just a very well trodden trail, a couple of metres wide. If the luggage wasn't hovering and was on wheels trundling along it would have got stuck or fell over on the bumpy trail. They walk, from where they docked, towards the coast then take a right. They have the seas to their left and grassland to their right. The grass looks so green and luscious which is such a new sight for them all.

'I'd love to be here munching if I was a cow,' says Cam innocently, as they walk along.

Everyone bursts out laughing. Cam is not amused or convinced that this planet can be called home for him, as he is so used to the ways of Earth no matter how bleak it is.

'Why are we and everyone else walking?' Cam continues looking about wishing he *was* a happy oblivious cow munching the grass.

'The only means of transport here are the research carriers, bicycles or your feet - Son. They are trying not to harm anything by keeping emissions low.'

'Great... well... we will get fitter, so maybe not such a bad thing.'

In the distance to their left, not too far away, the large islands give the illusion of tumbling over one another and can be seen looming closer. The first island is not so far off the coast but the third is the furthest away. The only other steel and metal work in use is for the bridges across the shallow seas to each island. The Goshles wonder which of the five islands they will be on. While they walk along a cliff top full of contemplation they take in the sea on the left. The Shallows are a lovely turquoise blue, very clean and clear. The Deep is very noticeable along the edge of the Shallows as the colour of turquoise turns to a dark navy blue. The Shallows look so inviting and they all hope that they will be able to have a swim in the near future. To the right they can only see grassland and again no roads. Gee says it is one of the most beautiful sights she has ever seen and her mother agrees. With her good eyesight Gee can just about see some blurry mountains on the horizon.

As Gee is walking along she is aware that she is walking differently and it is going unnoticed by the others. She is walking with an obvious spring in her step and it isn't because she is purposely doing a bouncy happy walk and this is what puzzles her.

She speaks up, 'The ground feels spongy to me.' She stands on the spot automatically stopping the others and taps her feet on the ground to try and alleviate the feeling.

'Feels solid enough to me love,' remarks Posall copying his daughter by stamping his own feet hard on the dusty ground.

'Odd – perhaps it's my footwear.'

'You could be right there honey,' says Ameel giving her daughter a hug, 'we will have a look at them when we have a minutes rest.' She keeps her arm around her daughter as they all start walking again.

The path leads them down so they are nearly level with the sea shore. They soon get to the first bridge and what appears to be a low key market with traders.

Everyone is wandering along following the luggage and then it suddenly turns left towards the first bridge. Gee, Posall and Ameel slow down realising this is the island they will be staying on. Cam doesn't look where he is going because he is too busy staring at a female Spognoff who is trading some fresh fruit, she had previously gathered, for some ground wheat. Cam bumps into his father which snaps him out of his gawping. He apologises for the accident and the explanation is written over his face for his father to read; while he continues to be mesmerized by the female Spognoff who he is looking at. He sees a beautiful woman of similar age with very long dark hair, a bronzed looking tan and simple clothing. She catches him staring from under her brow and then looks him square in the eyes and smirks. He looks away embarrassed because he feels like he has been rude. He can't help but look back and the woman is about to leave and she waves gently at him and he returns it wishing he hadn't been such an obvious and uncool newcomer. Gee notes her brother's posture has relaxed as it is not so guarded. She smiles to herself knowing that her brother is fascinated by females and mutters 'can't take him anywhere'. She lets out a chuckle which gets her brother's attention but she pretends otherwise not wanting to spoil his fun.

Just before stepping onto the bridge they read a sign saying 'Welcome to Isca Island'. Gee, Cam, Posall and Ameel all say the name 'Isca…' in unison. Gee really likes the name and it makes her smile uncontrollably. Isca, Diadent, Pacle, Curfe, Semindi are the islands named in order of their positions making up the shape of the crescent starting from the southern point. The family all hurry to keep up with the luggage which is already hovering along the bridge. The bridge is three meters wide, metal under foot and an extremely sturdy structure. It is under a mile long.

The Goshles are now excited and are walking noticeably faster at the thought of nearly arriving at their final destination which has taken over a week of travelling and a near death experience. Cam watches the luggage approaching the end of the bridge which is in the middle of the sandy shore of Isca. He can see a left and a right track and makes mental odds on which way they will head next. Then the luggage crosses the dirt track to the other side and continues, not turning left or right. He hopes to himself, that they will not be living so near to the bridge where it is clearly busier with people coming and going.

The Goshles manage to get through the hustle and bustle of people on foot. If ever a roundabout was needed it would be at the bridges entrance and exit on Isca. They catch up with their escort and the terrain is getting steeper and uneven as the other side of the island is at a higher altitude. A turn to the right, then left between already occupied houses leads them to higher levels. Ameel and Gee are slightly out of breath now. At last the luggage enters a front garden, which is grassy and fenced off, to a property and stops at the front door. It is a simply built symmetrical house made out of pre-fabricated material.

'Finally,' mutters Cam.

'It has been rather a trek,' agrees Posall.

They all turn their backs on the awaiting house and admire the view. The house is situated a third of the way up a mountain side amongst the pot hills that are all now in plain sight. Many other houses are strewn across the rugged landscape. The houses are not crammed into the vast space like rabbit hutches but are spread out with ample land surrounding each one. In the lowlands near the coast of the Shallows, on Isca, they can see people who appear tiny, going about their business. They hadn't realised just how high up they had walked. Beyond the coast lines and into the mainland the view is good because the sky is clear and blue. They can see more than just grassland and a smudged horizon. The different habitats are so distinctive that they all stand and point to the plains, forests and mountains. The planet of Teeria is vast and beyond belief unless you have seen it with your own eyes.

'Wow,' says Ameel, absolutely staggered by what is on her new front doorstep.

'I second that. Wow indeed love.' Posall is also in ore of the view.

'Let me take a photo. Stand in front of the view. This is a day to remember.' Gee hustles them into position and takes a picture, wanting the camera to capture the great expanse and beauty of their new home.

'Can we go in now? I need a drink, I'm so thirsty.' Cam brings them all back to reality as usual.

'Good idea Son. Now we need to unlock the door.' He looks slightly miffed as they haven't been given a key.

'Maybe it isn't locked?' suggests Cam.

With that he goes to the door and presses down the handle. It opens easily.

'Nice one Brov.' Gee isn't far behind and looks over her brother's shoulder as he opens the door and they peer in.

Posall steps past his offspring and takes the lead. All of them are stood on a hard wearing carpet in a large vestibule. There are stairs to the right leading the way to the bedrooms and bathroom. Off the vestibule are doors to a kitchen towards the back of the property, a dining and living area to the left and to the right, a large room with the dual purpose of a study and library.

The luggage that has been their quiet chaperone, moves into the property and comes to rest beside a side unit. The side unit stands to the right of the doorway. Posall notices that the luggage has stopped there for a reason. On the side unit is a binder with the words, "Welcome. Please read me on entering this property." Next to the thick binder are four strange looking objects reminding Cam of crash helmets worn when riding the old fashioned motorcycles his father has told him about.

'We best do as asked. Is there anywhere to sit down? My feet are aching,' says Posall.

'This way I reckon.' Cam gets the binder and then heads towards the door at the end of the hallway.

It takes them into an open planned kitchen. It has been kindly left with emergency provisions before their personal goods, appliances and larger luggage arrives.

Ameel fills up a pot of water to heat up on the censored hot plate and sets to work finding all that's needed to make a hot cup of tea for them all. She notices a very large cardboard box in a corner of the kitchen labelled "Trade". She initially ignores the box, as it is another puzzle to solve, knowing that all will become clear with time. Posall sits down at a table in front of a very large window and gazes out taking it all in. Cam fetches the strange objects and Gee's curiosity takes her for a quick look around the whole interior of the property.

Once everyone has sat down Posall opens up the very thick binder and starts at the beginning. It gives background knowledge of Teeria then the basics, like the amenities found on Isca. Certain protocols are in place for the first full day on arrival, which have to be followed. They have to stay in the property until they have had their inoculations and wait for the remaining luggage to arrive that's due anytime. The inoculations are given to all newcomers to help aid the immune system to get used to all the new germs. All the Spognoffs have also had a tailor-made vaccination appropriate for their own DNA type against human ailments.

The binder also informs them it is in *their* own interests to read about possible hazards before leaving the property. Their eyes are wide when they read the word "hazard". The hazard relates to one problem in particular, a vicious insect. The Neapi are a swarm travelling insect that attacks anything in their path. It is an insect with a sting and has similar characteristics of our killer bees and wasps. It is double the size of our wasp and has the same kind of striped body but the colour of it spells danger because it is bright red and black.

Everyone is shocked and the idyllic bubble has been burst with this bombshell. They wonder before reading more if they are allowed to go outside. They read further. The swarms are only active through the summer of the Teerian year, and are usually only seen once or twice during the season. The Goshles learn that the helmets are in fact for safety against the Neapi.

The helmets are silver, streamlined, light weight and to be worn with no exceptions. The helmet is to be worn by the individual when outside during the dangerous time of year. All bare skin is to be covered, if only in a light cotton fabric. If a swarm approaches, the person just touches the temples of the helmet and a safety visor comes down, covering and protecting the face. The swarms are also monitored and an alarm is sent to any helmet shown to be in their region, in the way of a vibration. The person who receives the alarm taps the helmet acknowledging the warning and again lowers the visor.

Another important issue they are made aware of is

the fact that there *is* another civilization present and the chance of them running into each other is high, as Cam well knows. The aim in years to come is that we humans will be living amongst the Spognoffs. It is made clear that they are a very friendly race and that we have absolutely nothing to fear. Two pictures of a male and female Spognoff and basic information are shown to help the new families adapt better in their different surroundings.

A buzz comes from the front door just as they are reading about the Spognoffs general statistics and culture. Posall gets up stiffly and answers it. There is a medic and two large loads holding all their travelled furniture and personal effects. They can't get over how efficient the personnel workers are on Teeria. The medic is invited in along with their belongings. Gee mentions the spongy walk to the medic and he books her in for some basic tests as a precaution. The medic assures Gee there is really nothing to worry about and probably due to the cleaner breathing conditions. Once the Goshles have had the all important vaccination they then all get to work by unpacking.

After unpacking the majority of their essentials they stop and go through the rest of the binder. Ameel loves their new home which is a relief for Posall. It is bigger than their home on Earth. The kitchen looks out into a large square garden. It has been left as a blank canvas with some mown grass and two raised bed areas filled with soil and some tiny weed seedlings attempting their chances of growing. The beds are for growing vegetables, fruits and salads. They and everyone else will have to adapt to growing as much as they can because there is no currency. This will help transform and change the lazy ways of the human civilization and what has become accustomed to, with a new appreciation to learn and be as self sufficient as possible. When the Goshles read this part in the binder it gives a mixed reaction. Cam turned his nose up, Gee is always willing to have a go along with her father, and Ameel likes the prospect of cooking with fresh ingredients. She even added herbs to the list of plants they wanted to grow. TRF provides the electric as long as everyone pulls their weight and work. The electric is gained from the water on Teeria. It is harnessed in the way of kinetic energy and sourced from the great waterfalls and the sea. The Spognoffs had very cleverly managed to find a way to attract and use a conductor to capture the abundance of energy which is then taken to an underground station. It is then converted safely for the use as a sustainable power.

Ameel learns what the "Trade" box is. As mentioned they have to grow edible plants to be as sufficient as possible. The box is a start and guide for them. It is filled with goods that can be traded for other goods. There are bags of flour, cartons of juice, tins, seasonings, blankets, shampoos and other personal hygiene items and so much more. On top of all the mixed up items is a small folder giving examples of what can be expected to gain by trading say a bag of flour. A bag of flour would be traded for many small or a couple of large items because it is a key ingredient and lasts a long time. Ameel knows that it will be up to her to get it right with a bit of help from her husband and feels for the first time she has a purpose and is of some use.

Posall, Ameel, Cam and Gee were all aware that Teerian days were going to be completely different to an Earth day, but they had no idea quite how much. The binder introduces them to the facts. One Teerian day is longer than an Earth day. A Teerian day is thirty six hours in length. They learn that their experiences and ways of life are completely different and are now turned on its head. The Spognoffs have shown and led by example of how to get through such a long day by working or trading in the early sun and resting or relaxing recreationally during the long afternoon. They will then continue to work if required until the onset of last light - dusk. The Spognoffs do not live by weeks or months but just by regular numerical counts of the days.

The morning and afternoon is early and late sun; noon is mid sun; with first and last light being dawn and dusk. Their year is different and it takes longer to orbit the sun. A Teerian year is four hundred and seventy six days. Their calendar is called a cyclic rotation. It is split into five climatic conditions like our seasons but unlike ours, which are now blurred into one another, theirs are distinctively different. The Spognoffs live by and respect what the Teerian weather throws at them and they do not wish to fight or work against it but accept it for all it is. It is the basis and at the heart of reasoning and logic behind their cyclic rotation and way of life. The five cycles are Sakoron, Amary, Ohioté, Nuvdeau and Ariak-deau. Each one has a specific meaning and obviously relates to the natural order of Teeria's uncontrollable forces. Sakoron is the first wintery cycle of each year. The second is Amary which is without fail the wettest, but graciously recognised for the wealth and abundance of water. Ohioté means prime because after all of the rain the lands are green once again and bursting with continuous growth. The fourth is Nuvdeau leaving behind the gorged plants, trees and animals to the heat of the sun. Lastly Ariak-deau means the moon. Ariak-deau is the final cycle for the Teerian year which includes autumnal conditions leading into the onslaught of darkness and the shortest sun lit days of the year. Each season or climate condition is ninety five days long. It is a lot for any newcomer to take onboard but very possible and easily accomplished only after a manner of a few days.

The Goshles can now work out where they are on the cyclic rotation. They have arrived on Teeria during the early Nuvdeau season. They are quite stunned and taken back by the reality and differences of living on a different planet. It is a lot to comprehend and the reality of it can only be experienced and not imagined. Cam instantly points out that the summers will be longer which will be a bonus but then Posall wearily concludes while rubbing his brow that the winters will be just as long too. Ameel can see how tired her husband and two children are after all of the excitement. Reality has caught up with them, now that they are all sat down in their new home and so Ameel decides to return to the important matters such as getting the sleeping arrangements sorted out so if anyone is tired they can sleep.

The upstairs has four bedrooms so one is used straight away for storage. Cam and Gee have a room each out the back, looking out over the garden and mountains. Ameel and Posall take the largest bedroom to the front with an en-suite. During the last of the essential unpacking Posall catches his wife looking out of their bedroom window looking at the new view. She admits it will take sometime to get used to it.

The living room is off to the left of the hallway. It adjoins the dining area with a partitioned door. In the wall just inside the living room from the hallway is a small cubby hole. It is shaped like a thick oblong letter box, back lit in a purple glow with an electronic book placed in it. The Goshles previously read in the binder that the book is a journal and for anyone's use to report any findings when they have been out and about. Once the journal has been returned and placed within the cubby hole the new information is copied and automatically downloaded to TRF's headquarters. Appointed researchers make a preliminary note of anything of importance, which is then looked into and researched thoroughly before being officially recorded. Gee can't wait to have something to write in it.

Cam was surprised how interesting the binder's information was when they were all reading it. He had found himself enjoying and engaging the binder with his family. On Earth he had a cavalier attitude but here on Teeria he has responsibilities and is needed by his sister and parents. He has a better outlook and is completely on board with the new adventure like his family and feels ready for action. He wants to make his father proud and so looks forward to gaining a better understanding by finishing his study's and to then help in the overall grand scheme of things.

Chapter 5

The Goshles have eighteen days to themselves; the human equivalent of two very long weeks. It is like a luxurious holiday so they can find their feet before they get to work and most importantly adjust to the new day length of the Teerian calendar. They are all ready for the siesta each late sun and have difficulty ensuring it is just a nap and not a night's sleep. The nights seem long and it causes insomnia in all of them for the first twenty seven days. They find keeping up as late as possible before tiredness prevails helps, giving them all longer evenings. The very clean air on Teeria helps them sleep and they cannot get over how fresh it is and how green the vegetation is. When they are out and about getting to know where everything is and taking in the sights, they are pleased to see people swimming in the Shallows. Swimming is a thankful rest from wearing the safety helmets in the heat because of the Neapi. The Neapi swarms stay clear from the waters of the Shallows and rivers, so going for a swim during the uneasy Nuvdeau is a bonus.

Out of curiosity they all went down to the trade market with two bags of flour to see what they could get. The trade market is opposite the entrance of Isca's bridge. Each bridge has a trade market and each one specialises in something different along with the essentials. The Goshles were all astonished when they walked home as each one wished they had another pair of hands so they could carry everything easily. Ameel managed to get some seeds for all the main vegetables, if a little late in the season, but she is determined to try and get some late crops. Posall was carrying some meat which would last out two to three human weeks, and Cam and Gee were carrying toiletries and basic staple must haves, such as eggs, butter, milk and bread. Two bags of flour basically got a good shop of groceries and more, who needs money?

Ameel made a rough plan along with the others, in order to be as sufficient as possible. Gee is going to find out how to bake bread which they can eat and trade on a weekly basis. Cam surprisingly volunteered his services to get a chicken coop up and running so they have access to eggs and meat for both purposes. Posall will help whoever needs it the most, when his workload isn't heavy.

Isca is a marvellous island with plenty to do and there wasn't any need or time for the Goshles to go onto the mainland apart from the trading. A hover lift is available to whoever is interested in going to the mountain tops on the island. Posall, Gee and Cam go one late sun while Ameel attended to one of her new pass times, which is gardening.

When the lift reaches the top of the mountain it feels like they are all on top of the world, well Teeria's world. The trio are above a few wispy clouds and have a very good view all around of three hundred and sixty degrees. Cam can't believe it when he sees Tiarla and Ven step out of the lift having had the same idea; he is practically jumping up and down. They haven't seen each other since they were all on the space shuttle. They all act like long lost friends because they're so pleased to see each other, even though the new friendships started under a month ago. In this situation and place, a familiar face is worth a great deal. It turns out that Tiarla and Ven live on Isca nearer to the bridge each in a smaller house, slightly further apart from each other than neighbours.

Once they are all reacquainted and caught up with each others news, all five have their first real view of the Deep. Little is known about the oceans especially the Deep because the Spognoffs didn't have much information to pass on; because they generally don't like to get their feet wet. All that is known by the Spognoffs was the areas of which the Deep covers on Teeria; small types of shoal fish that make good eating and the knowledge that it has its dangers from large aquatic life. Sightings have occurred of giant sea mammals but nothing as of yet has been researched properly and is temporarily out of bounds to humans. The depth and terrain are to be mapped first and then the cataloguing of the marine life. A completely different department are to be drafted in to tackle the giant and mind boggling task.

Posall invites Tiarla and Ven back to see Ameel. Ameel is thrilled to see them both. Ven also has some good news for Posall behind closed doors about their work. Ven admitted giving into his impatience for finding out, with whom he will be spending the next few years with. He had made some enquiries in the office on the mainland where they all arrived where the check points are. His reliable source works directly under General Carter. They are all down to work together – Ven, Tiarla and Posall. The three of them are all equally matched academically and are specialists in their own field. Each will have an assistant to help with the work, making up a team of six. Posall is over the moon to hear such good news and can't wait to start. As much as Ameel likes having her husband around more at the moment she knows he isn't completely happy unless he is in the thick of it.

* * *

The Goshles make the most of the summer like weather of the Nuvdeau. They go to the mainlands shore, not far from the entrance of Isca's bridge, and indulge in beach activities, swimming, sun bathing and delicious picnics that Ameel rustles up.

For their first swim Gee is first in the sea with her skimpy two piece bikini on. She dips her toe in first and discovers the water is lovely and warm. The Shallows were given its name because it is no more than five feet deep. Gee walks in and it steadily slopes taking her in deeper lapping around her ankles, knees, thighs then waist. She then disappears under and pops up again enjoying the warmth of the water. It is a soothing relief to her aching muscles because of all the walking she has had to endure. She compares it to having a salty bath because there is no variation in the temperature with the water and still remains warm the deeper she goes. Ameel joins her daughter shortly after, taking it steady to start with to avoid standing on any sharp or hard edges but to her delight it is just sand. She is glad to feel the soft sand between her toes and gives them a pleased wiggle. Posall and Cam follow, not being so wary. Cam does a lovely belly flop which makes them all laugh.

Gee floats in the calm, unmoving sea, enjoying the tranquillity and view of the creamy white sands. She finds it a relief from the springy motion when she walks. She has had a check up and was told to wear a heavier shoe. They concluded it is an individual case and Gee is sensitive to the slight difference in the gravitational pull on Teeria and her father found that nobody else had had the same experience. Her heavier hiking boots help but do not completely mask the motion. She is coming to terms with the strange sensation because she has gotten a logical answer back.

Gee marvels at the untainted sands that go off in both directions and into the distance up the coast line for miles. A male Spognoff catches her attention. He is stood on the bank at the back of the beach watching.

While standing up and wiping the salty water from her face she looks to see where his gaze falls and takes in every detail. He watches each of her family members in turn and his gaze stops at her for five noticeably seconds and their eyes connect across the water. He breaks the gaze first, realising he has been caught looking and moves on.

Gee feels intrigued by the male Spognoff and could see he was very handsome with his long black hair, chiselled jaw and healthy tan. He was minimally dressed and reminds her of her Ancestry and Culture lesson she recently took about Native American Indians. He had an olive green shirt on but was barely wearing it, with only a few buttons fastened and the sleeves rolled up as high as they would go. He wore the full length hollowed leggings similar to the researched Indians. The leggings had some detailed needlecraft and tassels up the side of each leg made from smoked yellowy buckskin. A cloth was attached to his waist band like an adapted loin cloth for comfort and practicalities. He had ankle high moccasins which were decorated with beads. Gee also noticed that he was only five to six years her senior and wished she hadn't been so far away. She would have liked to have talked to him. The chance or a given situation hadn't arisen to talk to a Spognoff yet and she is so curious. She lets her mind wander while floating in the water and wonders if she will see him again and thinks how grand he looked standing there with a wooden pole in one hand, relaxed in his fetching outfit.

* * *

After the vacation with a twist, it was time for Posall to do what he does best. He was officially assigned the small crew he and Ven knew about and a hover shuttle to start the never ending research. His PhD's were a priceless addition to the personnel of TRF (Terrestrial Research Federation). He would go out with his TRF crew every six consecutive days with three off. In the evenings he would tell anyone who was interested in his findings. Gee was the one who couldn't wait to hear about her father's adventures. She wished she could tag along but alas her father said "no", as he did not want to push all the protocols and get anyone into trouble.

Gee and Cam carry on with their studying even though they told the universities back on Earth that they were taking a break. Gee is interested in the Cultural side, involving people from far and wide. It is the reason why she had chosen the course Cultural and Ancestry Science. Cam is finishing off his last year of Ocean Science and his knowledge of engineering is an invaluable addition. He is also extremely keen to carry on and follow his own interest of the oceans, especially knowing that the oceans on Teeria are pretty much undiscovered. Gee's study of Cultural and Ancestry Science will also be an advantage for TRF because she is a young historian from Earth, who will want to learn the unknown and undiscovered Teerian history. She hopes one day she will get to work along side the Spognoffs to help write their history together.

Ameel has settled into working in a school on Isca, only a short walk from home. She teaches infants who are fresh from pre-school.

It is break time and the children are playing outside. She is in her classroom tidying up after a painting session which is always loved by her little pupils. As she is gathering up all the dried colourful pictures she daydreams looking out of the large windows at the bright beautiful day. She loves to hear the children running, skipping, screaming and enjoying their playtime. She can see a female pupil who she guesses is about eight years old playing with a small ball. She is dressed in a long sleeved red tunic, white skirt and tights.

All of a sudden Ameel drops the paintings which float and scatter across the floor. From out of nowhere she sees a speeding bright red cloud heading for the young girl. It is a swarm of Neapi and they have their target. The little girl already has her helmet on and manages to get the visor down in time before the Neapi ram into her. The Neapi knock her so hard she is flung clean off her feet and into the air, landing a foot away from where she was playing. The Neapi haven't left her alone. Ameel thinks quickly, along with the other teachers who also witnessed the terrible event. Ameel grabs her helmet and gets an extinguisher, which contains solidified carbon dioxide – (dry ice), on her way out to the defenceless girl. When the teachers reach the young girl she is already on her feet trying to get away from the swarm. Ameel tells her to stand absolutely still while her and the other teachers spray the Neapies with the dry ice. It works instantly and the swarm disperses immediately. Some of the Neapi got stuck in the girls clothing as their natural response is to automatically sting the target first. The teachers gingerly pull the dead Neapi out of the clothing and bag them for research. Ameel holds one in her gloved hand. She is staggered by how big it is. The sting is as big as a large rose thorn which hooks downwards. The body is fat and plump and decorated in jagged stripes of bright blood red and black. It *is* an insect because of its six black segmented legs. It has wide oval brown eyes and two antennae. 'You are a horrible and evil looking bug,' she mutters in disgust.

The head teacher takes the girl in who only has superficial injuries but is obviously shaken up. Ameel and the others take all the other children in who had watched the whole thing. The teachers don't understand why there was no warning. Ameel intends to find out, not wanting to witness such a distressing attack again. If the alarms go off the children are normally bought in straightaway to avoid such an attack. All the children look shook up and are unsettled so they are let out of school early.

Ameel gets home early and feels unsettled too. She contacts Posall knowing he will settle her nerves. He will also know who to talk to, and sort out the reason why there was no warning of the incoming Neapi. He returns her call within a human half an hour with some good news. The readouts from the monitoring systems had shown that the scanners weren't set sensitively enough for small swarms. It was easily readjusted and it shouldn't happen again. Posall is very aware that something like that can't happen again while his wife is in the proximity of young children because she can't handle the innocent and vulnerable being attacked in such a callous way. She would rather give up her job if it happened again and in their current situation that wouldn't do. She is soft hearted and that is why Posall loves her.

Ameel realises she has something of use to put in the journal and also adds the course of action she took and the problem with the scanner's sensitivity and how it should be avoided again. She also asks a simple question, 'How do the Spognoffs cope with the Neapi?'

Chapter 6

Gee crouches and takes in her surroundings. She is hiding her presence amongst some undergrowth on the edge of a glade. To the right of her is a clearing. On the north side of the clearing is the entrance to a cave; the home of the local Gladestine tribe of the Spognoffs. She watches the shuttle leave with her father onboard and a fellow Spognoff who is their guide. The shuttle is an open topped vessel holding up to eight people. To the rear behind the seating is a large storage area for all of their equipment. This is where Gee managed to hide. She snuck in when the shuttle came to pick up her father, Ven and Tiarla to take them to work. The pick up point is at the Isca Bridge entrance alongside the early traders. She went unnoticed because of the amount of people going about their duties and trading. It was easy to slip in amongst the equipment; making the most of her father and the others, who acted unknowingly like a diversion. She was concerned it would be harder to get out unseen but she kept one of the doors slightly ajar. She threw herself out into the undergrowth once the opportunity arose when the shuttle slowed down to turn into the clearing. She was very pleased at pulling off such a plan.

Gee had pleaded with her father to let her join him last night as it's his last day of work of his long working week. Every sixth, seventh, eighth and ninth day is free for her from studying. He wouldn't give into her persuasive arguments of wanting to see the mainland. She wanted to see more than the grass plains and seas. Beyond the plains is where her curiosity lies. To start with she loved the sight of the flat plains and nothingness that went on for mile upon mile. The plains are like a vast meadow filled with different grasses and wild flowers that are very untouched. She is like a sponge, always wanting to know and see more, and so this is why she took the risk of being caught by her father or even worse by TRF personnel who are very strict. The grounds amongst the trees are no longer flat and uninteresting. She had known when she was back in the cargo area of the shuttle it was no longer flat, as she got flung hard into the doors when they started to travel up hill. The ride was very bumpy and uneven for her, but she didn't mind.

All is quiet in the clearing again. The clearing is surrounded by wild shrubs, brush and trees that are the tallest she has ever seen. The entire flora is unknown to her which gives her an odd feeling. She knew of many floras such as trees and wild flowers on Earth but here, she has to learn again like a young child would do when growing up. She looks into the clearing and sees a stone circle that has been made up with oblong, smooth, grey boulders. In the center of the stones is ash and charred wood of thick branches that haven't quite burned from the remnants of an old fire. There doesn't seem to be any way out of the clearing but she had seen the shuttle go through a small gap in the thicket that is easily missed, up a narrow track.

While hiding and getting acquainted with her surroundings, she sees a huge rock face above the cave opening. The rocky surface of the exterior to the cave disappears in all three directions left, right and up, amongst the forest that camouflages it. She can't see where the rock face ends. She takes in her immediate surroundings and her senses come alive, noticing the fresh smell of the air and hearing an abundance of song from the native bird like creatures. It is very dry under foot with it being late in the Nuvdeau. She watches the cave entrance as a male Spognoff exits and heads towards her side of the clearing. As he gets closer she recognises him from the beach, the one who had briefly been watching her. He is minimally dressed as it is hot and carrying a carved wooden pole, six foot in length. He has many similar human features and his skeletal structure is more or less identical. Both the male and female Spognoff's stand tall and slim. The male Spognoff has a smooth and light walk without making a sound as he enters the tree canopy.

On deciding to follow him Gee picks up her cloth shoulder bag and slings it over her head and shoulder so it sits to the back of her hip. She has her helmet with her but leaves it in the bag knowing she will feel the vibration through the fabric should there be any warning. She moves with stealth and grace and places every foot with care. Without hurrying not wanting to get too close to the stranger she keeps one eye on him and enjoys her new surroundings with the other.

There are times when she has to hurry because she is slow on the rocky terrain. He leads unknowingly up and down rugged slopes and in and out of the forest canopies. Her energy is starting to wane and is pleased when he uses a dried up stream bed to walk along. She manages to keep up from a distance. She isn't used to hiking and her legs are now tired and heavy making her feel like she is a lumbering elephant compared to the stranger who moves in silence. He doesn't cause any disturbance and his presence is unknown to the wildlife. Despite being tired she still manages to take it steady and sips some water and keeps up.

It doesn't bother her that she is in the middle of nowhere, the middle of the complete unknown. She has a streak of fearlessness running deep within and always pushes the boundaries, much to her mothers and fathers concern and annoyance.

The stream bed is so dry it is chalky in texture and dusty. Either side are gradual sloping gravel faces all tripping over each other. Over time, dirt and decaying debris had settled on the slopes giving rise to young sapling trees and grasses.

After ten human minutes the Spognoff starts to disappear down an incline of the stream bed. Gee hurries along not wanting to lose her secret guide. When she makes it to the top of the slope she is suddenly faced with a pool and the Spognoff sitting on its edge. She dashes into a thick bit of shrubbery and hopes she hasn't been caught. Her heart is pounding so loud she worries he can hear. She concentrates on her breathing to settle her nerves.

The male Spognoff is a lot closer than she had intended but he doesn't seem to be aware of her presence. She notices the long black glossy hair down his back, his muscular tone and perfect stature. Now she is closer she can see his skin has different shades of brown making it look almost mottled by coloured freckles. As far as she can see from her distance he is mottled all over.

She watches him get his wooden pole and remove a concealed, hollowed out long cap. It reveals a deadly looking spear. He wades into the pool which looks ever so refreshing to her overheated feet. He stands still and quiet for some time. While waiting for him to move she decides now is the time to eat. She quietly gets an apple out of her bag and enjoys the juiciness from it.

All of a sudden he moves his spear so quickly that Gee nearly misses it while taking a bite from her apple. He has caught something.

Every muscle in his arms are used to heave the scaly, slimy, gilled creature, he had so patiently been waiting for, out on to the grass bank. It is not too dissimilar to one of Earth's fish. The fish is very large to Gee's standards and she is impressed by what she just saw. The fish is flapping about on the bank helpless out of the water. The Spognoff splashes through the water and clonks it on the head within seconds of it being caught.

Without realising Gee had edged further forward and was no longer completely hidden. The stranger looks up from attending to the fish and looks at her. He stands and takes one step towards her saying nothing.

Gee is shocked that he has seen her and all of a sudden feels foolish and embarrassed. She turns and grabs her bag; gets up and runs.

She doesn't look back but heads the way they came. Adrenaline kicks in from the shock of her stupidity and possibly dangerous situation, moving her on. The wind whistles past her ears because she is running so fast and has the advantage of being light footed because of her gravitational difference.

She makes it along the dried up stream and into the rugged terrain in a very short amount of time. She stumbles up and down the slopes trying to get ahead.

She turns to see if she has been followed and then loses her footing and wrenches her ankle on the uneven ground. She falls down quickly and hard, and hits her head on a nearby rough tree trunk. She is sprawled on the ground nearly unconscious and unable to move.

Drifting in and out of consciousness she doesn't care if the Spognoff had followed. After trying desperately to fight the heavy sleepy feeling she gives in and passes out.

* * *

There is no hurry to the young male Spognoff. He didn't pursue the human. He had merely gathered his belongings and the fifteen pound fish he had caught and ambled back the way he had come. In time he arrives to where Gee had fallen. He puts down the fish and his spear very calmly and goes over to her. He notices a cut to her head which is still bleeding a little. She has fallen and landed on the rocky ground trapping her leg underneath herself. By the way she is laying he knows she had tripped. He gently moves her hair from her face and checks her pulse. Once he has found a pulse he seems satisfied and looks at her face again. He hasn't seen a human as close as this before let alone touched one. He is struck by how beautiful she is with clear skin and no markings.

Knowing that she is hurt and that he is unable to carry her, and the fish, he whistles in three short bursts. While he waits, he tries to sit her up but she lies limply in his arms and is hard to manoeuvre. He puts pressure on the head wound with a piece of cotton cloth. She murmurs, not making any sense which startles him at first but then ignores it knowing he must stop the bleeding and keeps the cloth in place. He sees that her shoe is scuffed badly where she had twisted her ankle.

A short amount of time passes by and a thudding noise can be heard coming closer. The Spognoff doesn't seem worried and checks on the humans wound that has now stopped bleeding. Appearing from behind the stubborn tree that hadn't moved when Gee had hit it with her head, is what looks like a strange horse. It is a Leeaque. The Leeaque is very tall and much, much bigger to what we are used to. It is strong and sturdy in its legs, neck and back. He is a magnificent beast and pure black with a glossy coat. He has a thick mane and tail with long hair across his tethers leading down each side of his strong front legs.

The Leeaques are friends to the Spognoffs because they have never had anything to fear from them. They have a gentle and very inquisitive nature and love a fuss from their individual friends within the Spognoff community. They are wild but come if they hear a whistle hoping for a tasty treat.

The Spognoff greets the Leeaque by reaching up and stroking him on the nose. The Leeaque nuzzles the Spognoff, greeting him gently making the young Spognoff smile. The Spognoff returns their mutual understanding by stroking and patting him around his neck. The Leeaque hints for a treat by taking two small steps forward and then sniffs the lifeless fish. With that the Spognoff gets acouple of scrap treats from a pocket in his waist band and holds it out to the Leeaque who takes them gently. One wrong move from the mouth of a Leeaque would cause loss of fingers or even the whole hand. The Leeaques are generally herbivores but also eat the odd fish if clumsily grabbed in a lengthy battle of wills, or if one is kindly caught for them.

Saying nothing the Spognoff points towards the young woman. The satisfied Leeaque sniffs her head and her hair gets sucked up and tickles his large nostrils. The Spognoff then taps the Leeaque on the leg and the Leeaque lays down coming to rest on his knees. Then the Spognoff picks up the human and temporarily lays her on her front across the Leeaque's broad shoulders. He covers the fish in some cloth and straps it to his back and gathers up his possessions then swiftly jumps up and straddles his legs astride the Leeaque. Now that he can support the human, he sits her up in his arms. He nudges the Leeaque who then stands. The Spognoff holds the human with one arm along with the spear and wraps a tuft of long hair from the Leeaque's mane around his hands so he can steady himself. A squeeze and grip of the rider's strong legs moves the Leeaque forward and then they are galloping off to the Spognoff's home. The ride is short because of the animal's great size, making light work of the journey.

Chapter 7

Gee wakes and realises she is laying on her front on a hard covered surface. It is dark and gloomy and hard to make out where she is. It looks like a cave. She feels something tugging at the back of her shirt. All of a sudden the shirt fabric is pulled up a little way. She jumps realising she isn't alone.

'Please don't hurt me!' Gee shrieks, trying to get up, but feels a strong weight across her shoulders and legs. She is unable to move an inch. A female speaks who Gee cannot understand as she is talking in a different language. The grip is tightened much to Gee's alarm. Gee squirms and pleads with the unknown voice. There is now only silence in the air. She flinches when she feels something gently touching her back. Then she feels a warm wet dabbing motion then something drying it. Gee manages to strain her neck now that her captor has relaxed a little to see who has pinned her down and her eyes are wide.

'Please, please... let me go.'

A male Spognoff, who she recognises from her disastrous sight seeing trip, and an elderly female Spognoff look at her, and then without saying anything they let her go. She moves so quickly it takes the Spognoff's by surprise. She launches herself at the male who is in her way of escape. She pushes against his chest to unbalance him with all of her strength, in hope of taking him by surprise, but he doesn't move and is stood fast to the spot. He grabs her by the hands and restrains her. Gee screams, so desperately wanting to escape. He puts one hand over her mouth, and holds her hands with the other then speaks.

'You are still delusional. You were hurt. We have been looking after you. You had a cut to your head and a bad graze to your back,' the male Spognoff says with a deep tone.

Gee can't help but think if he is helping then what's the reason for being so rough? This approach frightens her. His hands are like iron grips with no give. If her eyes were any wider they would pop out of their sockets and she is breathing so hard she feels like she may pass out.

The female leaves knowing he has the human under control. The male Spognoff pulls Gee close to his face leaving her standing limply on the tip of her toes. He gently takes a lock of her hair in his large rough looking hand and brings it to his nose to smell the scent, pausing then takes another sniff. He turns her head with the hand that was over her mouth to look at her cheeks and ears. They are stood right up against each other and she can feel his body warmth through her clothes. He lets go of her hands and touches the soft skin on her face. Gee dare not even try to escape again and stands still. He moves her hair over her shoulder and his face comes close to hers looking briefly into her eyes, but then looks over her shoulder. He looks at her back but cannot see her skin because of her clothes and then places a hand around her waist and touches the skin on her lower back under her shirt. He moves his head back slowly. His gaze comes close, back to her eyes which are still startled and afraid.

Everything unthinkable is running through her mind.

'I am Lellan Weebwra. I will not hurt you. You are amongst the Gladestine tribe.' He lets her go after being satisfied with the uninterrupted viewing of what is in front of him.

'Lel…Lellan, I'm… G…Gee,' she says just about audible. 'I have heard about your tribe. You have helped our people,' she says trying to be more

77

composed.

'That is correct,' he says evenly.

'You can understand me? And you speak our human language very well?' she says surprised.

'Some of us have learnt your language. We hope your kind will try to learn ours,' he says shortly.

Gee desperately wants to gain her way out of this unsure situation, 'If you show me the way out I will put your wishes forward?' She is still stood on the spot where he left her looking like a rag doll in comparison to him who is stood tall and upright.

Lellan just nods, never taking his eyes off her and it is not the reaction Gee had hoped for. 'Can I go…? I need…'

'Why were you following me?' Lellan ignores her plea.

'It was you who found me?'

'Yes. Why were you following me?' His tone is firmer now, wanting the answer.

'I… I was curious about the mainland and wanted to see more. I then saw you come into the forest and curiosity got the better of me. I felt safe not being alone, knowing there was someone close by. Bloody stupid trusting a complete stranger,' she mutters, 'but then you saw me and well, I ran and I fell… How did you know I was following you?'

'The fruit you eat would have been a certain giveaway if not for the walking. You are a very noisy walker and I heard every mouthful eaten.'

'Oh…' Gee is amazed at how good his hearing is and thought she was quieter with her own walking now she has a spring to her step.

'You are not supposed to be over here!' Lellan's tone is firm, gruff and vibrates through her.

Gee jumps. He is concerned that she isn't taking the situation seriously and missing the point.

'Let me leave then,' says Gee in a matter of-fact manner. She suddenly turns and makes a run for it, heading out of Lellan's cave.

Lellan is in close pursuit and reaches for her clothing but she just shrugs off the unsecure hold. Gee comes to an abrupt stop when she exits Lellan's cave chamber only to learn that she is in an even larger one.

Gee is now faced with a growing crowd of inquisitive Spognoffs. She steps back and bumps into Lellan who is directly behind her. She forgets why she was running and hides behind him - frightened. She is even more panicked by her situation.

She stands behind Lellan trying to work out her own escape then hears the other Spognoffs and Lellan in deep conversation of an even tone. Gee cannot understand a word they are saying because they are speaking in their mother tongue. Their conversation doesn't last long and abruptly stops. Lellan then moves to one side revealing Gee who is looking more like a cornered wild cat with torn clothes, a grubby appearance and hair out of control.

They are all looking at her intensely as some have never seen a human close up. She doesn't wait to find out what will happen next and makes a run for it again, running towards a small opening to the right of the ever growing group. She charges her way through, running towards the natural light ahead in the distance.

All of a sudden her feet are not in contact with the stone ground. She is being held by her waist like the weight of a feather and supported against a Spognoff's side. She manages to look up to see it is Lellan *again*. She struggles with all of her might to get free, punching, kicking and screaming – completely losing control. She ends up on the cold floor in a heap with a thud, only to be picked up again by Lellan and thrown over his shoulder. She gives up fighting because she feels defeated and weak.

Lellan walks away from the freedom of the bright yellow light. She tries to grasp at it in a final attempt of pathetic desperation. Lellan and Gee are followed by the group of Spognoffs. One comes close and tugs her hair - she shrieks. Lellan spins around and growls at the Spognoff that is too close. Lellan moves Gee into the cradle of his arms as if to protect her and then carries on in the direction they were going. She surprisingly feels comforted in the safety of Lellan's arms as he could have let the others taunt her. She hides away and nestles down into his chest which is covered in soft downy hair, similar in texture to a black rabbit. Lellan loosens his grip feeling that the human in his arms has relaxed.

Lellan keeps up the momentum and doesn't waver with the extra weight he is carrying and walks for a lengthy distance deep into the cave then comes to a stop. She looks up from her silent sobbing through bleary eyes. Before them is a large hall carved out of the rock with the walls rounding and disappearing into the ceiling. Like an old Roman amphitheatre in the center of the room is a sunken circular area with five tiered ledges all carved from the stone. The ledges are covered in fur hides and Gee presumes they are for sitting on so the Spognoffs aren't sitting directly onto the cold stone. Lellan lets her take it in, in order to keep her calm. Once she seems acclimatised with the surroundings he then continues and walks to the center of the sunken stone stage to join another Spognoff.

Lellan puts Gee down and then has a brief conversation with the Spognoff in front of them. Lellan encourages Gee by giving her a gentle nudge to go and stand in front of the other Spognoff. Gee stands upright in front of a Spognoff who is older, clearly respected and wiser than Lellan. His long dark hair has pure white flecks and his brown skin looks aged with deep lines on his face. He has a kind, approachable appearance. His clothes are much grander compared to Lellans, whose are more simple for practical needs. The older Spognoff is wearing furs, plant and cotton looking fabric which interests Gee.

'Don't be afraid. We welcome you. We are the Gladestine tribe. I am Mogue. You have already met Lellan and some of the others.' He gestures to the crowd that has appeared around them who are now sitting on the steps.

Gee nods, stuck for words.

'Lellan tells me,' Mogue continues, 'that you fell down in the rocky forest and hurt yourself. You were not awake when he got to you and he did not want to leave you alone to the dangers, so he bought you back here. What is your name?'

'Gee. My name is Gee Goshle.'

'Well Gee, you have caused much interest amongst us. We want to help you get back to your family,' he leans in close… 'I'm sorry if Lellan was heavy handed but he was just trying to keep you safe and attend to your wounds, with one of our healers. He does not know his own strength at times and has not had personal contact with a human. We did not want to send you back unconscious that would not look good from either point of view.'

'Thank you, I really don't want to cause any more trouble. How long was I asleep?' says Gee still looking at Mogue.

'One night passed.'

'Oh no my family are going to be so worried. I hadn't told them of my plans. You see – I… I… snuck out.' She shakes her head with embarrassment and bites her bottom lip. She turns to Lellan looking very, very sheepish and close to tears again.

'I wish to thank you for your hospitality and I'm sorry I...I hit you. I didn't understand. Did I hurt you?' Gee looks so concerned it makes both Mogue and Lellan laugh.

'There is no need to apologise. You woke up in unfamiliar surroundings and I apologise for my nosey behaviour. I am not at all hurt, not even a scratch,' smirk's Lellan.

'No need to boast,' says Gee quietly.

'Well we will send word by the particle link communicator to TRF head quarters of your safety and send for your Father. You will have to stay in Lellan's care in the mean time, as he is the one who found you. Your Father will not be here until tomorrow mid sun.'

Gee can't believe that her simple walk has turned into such a situation. She worries about her parents fretting needlessly and she knows Cam is going to be really annoyed with her for being such an idiot. She thanks Mogue and is advised to go back to Lellan's dwelling in order to keep the peace and away from prying eyes. With that Lellan steps close to her and is about to pick her up again but she stops him. She feels she can manage and doesn't want the fuss. She starts to walk but feels shaky and limps because her ankle hurts from the sprain. She hadn't noticed it earlier because of fright and adrenaline. Weakness takes over and her thoughts turn to food and drink knowing she hasn't eaten or drank anything in the last day. Lellan is soon by her side and helps by supporting her weight against his. Lellan is taller as she only comes up to his shoulder.

They walk down the long corridor tunnelled through the heart of the mammoth cavern. The cavern has three levels all with low ceilings. Off the main cavern corridors are smaller cave chambers all carved out of the rock. Each home is individually carved to the occupiers specifications.

The corridor is lit with lights as far as Gee's eyes can see both left and right. She looks at the lights to see that they are in fact shallow dishes, with a small amount of liquid in them. Unknown to her the liquid is water, with a drop of illuminating rubber, added from a tree. The rubber alone is dull grey in colour and thick in texture. By adding it to the water a reaction takes place and it gives out light.

Gee is glad to get back to Lellan's cave chamber. She asks for some water because her mouth feels so dry. She sits down on a wooden bench covered in animal hide and fur for cushioning. It is very comfortable. He disappears towards the back of the large oblong hollowed out cave and retrieves a tall wooden jug and cups. He pours some water into the cups and he sits down beside her. They are both silent for sometime enjoying the freshness of the water. She feels dirty when she catches the sight of her hands and the dirt under her nails. Lellan watches her.

'Come with me.' Lellan extends his hand to help her up.

'Oh, can't I just sit.'

'Trust me,' he assures her.

He looks at her with such kind and gentle eyes. She gets up and follows him without question.

He leads her towards the back of the cave to a wooden partition. He opens it to reveal a very stylish looking bathing area carved out of the rock. She is so surprised she forgets herself.

'But you live like cavemen and you have a bathroom!'

'We are not "*cave men*",' says Lellan quite calmly much to Gee's surprise. He continues, 'We are as advanced as you if not more so and this is how we like to live. Now please take your time and relax. Here are some fresh clothes. Help yourself to the lotions under the mirror. The pale pink is Quwacum and very good to use for cleaning hair.' He points towards the mirror.

Lellan shuts the partition and leaves her to it. She looks around in disbelief and heads towards the mirror on the stone wall. The stone walls are a rich brown with an almost ruby red depth to them. She touches the wall, drawn to its beauty. It feels so smooth and soft like a car that has just been polished. It surprises her that it is not cold as you'd expect but lukewarm. She takes a look in the mirror and hardly recognises the reflection in it. Her once pale and flawless complexion has vanished behind a mask of dirt. She looks like she has had a roll in some dry dusty soil. Glad of the opportunity to clean up and have some brief time alone she looks for the Quwacum.

Beneath the mirror on a thin ledge are three wooden bowls. Each one has a thick gloopy liquid in it. The first smells like leaves, giving no clue what it is used for, the middle has the pale pink Quwacum shampoo and the third has a soapy scent. She picks up the second and third dish and puts them down by the side of the taps protruding out of the stone floor, next to the side of a large hollowed out stone bath. She runs some water, and then after looking around to make sure she is completely alone, she undresses and climbs in. She has a soak and washes her hair. She is grateful and relieved when she has freshened up. She puts the clothes on that Lellan gave her. They smell clean and fresh. She tries to work out what to do with the top. She ties and wraps it around her body the best she can. It is hand sewn and made from a soft salmon coloured cotton fabric. Next she puts on a cream skirt that comes just above the knee that is made in a similar way to the top with panels of fabric.

Gee heads back to find Lellan and her drink of

water. She sees him with fresh eyes and he sees her with his, now that she is clean. He is astonished by the attractive human before him. Lellan looks down at what he is doing and finishes off with a smirk. He gets up and walks over to help her tie her top properly. He is so quick she still doesn't know how it is fastened. He notices how much more relaxed she looks. She runs her fingers through her long wet hair to detangle it and sits down once again.

With a new and fresh perspective Gee decides to broach the subject about their first encounter of when she woke.

'Can I ask you a question?'

He looks up and gives her his full attention, 'Yes – anything.'

'Why did you t… touch my back earlier?'

'Like you, I was curious.' Lellan eats some fruit from the low table, in front of them where they are sitting.

He encourages her to eat something.

'Curious?' she prompts.

She then takes an identical bit of fruit that Lellan is eating. She has never seen any of the fruits before and wouldn't know what to do with them. They are both eating a bright purple fruit about the size of a pear but the taste is completely different. She concludes it is honey flavoured and very moreish. Lellan notes how much she is enjoying it.

'I had to see for myself when your wound was being dressed. I am afraid the opportunity had presented itself; I could not pass it up. I could not believe what my eyes had seen, so that is why when you were stood up I looked again.'

'I still don't fully understand.'

'Your skin is so clear and of an olive tone whereas we, male and females, have freckled skin. The male freckles are more pronounced in colour. You do not have any body hair to really speak of, that is what I was looking for. You are bald! It is amazing.' He touches the skin on her cheek to emphasize his amazement.

'Bald...thank you Lellan.'

'I cannot think of any other word to describe what I have seen. I am not used to your kind.'

'Me neither. I'm sorry I fought you. I had no idea of where I was.'

'It was not my intention to scare you, I understand your reactions. You did not hurt me, you could not, because you and your kind *are* weaker than me - us.'

Gee nearly chokes on her second piece of purple fruit. She mumbles to herself, 'That wasn't in the stats.'

'What stats?'

'When my family arrived we were given a folder of general information of where we were living and about your kind. It said nothing about your formidable strength and the differences like me being "bald",' she laughs. 'And that you are not. How are we supposed to settle amongst you in time, if we do not know all the facts? It makes us look like fools.'

'We can help each other. This is new for both of us.'

'How?'

'Let us start right here. Look at my back.' She shyly looks up and is about to say hang on a moment but Lellan jumps to his feet, strips off his top garments and turns around to show his back.

'Wow your back is covered in fur; I thought it was just your chest.' She is now on her feet and pleased she hadn't stopped him.

'Fur... it is our body hair. Fur is what your kind would associate with a pet animal. I am not a pet.'

Gee chuckles, 'Well being "bald" or having "fur", what does it matter? May I?' She steps closer and wants to touch the hair.

'Fairs fair,' concludes Lellan standing relaxed.

She gently touches the hair on his back to assess the texture and it does feel like fur. She smiles to herself. She then starts to run her fingers through it. The hair is jet black and has a glossy shine. It is very, very soft and fine but densely thick. It covers his broad shoulders and tappers down following the shape of his back. The hair is thickest in the middle, down the length of his spine, giving a tufty ridge. She can see why she was over powered by this creature stood before her because his torso is pure muscle. She moves his long black hair to one side to see how high the tufty ridge goes. It goes up into his hair line. Lellan turns to stop her. She doesn't shy away this time and they hold each others gaze. His eyes are vibrant with the colour of magenta and cyan. Her eye is then drawn to his skin on his cheek bones. They are noticeably a different colour. A blush of light blue fades quickly to its original colours of brown.

'Your face?' She tries to touch but again he stops her and turns his face away from her so she can't see. He doesn't speak.

'Why did you stop me? You didn't give me a choice when you wanted to look.' She isn't at all worried about pushing him for an answer.

He turns back to her, 'The touching between a male and female Spognoff, however slight, is sacred. I haven't been touched by a female before and *you* are not our kind.' He looks uncomfortable with a deep look of fire in his eyes.

'I'm sorry, I didn't know.' She sits down to defuse the situation, alarmed by his change and the look in his eyes.

He sits beside her. His chiselled jaw is set and every muscle in his arms are tensed and strained. She notices that he is blushing red now on his cheekbones but says nothing about it.

'I really didn't want to make you cross again.' Due to his revelation she decides against bravely patting his hand and giving moral support this way.

'I... I could have let you carry on but... we... are not used to it. When we partner up it is different, but when we are not we do not like to get distracted with the opposite sex.' He struggles with the delicate subject.

'Oh I see. Ah ha. So... because I stroked your hair it caused a distraction and that's not good - right?' A sound comes from his throat of a low rumbling growl at her comment. She jumps a little at the powerful noise but sees that he isn't so troubled and tense.

Gee thinks it is odd that her touch was a distraction but does not say any more on the matter and doesn't dare ask about the colour change of his skin. She changes the subject.

'Why were you so intent on sniffing my hair?'

'It smelt like nothing I have ever come across before. The depth of it was intoxicating.'

'Depth?'

'Yes depth. We have very sensitive noses. We can recognise many scents *within* a smell giving it depth. Your hair had a peculiar smell. I could pick out an unknown plant leaf and some sweet pollen. It now smells of the Quwacum plant. It is made from the Quwacum's swollen leaves, and when snapped oozes the thick pink liquid you used.' He takes a dry lock of her hair in his hand and sniffs, adding, 'I can still smell your previous wash as it was very strong. Quwacum has a milder smell and washing properties.'

Gee is taken aback by how much Lellan can learn simply by smelling her hair. Reality obviously hasn't dawned on her. He senses that she seems dazed and asks if she is alright. She explains that the reality of meeting him and the others has not sunk in yet. He attentively strokes her hair then stops himself again and gives her a shoulder to lean on instead. She closes her eyes and thinks about everything she has seen and learnt. She wonders if she is dreaming. She wants to know more and has to figure out if there is a way to come back again once she has been picked up. Gee falls asleep leaning against Lellan's shoulder during late sun. He manages to move her into a comfortable position on the bench. Quietly he covers her up with blankets and furs to keep her warm. Lellan had sat at the end of the bench for sometime looking and watching her while she slept. To him she is the most beautiful creature with fire and spirit. He remembers her from the beach many days before and was stunned by her beauty then, and this is why she had caught him out looking. He has never really been interested in females because he loves what he does. He is a hunter of great standing for his young age and has favoured his own company to enhance his gift. He is his father's successor and his name "Lellan" means 'leader'.

Chapter 8

Lellan is back at the end of bench again for when Gee wakes after her nap. He braces himself for the same of the earlier sun's saga. Instead she sees him and smiles. Lellan has become very fond of her smile. She is glad it wasn't a dream. She stretches and groans because she feels stiff and aches all over. He helps her sit up and then gives her a warm drink of tea. This she recognises and she smiles to herself knowing all isn't so different.

Lellan also seems well rested after a sit down in his favourite chair while she slept. After some time alone he is now happy to oblige in telling her anything she wants to learn. She asks about his skin changing colour and explains that her skin only blushes pink or red in embarrassment. She had never seen anything as remarkable before. This prompts him to show her, 'Give me your arm,' he asks. He runs his finger down the inside of her wrist. It tickles and gives her goose bumps. 'It is giving you skin bumps,' he notes.

'Goose bumps.' She corrects even though it doesn't theoretically make any sense.

'Yes… goose bumps…and this?' He runs his finger along her skin again.

'It gives me a sensation that tickles too.'

'Now you do it to me,' he says and she does very gentle on his soft brown freckled skin.

'Can you see? My skin works as yours does and has similar sensations it seems, but mine shows colour.' With each move of her finger a pale blue trail is left that shortly fades.

'Why is it blue? And…why…?' He laughs he isn't used to her being stuck for words and so he explains.

'The blue that appears is a pigment that reacts in the same way as when you get the tickled sensation which

90

gives you the goose bumps. It means it feels nice, even relaxing and the bumps or blue appear where the sensation occurs.'

'I saw you turn red earlier though.' She just has to ask.

'Yes. Blue and red are the two colours that our skin flush. The red is due to anger, frustration or ill health. Our skin is mottled for this exact reason and we do not have to speak to communicate because of it. It can be very useful and sometimes... very embarrassing.'

'Let me get this straight...' She presses against her forehead as if it helps her to think, 'When we touch each others skin and I get goose bumps and you turn blue; we really like each other's touch.'

'Yes – embarrassing like I said.' He bows his head.

'You were blue in the cheeks earlier when I was looking at your back... Oh... Now I get it...' *She* now blushes and looks away as she has full understanding and the added similarity, knowing that she has never slept with a male.

Lellan is about to press her obvious coherence due to the long pause and look away when they both hear a 'hello' from the cave entrance making them both turn to look. It is Mogue.

Mogue pops in and has a drink and some fruit. He informs Gee that her father has been notified and all is well. He notices and is pleased to see that she has cleaned herself up and Lellan is looking after her properly. He also hopes that she can put up with their company a little longer while she waits. Gee is now happy in her surroundings and is eager to learn more about the Spognoffs. Mogue is the leader of this settlement and will be silently pleased to have Gee back again under better circumstances to learn more of their existence and chosen path. Mogue leaves after a human hour has passed not wishing to interrupt Lellan and Gee anyfurther as they appear to be getting along just fine.

After telling Lellan of her own family of four she asks if he has family. She notes he didn't like to talk about it. He simply informed her that his mother died during childbirth, when she had given birth to his brother, whom had only taken a few short breaths himself and hadn't lived either. Gee didn't press for anymore information about who his father is as she felt it inappropriate after learning of such a sad loss of his mother and brother.

Gee has been fed to the point of bursting. Many of Lellan's neighbours have bought in food to welcome the visitor, from cooked meats, to fresh or stewed fruit. The meats are delicious and Lellan gives her all the encouragement she needs to try their foods. As we know the Spognoffs don't go to a shop and buy groceries like we do as there is no such thing as money. Instead they barter and swap goods, such as food or even simply help each other out. Gee likes their way of living and finds it fascinating and has plenty of questions which Lellan is all too pleased to answer. The more they talk and get to know each other the more he wants to learn about her. He wants to know what makes up her center core of morals and personality. He would love to know what makes this curious human tick who is sitting with him, as she has certainly caught his attention. She is more than willing to answer his questions but always gets back to her train of thought wanting more answers.

Lellan shows Gee where she is to sleep for the night and it is where she had woken up during early sun. As Lellan helps her settle back into the bed, she feels guilty about how she had behaved and a bad feeling of guilt keeps tugging at her sub consciousness. Lellan senses the difference and assures her that all is forgotten and she is very tired and should get some rest as she has had a busy day. He kindly tucks her in like a very tired child and pats her on the head for reassurance. Before long she is sound asleep again and Lellan watches over her for sometime before he goes to his own bed himself. He hopes that she sleeps well through the night as she has looked deathly pale all day.

* * *

Both of them have had a good nights sleep and wake when the new first sun arrives. Gee watches the young Spognoff, from her comfortable bed, as he goes about his morning routine. Gee notes he has changed his clothes into some very fresh looking cream leather leggings and a waistcoat which are highly decorated and set off his tan. He looks incredibly handsome in his smart outfit which is a big contrast from his hunting gear. Gee would like to watch him all day as everything he does is new and different to what she has become used to on Isca.

Lellan sits on the edge of her bed and is pleased to see Gee with colour back in her cheeks. Gee gets up and dresses into her new Spognoffian clothes. She is glad to have the morning with Lellan and savours every moment in the company of her new found friendly Spognoff. She has learnt a great deal already about the Spognoff community within the short time she has spent with Lellan and in hind sight, despite the trouble she is going to be in, is glad that she snuck out. She has a good feeling about Lellan and hopes to herself that she will see him again around the market near the entrance of Isca's bridge trading his hunted goods.

Once they have had time to eat, Mogue arrives to escort them to the clearing in front of the cave to meet up with Gee's father. Gee and Lellan follow Mogue slowly. Gee isn't looking forward to what's coming as she knows she has worried her parent's sick and made herself look like an idiot. Lellan doesn't want to send her on her way like a scolded animal after getting to know her and feels uncomfortable with the uncertainty that he may not be able to see her again. When they get to the cavern's mammoth mouth, Posall and Cam are both waiting to the far side of the clearing for her arrival. They both look tense.

On leaving her chaperones, Gee walks past the stone circle and then turns to look at both Mogue then Lellan who are watching and slowly following her reluctant steps. There is a connecting look between Gee and Lellan.

'Can I have a word please?' Instantly she can hear that her father has a sharp tone.

They take a couple of steps away, out of what they think is earshot of the two Spognoffs.

'I'm sorry Father. I was wrong,'

'What the hell were you thinking?'

'Could we do this later...? At home?' She is conscious of being watched by Lellan and Mogue and doesn't want an embarrassing scene.

'No - this can't wait. I will have calmed down later and I don't want to. Your Mother has been having a terrible time and the worry you caused us both – well you couldn't imagine. I have never made so many cups of that blasted camomile tea before. We were at our wits end and then thankfully we hear that you are alright. Your Mother then begins chirping in my ear all night. We are both very cross. You could have jeopardized my work here, and hers. I know that you, out of all of us, was very excited to come here and learn, but that was not the way to go about it Gee.'

'I'm ever so sorry. I realised when it was too late. I feel terrible. How can I make it up to you both?'

'I don't know, but you are grounded.'

'Dad I'm twenty three. I promise I will make it up to you. How about I do everyone's chores for a week?'

'A month!'

'Two weeks – come on, I know I done wrong and as soon as I was out on my own, I knew I had made a terrible mistake – please… Father.'

'Ok… but you are not coming back again – do you hear!' Gee is about to disagree but is interrupted.

'We couldn't help but overhear. We would like to see Gee again,' Mogue intervenes, with a relieved smile from Lellan.

'I don't think that is such a good idea – Sir. She has caused many worries for us back on Isca.'

'Even though the circumstances could have been better we have learnt a great deal from your Daughter – haven't we Son?'

'Yes… we have,' smirk's Lellan.

'He is your Son?' Gee splutters in surprise looking at Mogue.

'Yes we both take the name Weebwra. We do not make it public knowledge because of my position. But hear this - I do understand the need of being patient with the youngsters and… the more we learn from each other, the more misunderstandings will grow further apart. If it is alright with you and your Daughter she can come here in her free time the day after each of her study sessions and spend time with my Son while he goes about his routine.'

'Sounds like a pairing,' Cam finally interjects.

Everyone had forgotten his presence.

'Cut it out Cam. I understand what you are saying Mogue, I don't want her to be let off the hook so easily.' Posall is now very interested to hear what Mogue has in mind.

'Don't worry about that my friend. My Son will set her to work. She will be worn out by the time you pick her up at the end of your day.'

'Maybe I can encourage my Daughter to use her sharp mind to decipher and learn your language?' says Posall eager to please; knowing all to well it will go down better with General Carter.

Gee winces with embarrassment at the reminder of yesterdays situation of her offer to learn their language, when she was desperate to leave as she would have said anything. She also works out that she has lost some of her free days and is back to studying the day after tomorrow and so will be seeing Lellan again quite soon.

Posall and Mogue laugh as the situation between the two parties have easily been dealt with. Posall is relieved to see that Mogue is an understanding leader and sighs with relief as it could have easily gone a different way. Gee is now stood to one side with her arms crossed as the conversation has been taken on a different course and she has nothing to add. Cam has gone back to the travel vessel and patiently waits. Gee glances up from under her long black lashes to see that Lellan is looking directly at her. He has meaning in his eyes and if they could speak his eyes would have spoken volumes. They are full of care for her despite him making light of what has come to pass. He wants to see her again and get to know her properly. She has touched his heart in an innocent way and he just wants to enjoy and follow the feeling he has when he is in her company. Her eyes are still enchanted by his because of the sympathy they hold for her. She doesn't hear her father talk anymore just hears her own thoughts while they look at each other and wait for the elders to stop talking.

Lellan starts walking towards her not breaking the contact between their eyes which makes Gee feel self conscious to the point where her cheeks warm up and flush a soft pink.

'We may aswell sit down for a bit. I know my Father; he will talk to yours for some time yet.' She sits down beside him.

'Are you alright Gee?' he asks softly.

'Yes I'm fine. I deserved my Fathers wrath, I was very stupid. I want to say it again. I'm very sorry for causing you this problem. Are you sure you want me to come back? I would fully understand if you didn't want me slowing you down and becoming a hindrance.'

'I told you before you have no need to apologise. You had hit your head and did not know where you were when you woke, and you had never spoken to us before. I completely understand Gee.' He sounds so sincere it puts her mind to rest, 'And as for you keeping up with me, we have to pretend to work you hard to appease your Father. You can help me out if you are able. How are you with a spear?' Gee laughs out loud but then gathers herself quickly, as she is supposed to be full of remorse.

Lellan grins and runs the back of his hand down her cheek and says, 'That is better. It is good to hear you laugh again.'

Mogue, Posall and Cam are all looking in their direction and notice how well they get along. Cam sees the way Lellan looks at his sister and isn't sure what to make of it. He scrubs out any unnecessary conclusions and instead he goes over and takes hold of her arm a bit too roughly for Lellans liking. Lellan lets out a growl sounding like a low rumble and feels instinctively protective of her. He doesn't understand his emotion and the growl is over as soon as it begun. Gee tells him it is ok and that she will see him in six days. As she is marched by her brother to the vessel she turns and mouths 'thank you'. Instead of Lellan taking his own leave and because of her brother's reaction, he waits from a distance watching her carefully until she leaves. He is puzzled by his instinctive need to protect her when he only knows her as a new friend. He can understand her brother's response after all he was simply being protective of his young sister.

Lellan and Gee both miss each other once they have gone their separate ways. Gee misses Lellan. She cannot put her finger on *what* exactly but she knows there is definitely more than one likeable quality about him; his looks, mind and his kind and caring nature – even if she had misunderstood it in the beginning. Lellan wishes he could watch her all day to satisfy his own curiosity of humans. He openly admits to himself that his interest in Gee run's deeper and it is not just because she is a human.

Chapter 9

A door of an office is politely knocked upon and a firm voice says, 'Come in.' A man then enters the office carrying some documents.

'Here are the images you requested Sir,' says a uniformed man.

'Thanks Bryne,' says Aidy Campion dryly.

He looks at the photograph images given to him. He is a polished man in his early thirties and of average height. His shortly cropped brown hair helps present a man who is manicured and clean shaven. Aidy is sat in a black leather chair behind a desk with an array of touch screen technology in front of him in a neat office in the heart of EMMA. The office has a glass front with the door to the rear which is where the uniformed man had entered. Aidy's office is beside others alike in a row, but his is double the size and positioned on the second floor overlooking the staff below. The employment includes the key workers for recruitment; allocated campaigners; and of course some are in charge of settling newcomers into their new and permanent homes. Aidy isn't in uniform but is smartly dressed in a crisp white shirt, black trousers and jacket.

'Anything else Sir?'

'Wait one moment.' Aidy spots what he was looking for, 'Who gave the orders for the fire strike on the Teeria shuttles?' He touches the picture.

'The Command Centre, Sir. They were carrying out Wardelf's orders,' replies Bryne evenly.

'Well it's certainly a good job that we missed and didn't destroy the first one on this take off.' He stabs the photo with his finger.

'Sir?'

'Because…' Aidy bellows, standing up, 'Gee

Goshle and her family were on that one!' He waves the images in front of Bryne.

Aidy hasn't heard from Gee for months. He needed to know why she had mysteriously ceased contact with him. It was unlike her not to return his messages and she certainly wasn't one for being evasive. Now he had his answer.

'Get out!' he snaps making Bryne jump on the spot who then takes his leave quickly.

Aidy sits down and looks at the photos again. They were taken by the protesters on the day of Gee's leave. She looks so happy and excited in the picture and so does her father. This makes Aidy all the more cross and he slams his fists down on the table. He now feels like he has lost Gee, she was and still is everything in a woman he wants. He had been keeping in touch by email and had even told her about the EMMA movement and was relieved when she had seemed interested in it. Long ago since she had shown an interest in EMMA, Aidy had decided that when the time was right he would ask Gee to join him on EMMA. He hadn't asked her sooner because he didn't want to rush her and he was also very busy arranging a future his end and working damn hard for it. He had had his suspicions that her father would be eventually chosen to leave for Teeria and wishes he had asked her instead of waiting but it had all happened sooner than expected and he has sadly missed out.

* * *

Wardelf Shooper had eyes and ears on the ground but nothing was found out, of whom was being evacuated. As a consolation prize, a rough time estimate for departures was obtained from a reliable source that needed some tortuous persuasion. It was then decided that the protesters were to be put in place as decoys to side track the authorities while secretive images were taken to ascertain names to faces near to where the shuttles were to take off. NASA had made it nearly impossible to infiltrate the proceedings but the underhand persistence of Wardelf's men, who were always lurking in the shadows, had paid off.

Over the years a lot of evidence was accumulated by the US government who finally proved that Wardelf's devious men were in fact now associated and connected to EMMA. Wardelf's men did what they were told with no questions asked and returned with their orders completed. His men had committed many crimes from theft to murder to get what Wardelf had needed to create and run EMMA.

The great Wardelf Shooper is now dead and has been for several months. The US government had tracked him down and ordered his assassination for terrorism and treason against the connecting countries of his terror. Even though Wardelf was responsible for many underhand methods to get what he wanted he had a huge and diverse following because of his goal. His goal was to create a safety net for earthlings in their hour of need and many praised him for his efforts in his remaining years.

When Aidy Campion had first arrived many years ago in the North in Russia, Wardelf had taken the young man under his wing as he could see he had promise and potential. Wardelf mentored him and moulded him into what he is today. Aidy was his chosen one should something bad ever happen. Aidy was to take his place and was always second in command when Wardelf was off EMMA on the ground. Wardelf knew of his enemies and had always made contingency plans when he was away.

With the loss of his mentor Aidy had a lot to do and

had given the order to the Command Centre to follow as Wardelf had instructed until he had a handle on everything and was up to speed. He was devastated by the loss of Wardelf, like many other followers, but he had to keep everything running smoothly. He had been continuing Wardelf's work and at the time, the Teerian shuttles were not a priority to him and he was too busy to care. The air attacks could have been a catastrophe and he could have lost his love – Gee. Aidy has had to grow up a lot in the past few years which armed him for the death and departure of his mentor. He is beyond recognition and has made, and done, some terrible things to get where he is today. Today Aidy gets what he wants and demands respect.

* * *

After three months of Aidy's full attention, EMMA is now running smoothly. While looking over the images to gain the names of whom has left Earth, Aidy thinks about getting Gee back. To him it is a positive sign that she had survived such an attack. He is positive in his own mind that she should be by his side so no more harm may come to her. He is however a little disappointed in her because she hadn't told him she was to leave and this has left a bitter taste in his mouth and he now plans to get to the bottom of it. Now that he has everything under control on EMMA he can afford to do his own investigations. He starts tapping the touch screens in front of him with his brain firing on all cylinders with the thought of getting Gee back. He hacks into what are supposed to be secured government files. He cannot get in too deep but is satisfied with what he finds. He researches Teeria and its inhabitants and learns about the ways of living to give himself the upper hand. He finds out that an off shoot of NASA is the Terrestrial Research Federation (TRF), who is running the show on the Teerian soil for the earthling's representation. He gains knowledge about the Spognoffs and is astounded to learn that they are very capable in the wonders of technology because to him they look like ape men. A smile appears across his unemotional face because he knows he can now use the Spognoff technology to his advantage. He finds out how they communicate and discovers the particle link up system. He is unperturbed when he finds out that the particle link can only be used on Teerian land.

'If only I could patch into a signal with the human federation on Teeria then... maybe piggy back off its signal into the particle link to an unsuspecting Spognoff?' he mutters to himself, 'Yes... That just might work – longshot. If I can get hold of a young Spognoff who is easily persuaded by staple goods I can make a deal.'

Aidy presses a button positioned underneath the edge of the table where he is sitting. Immediately there is a knock at the door and Aidy tells the person to come in. Bryne opens the door and enters.

'Bryne bring me your reader. You have a new and urgent assignment,' announces Aidy.

'Yes Sir.' The young uniformed man takes out a small object from his pocket.

It is the size of a playing card and nearly as thin with a shiny silver casing. Bryne hands the reader without question to Aidy. Aidy slots the reader into a docking feed under his desk and copies across the information he has found out himself. It only takes seconds to complete the transfer and then he hands it back.

'This takes precedence over any other work you are doing for me at the moment. It is imperative that you only report to me about this matter. Nobody else needs to be involved. Do I make myself clear Bryne?'

'Yes Sir,' says Bryne with no emotion just like his superior.

'If you stick with me and do your job properly, I can promise you it will not go unnoticed.'

'Yes Sir,' says Bryne again but noticeably with an appreciative tone.

Aidy brings him up to date with the matter at hand. Aidy has had many EMMA agents who have worked personally for him but they have all failed in one way or another. He is a hard man to work for and demands precision in all areas. He expects his personal agents to comply. Bryne reminds Aidy of himself when he was new and can see potential like Wardelf had seen in himself. So far Bryne's work for Aidy had been exceptional and he has always delivered results as if his life had depended on it.

The young man leaves and Aidy sits back in his chair looking out of the glass window. He sits deep in thought for sometime unmoved, with his elbows resting on the arms of the chair with his finger tips pressing together so he can feel the pulse in each one. He is pleased with his findings and knows it will not be long before Bryne gets him a positive result.

'I will be seeing you soon Gee,' he says quietly; confirming the reality of his morning's work with a sly chuckle.

Chapter 10

Gee hitches a ride with her father on his work shuttle after counting the days to see Lellan again. She can hardly contain her excitement. Posall is pleased for his daughter knowing she is old enough, at the age of twenty three, to take a healthy interest which will also benefit TRF. The information she recorded in the journal at home after her mini adventure was of great interest to TRF and they agreed there is no harm in her spending time with Lellan while he hunts. Lellan and Mogue were both pleased to hear of the news and even more so because they would get to enjoy her quirky company again.

Mogue understands her curiosities and thrives at the thought of the new knowledge that will be gained by her eyes. He welcomes fresh minds, especially hers because she is a young, untainted human. He looks forward to her views in time and welcomes the friendly addition.

The shuttle pulls up and Gee waves her father goodbye for the day. He is working north east of Roudruom where the Spognoff's live. Tiarla and Ven are in ore of Gee getting a free insight into the Spognoffian ways of living and of course the new sights. When they are no longer in view she walks past the stone circle and enters the mouth of the cavern. It takes her eyes a few moments to adjust because they had become accustomed to the bright and glorious fresh early sun light outside. Her eyes become aware that there is someone in the shadows to her right. It is Lellan leaning against the smooth wall. He had been watching out for her arrival. He didn't go to her and wanted to wait for her to come to the cave. He likes to watch her, like he would a shy animal that he hasn't seen many times, because she is new and different to him. He is not sure if it is her kind he is more interested in or her. He cannot deny that he had liked her company, her ways and her thinking had interested him, leaving an impression. She smiles at Lellan who hasn't moved. He looks thoughtful, then his distant eyes come into focus on her face and he returns her smile. It is so apparent that they are pleased to see each other by anyone who passes because they are caught in a very brief moment that leaves them standing in front of each other motionless. Each is feeling awkward in how to greet the other. Gee wants to give him a friendly hug hello but doesn't want to turn him a funny colour and he doesn't want to embarrass himself for the same reason.

They make their way back to his home to get ready. She has the same bag as before with the helmet just in case of the Neapi. He tells her she can leave the helmet behind but she feels a little apprehensive about leaving it. He shows her why. In the bathroom he retrieves the wooden dish with the pale green leafy mixture, which is the one she had no idea what it was for when she first smelt it. He dabs it on sparingly in spots on his temples, his neck, chest, his wrists and ankles.

'Wow that really stinks,' she giggles screwing up her nose. Then she sniffs the gloop in the dish. 'Why do you smell so bad and the lotion doesn't?'

'Thank you Gee; but you will smell just as bad as me when I am done with you!' Lellan has a devious twinkle in his eye and continues, 'Seriously. The body gives the reaction when the solution touches the skin – all to do with our own natural oils. It is a fantastic repellent against the Neapi and after a few moments the smell is not a problem.'

Gee isn't sure about having such a smelly goo applied to her but she gives in when he threatens to cover her from head to toe if she doesn't do it herself. She copies what he had done then ceremoniously covers her nose which makes him shake his head.

Lellan explains its origins, 'It is simply called the Neapi repellent and is made from ground up leaves from a Rue Tree. The tree has no other purpose and is very abundant across the mainland. Our ancestors would grind it up and then add water, making it into a sticky paste. It has hardly changed over hundreds of our years.'

Gee is side tracked from the smell while listening to Lellan and then realises he is right and after a few minutes she doesn't notice it. She likes to listen to his voice which is deep and tantalisingly charming. Lellan gathers a narrow rawhide bag with a long handle and his spear and Gee takes her helmet out of her bag, leaving it behind and then slings the bag over her shoulder.

They head out on foot bearing west of the cave mountain. Gee suspects Lellan has slowed his own pace so she can keep up. She does her best and manages quite well and keeps up with his pace which he has gradually quickened. He is impressed by her stamina. After an hour of walking they sit and have some water because the weather is hot. Lellan whistles in three short bursts then settles down with his water. She asks him why he is whistling and he simply says he is calling the wildlife, giving nothing away.

Within a few quick minutes they hear a thud-thud, thud-thud approaching from the dense thicket behind them. Gee quickly hides behind Lellan who laughs. She peeks over his shoulder still not daring to stand alone. The thud-thuds get closer then a Leeaque appears. It is the same one that helped Lellan the week before.

'W…What is he? He…is…gorgeous and so… big,' stammers Gee who is still hiding behind Lellan and grasping his shirt.

'This is my friend Han. He is a Leeaque. You have no need to be afraid, just careful because of his size.' Lellan moves forward and touches Han on the nose. He encourages Gee to do the same. Her petite hand looks like it should belong to a miniature doll when she strokes Han on the nose. Han gives her a gentle shove.

'He is reminding you he helped you nine suns ago and wants something of yours,' smirk's Lellan.

'Oh… he helped me? I don't have anything.'

'Yes he helped carry you back home. He wants a treat. I always have a little something for him.'

Lellan gives Han some welcomed treats and Gee gives him some too, all too aware she could lose her fingers if she doesn't pay attention because of his enormous mouth. She decided before she even left during first light, that as she was coming out into Lellan's world, she would trust him and be as open minded as she safely could. Gee is surprised to here that Leeaque's have become very partial to the taste of fish. The treats Lellan gives Han are dried scraps of fish. Lellan informs her that they indeed look very comical and clumsy when in a river trying to grab one. It takes them more goes than it does himself but they are surprisingly successful in the end.

'If it is alright with you we will ride now. I want to show you something else of our world before I fish and it is quite a long way to go by foot.'

'Yes, I'm here just to tag along. I don't want to slow you down Lellan,' she says bravely.

Her head barely comes up to Hans under belly.

Lellan admires her courage. He gently taps Han on the leg, making him come down to rest onto his knees. Gee can't help but make more of a fuss of him now he is easier to reach. She strokes between his eyes on his forehead and then behind his ears and then whispers into one ear, 'Thank you.' Han seems to enjoy the fuss.

Gee hops on first with Lellan jumping on behind her. He wraps his arms around her and gently nudges Han to stand. She says nothing about the rocky movement of just standing up, and hopes to God that Lellan won't let her fall off. She has to really lean out to the side to see the distant ground. Lellan instructs Han to start with a walk while she gets used to it. He tells her to grip with her legs as tight as she can and to wrap her hands in the long hair of Han's mane. It is course and dusty in her hand but she doesn't care because she knows she is going to have the ride of her life.

After walking and coming out of the rough and uneven rocky area, Lellan asks if she is ready to go faster on the stead beneath them. He squeezes his legs and Han moves into full motion. He thunders along the ground. Gee feels like she has no control of her body as she is being bumped and jostled about. Falling off seems inevitable to her. Lellan sits close against her body and holds her securely then whispers gently into her ear, 'Move with him'. He steady's her body against his. She understands what he means and synchronises her body with his. She moves with him and Han's rocky rhythm, and the three of them move as one.

Once she has mastered the ride she starts to look about instead of just looking directly ahead between Han's upright ears. Lellan has a firm hold of her and they are sat at very close quarters but it bothers neither of them. They head out of the lower rocky pot hills and undergrowth and head north-westerly from Lellan's home. Lellan guides Han with his legs. He takes them through a forest using a wide, well used trail. Gee wonders what has made such an apparent trail and then realises that each of Han's hooves are nearly a foot wide; they could have easily made it alone. They come out the other side of the forest and into a wilderness and grass plains that cover rolling hills. To the far right in the distance behind the gentle slopes are more mountains and forests.

A smile is plastered to Gee's face because she feels so free and exhilarated. This is better to her than any dream and beyond what she could have imagined. She is riding bare back under the watchful eye of her friend Lellan. She is now aware how close they are sitting but to her it is harmless and also in a wondrous way - a comfort. He asks if she is alright and she is. Han is very fast and hasn't even broken into a sweat.

They see many separate herds of other Leeaques. It is a beautiful and breath-taking sight to see their freedom. The herds are very large in size and have numbers far exceeding one hundred strong in each. Lellan steers Han towards one of the herds and gradually slows down. They join the rear of the herd and then walk along amongst them. It gives Han a well deserved rest because they have travelled many miles. While they walk along, Han grazes by taking in huge mouthfuls of grass each time, which is still slightly damp from the fresh first light dew.

Lellan and Gee chat idly when Han has settled into eating. She spots some young Leeaque foals which are the size of an adult pony from her world. Her mind wanders and she quietens. Lellan seems to understand that all he has shown her so far, is vastly different and a lot to take in. He has read and researched books and seen what Earth was once like and how it is now. He doesn't get into the politics but can see the differences between the two civilisations and cannot even comprehend what it must feel like to her and others alike. They amble along in a comfortable silence deep in their own thoughts and views.

Gee is still getting used to seeing the different

animals and plants. She compares it all to her own world. If a new discovery of an animal or plant was made on Earth it would have been an exciting prospect, but nothing new had been found for hundreds of years. Even before the loss of Mercury, Earth was certainly past renewal and has been brewed and rung out so many times like an old tea bag that all its strength had long since gone. It still isn't known why countless species were lost and catastrophic geographic events happened. Was it because of Earth's natural cycle or of man's intervention and hindrances, or both? The question is still open, and Gee's father and crew are only at the tip of the enormous ice burg of answering such a fundamental issue. Along with the help and a joint goal from the Spognoffs and their collaborations the long asked question of man *will* be solved.

Here on Teeria, and particularly to Gee's race, a new discovery is seen every day and it is hard to come to terms with. Due to failed attempts to save the longevity of Earth and its species, she would never have had the experiences she is having now. This saddens her. She feels that her people have let nature down on Earth and guilt consumes her. She feels very strongly about living amongst and not against and believes each action has a consequence. She is far too young to feel guilty as many of the losses happened before her time and through nobodies direct fault. She cannot help but feel disappointed and let down because of the defeated fauna and flora who lost their fight of survival on Earth. There was no compassion long ago and so many humans just did not care or seemed to have a true conscience. She feels very deeply and is a compassionate person and extremely intuitive for her age.

Lellan wonders what is troubling her so much, but does not intervene and instead tries to bring her back to the present, 'I read that on your planet these animals are named horses. Do they graze in such large numbers?'

'Yes they are horses but a lot smaller than Han here.' She pats his neck but has a sad tone.

Lellan senses the sadness in her voice and prompts, 'Tell me.'

'There once used to be herds of unimaginable numbers like here...' She gestures at the Leeaques. '...but now only small pockets exist and have been protected for thousands of years. We may have been responsible for their decline. We took away their freedom, their lands and erected fences so they couldn't roam freely and they never recovered.

You and your people have the balance right and that is why our people are trying to learn so much from you. It kind of haunts me somehow and the guilt far out ways anything else,' she pauses, feeling like an idiot for talking so freely to a stranger. 'Would you just *listen* to me?' She smiles to make light of her confession, 'I'm sorry to burden you. It isn't your problem.'

'It is ok. I have read about Earth's history and things could have easily have gone the same way for us. It is extremely unfortunate your planet has had a run of bad luck. We have had to learn along the way and very quickly in some cases. We are a different species at the end of it all and would obviously deal with a situation differently. Where we have failed in say - space travel - you have gained and that is why our two races are set on learning from each others negatives and positives – a win, win. I am a believer that good can be taken from the bad and in your case that is space travel.' He squeezes her shoulders which she appreciates and takes comfort in what he says to be true.

'You're so right. It is impossible to get everything right and especially circumstances out of our control. My aim is to learn and help as much as I can with your help.' She turns and her brilliant happy smile is back which is settling for him. 'Mogue spoke of "dangers" when I had had my fall. What did he mean? Everything seems so perfect.'

'We have the same kind of dangers as your world. My Father was talking about our wildlife in particular. We have many friendly mammals, birds, reptiles and insects but some as you know are not.'

'Like the Neapi?'

'Yes. Other insects, mammals and reptiles are deadly whether provoked or not. Some mammals make a snack out of anything that moves.' He feels her shudder while they saunter along on Han. 'We are safe riding on Han and amongst the others.' He gestures to the herd they are in the middle of now, 'However... they do not linger and it is not safe for us to come here alone on foot and the same goes for the smaller animals. There are deadly insects amongst the grasses. The Leeaques have very thick hair around their lower legs so if they accidentally come across a biting or stinging insect it doesn't penetrate as long as they keep moving. A single bite or sting from a spider-like Weegle or beetle-like Scurrier would kill one of us easily.

Other areas and habitats are home to deadly reptiles such as the Froudge which is similar to your Earth like lizard. It squirts a very nasty liquid from the pores of the skin if disturbed. Like your world we have felines. The Manga is our largest cat and of large proportions like the Leeaque. A single pair can take down an adult Leeaque quite easily – a big accomplishment on their part.'

'What do the Manga look like?'

'They appear from a distance to be only one colour – rustic, but close up they are many colours from browns, greys and a dull yellowy-green almost the shade of the grasses that have been dried by the sun. They have retractable claws on each paw and very large teeth that tear through any meat they hunt down. Their faces are marked with solid black lines against the overall rusty colouring of the hair. Each one is differently marked from another. We have had some close encounters with the Manga – some go rogue and two have entered our cave on separate occasions. We had to take drastic measures to save our people. We are a mere snack to them. I'm sure my Father will show you their hides if you wanted to safely see a Manga up close.'

'Well I may have to think about that – I'm not used to animal skins, but it does sound safer than the alternative of going out and meeting a real one in the flesh. There is something I have experienced since I have been on Teeria.'

'Is it about our wildlife, something I have not mentioned?' says Lellan hoping his surprise isn't ruined.

'No not at all. It's… well it's when I walk…'

'Go on…'

'The ground feels spongy and I feel light footed.'

'Have TRF checked you over?'

'Oh yes. I'd mentioned it on the day I arrived and then had a check up. In the end I was told it is simply to do with my sensitivity to the gravity here and would be better off wearing my heavier hiking boots. The reason I am telling you is I wondered if you experience a spring in your step or if you know of anyone else?'

'Well I am glad you have told me Gee,' says Lellan clearly puzzled. 'I have not heard of anyone with this "spongy" feeling. If it is alright with you I will tell my Father and maybe get one of ours just to double check with our different technology. I am sure TRF are correct and it does sound plausible.'

'It does, doesn't it. I would be very grateful for a second opinion. I'm glad I told you it is something that seems to be with me each day now. Thank you Lellan you are a good listener.' Gee sighs with the relief for telling her new friend other than her family and those of a human origin.

'You can tell me anything Gee, anything, not much can surprise me, except well keeping me on high alert that is,' he says with a comical smirk knowing that Gee will always keep him on his toes when they are in each others company. 'Now then, we are getting close to my surprise.' He nudges Han who has been happily listening and stopped grazing. The trio head out of the herd and away at a fast speed and make for the trees in the near distance. Once they are relatively close they slow down to a walk again.

Gee is happy to be in the shade of the trees because even though the early sun is still young its heat is strong. After a short time they stop and Han lowers down onto his front knees and they slide off down the front. Gee lands hard on her bum because her legs fail her and are left feeling weak, Lellan helps her up and tells her to walk it off. She follows him and so does Han. Han nuzzles her head frequently because he wants a treat or a fuss, making it impossible for her to walk in a straight line. She hears snuffling then feels her hair disappear up his nostrils which tickles him and makes him sneeze, unsteadying his whole body. She doesn't mind because thankfully, he has dry nostrils so her hair remains mucus free. She can't help but laugh at the giant's funny ways.

Lellan whispers to the pair of them to be serious and to cut it out to minimize any disturbance. Gee manages a straight line and Han walks along heavily with each step, like a scolded child. She can barely contain herself and has to keep her lips pressed tight together in order not to giggle. After walking in a concentrated silence close behind Lellan for a small distance, she is told to crouch down and Han is told to wait and to her surprise he does. Gee follows Lellan copying each step, keeping low and not making a sound. He stops behind a very wide tree trunk and tells her to peep around it. He watches for her expression then smirks because her eyes are wide and he see's, for the first time, a childlike innocence. She see's a creature. She looks at Lellan and then again at the creature, not believing what her eyes have shown her. He introduces the creature to her with a whisper, 'She is an Aterfly.'

A long and wide clearing is surrounded only by tall mature trees, bare soil at their bases and no ground dwelling plants. Lellan and Gee are stood in front of a tree right on the edge of the clearing where the Aterfly is happily grazing. Gee is astounded and can only achieve silence because her vocabulary has escaped her. Lellan takes her hand and guides her closer. They are looking at an enormous winged creature, predominately light green in colour with pink stripes running vertically along its body. Its long body, including the tail, is a staggering nineteen metres in length with a looming height of three metres. The thick stripes occur regularly with the same distance between each, starting from behind the fluorescent blue wings to the tip of the Aterflies tail. There are four wings centred behind her head, two on each side. They are very long and slim in width by comparison and are over half the length of the body.

Lellan speaks very quietly not wanting to disturb the shy creature, 'So…what do you think of her?'

'She is gorgeous. Is she an animal or insect? She looks like an oversized caterpillar because of her long shape and oh… she has suckers on her under carriage too, oh… yes… and, and a dragonfly because of her wings. Can she actually fly?'

'Oh yes. She is very graceful and less cumbersome in the air. And she *is* an insect. Would you like to feed her with some leaves?'

'Can we? I feel so overwhelmed by her it would be an honourable treat for me to feed her.'

Lellan goes and gets some very large leaves which have freshly fallen from a nearby tree. The leaves themselves are a couple of feet in width. They are now standing directly in front of the Aterfly with the gathered pile of leaves on the ground between them at their feet.

The Aterfly has an oval face with a wide thin mouth and a pair of perfectly round eyes. On top of her head is a pair of antennae with a small pink orb on each. Directly behind the antennae are three coloured upright tufts evenly spaced and identically shaped. The tufts are false replicas of the antennae that run along the ridge of her neck. The surface of her face and body is covered in soft bristly hair making her look very cute and affectionate. Lellan and Gee are dwarfed by her presence. Lellan holds up a leaf and waves it in front of her. She moves with a shuffle forward and takes it. Gee next gives a leaf not taking her eyes off the Aterflies adorable symmetrically oval face. When Lellan feeds her the next leaf he strokes her big cheek. She enjoys the petting because a contented low thrumming comes from her like a purring cat.

'How did you know she would be here?' asks Gee, nearly in a whisper.

'This is her spot every first light and early sun, and then at last light. She sleeps here. Once she has eaten she will take to the skies and will not come down until later with the onset of last light. She does not like the heat of the Nuvdeau at mid sun. She prefers to fly, catching insects on the wing and then drifting on the cold currents to get away from any heat. In the Ariak-deau she finds the warm currents and a warmer home but she seems to like it here during the warmer weather – plenty to eat.' He points to all the grassy vegetation in the large clearing at her disposal. 'This area is nice and open for her, the trees are spread apart and she keeps the brush down as she tramples.'

Once the pile of leaves have been eaten they go and lean against Han's chest; he had appeared quietly and had taken the weight off his feet and laid down. Gee pulls out two apples from her bag, one for Lellan, who is interested in the taste and one for herself. They watch the Aterfly who decides she fancies some more of the leaves. She shuffles along like an enormous caterpillar towards a tree. She then lifts up her front half and coils her tail to steady herself then carries on eating. Gee is so thankful to Lellan and Han for travelling such a long way and bringing her here. She enjoys this wonderful and enlightening moment and relaxes back further into Han's broad chest. Han purposely looks at her apple and makes her laugh. It is like having a cheeky and mischievous puppy about. She gives him the apple core which is gone in one crunch and she suspects it didn't even touch the sides. The Aterfly has had her fill and shuffles over to the three of them. She comes very close so they can stroke her oval face. Han just lifts his head then flop's it down again having seen it all before from previous visits. The Aterfly has a purpose to her brief linger as if she is saying 'goodbye'. She turns and makes her way into the center of the clearing. Her wings haven't moved, remaining tightly shut during their visit but now she has stretched them out to each side. She then flaps them gently at first then all of a sudden they are beating so quick she is starting to hover upwards like a helicopter. There is a lot of dust and debris kicked up into the air and Gee feels a little wind swept, but happy she didn't get anything in her eyes. When the Aterfly has hovered past the top of the tree line her wings do not move as much and she now flutters them effortlessly and periodically, gliding along in the direction of the faint breeze. They watch her until she disappears behind the distant rocky horizon. It is now getting close to mid sun and Lellan suggests that they had better make a move so he can earn his keep for the day and catch some fish.

* * *

It doesn't seem to take as long to get back to Lellan's favourite fishing spot which is where Gee had first seen him make a catch. Before Lellan fishes, he goes and finds a fresh water spring nearby and fills up their water flasks. Gee waits looking at the pool thinking how inviting it looks after the dusty ride back. Lellan gets back and sees she is cooling her hands in the water and tells her to go in. She doesn't dare go in and swim alone because she isn't so sure about what may be lurking beneath the surface. Lellan persuades her by arming himself with his spear and then leads her to the water's edge by taking her hand. Together they enter the water which is refreshingly cool for both of them. Lellan dives in, disappearing and then reappearing on the other side of the pool to clearly show she has nothing to worry about. Gee has a swim and then lies in the water on her back. Because of Lellan's colouring and skin tone she cannot help but notice his skin glistens now it is wet from the water. The sun adds to the effect making his overall appearance look polished like a pretty pebble in shallow water on a sea shore, which you would want to varnish to permanently expose the true colours. The muscles of his body, arms and legs seem to look even more enhanced than they already are.

Gee thinks to herself if he was human he would be classed as a gorgeous looking man who would be very, very popular with the women. Instead she is gratefully here with him in his wilderness and back yard. Her first impressions from the beach when she first saw him were right, he is very handsome. She wonders if it is wrong to fancy Lellan. She actually shakes her head trying to deny her thoughts because she knows absolutely that their friendship is special with no room for error. They have so much to learn from each other which may also be a benefit for others.

Even though she had banished such thoughts between her and her friend, she still wonders if it would be allowed in the future for a human and a Spognoff to be more than friends. In time of course the inevitable would happen but how would it be regarded – welcomed or frowned upon? If it was frowned upon – surely it would be a racist act. She thinks that surely if two people got along and loved each other, then they would be seen in the end to have chosen beyond race and colour, hairy or bald. She concludes that looks are what we are drawn to at first, then the personality, and then finally the compatibility if two people are to enjoy each others company or not. She decides she doesn't want to indulge in the politics but again is very certain that the questions have already been asked. She contemplates her questions, glad that Lellan isn't telepathic.

Gee lays in the water looking up at the clear sky and Lellan is poised with his spear not too far from her, like a protector from the fish. All of a sudden he stabs his spear into the water, creating a massive splash. Gee loses her ability to float and turns wondering what on earth has happened. There is definitely something attached to the spear as it is lethally being shoved about and if it wasn't for Lellan grasping it with both hands it could have easily have got the better of him. With every ounce of strength and muscle Lellan heaves the catch towards the bank in short but persistent bursts. Gee just stands and watches the action then snaps out of her daze and makes her way over to help. Lellan has just caught the biggest fish she had ever seen. It is so big she tries to help and gives him a hand to get it further up on to the bank. When it is laid out on the bank Gee can see it is easily the length of her. She is glad to hear it isn't a meat eater and there are no meat eating fish in these parts, fore she feared she might have been swallowed whole. Lellan finds it amusing and it tickles his humour when she doesn't want to return to the water. Han is eyeing up the monster fish. Lellan is happy with his catch for the day but has a soft heart and goes back into the water and gets some smaller fish for his Leeaque friend.

By mid late sun they get back to the caves. Gee is sad to say goodbye to Han but knows he is wild and happy and will hopefully be seen again. Gee tries to help Lellan by sharing the weight of the fish by carrying it into the cave but struggles and is left feeling like she hasn't participated much. After the struggle with the heavy fish, it is dropped off to Jjaym who is one of Lellan's friends. They have a deal between themselves. Lellan hunts and gathers the food daily then Jjaym and his female partner do the cooking for him and others. Jjaym is very pleased with Lellan's catch. Jjaym is about the same age as Lellan but a little shorter with more facial hair and a rounded face. He appears slightly stockier than Lellan giving the look of a chef rather than a hunter.

Gee is pleased to get back to Lellan's home to take the weight off her feet. His cave is cool and welcoming from the heat outside. He goes to get some cool drinks for them both and Gee slumps down into one of his single arm chairs. On first impressions of the chair it didn't look so inviting because of its wooden frame and imposing tall back, but it is cushioned and moulds to her body well and is very comfortable. She curls up in it after taking off her shoes. Lellan returns and smiles to see that she has made herself comfortable and gives her some freshly squeezed fruit juice which peps her up a little. She feels tired after the day she has had because she isn't used to being out and about nearly all day and on the go. For a Spognoff it is how they survive. She feels pooped and unfit at the thought of hunting on a daily basis.

A pitta patter comes into the room from outside of Lellan's cave through the opening of the hanging animal hide door. Gee looks around to see who or what is there but doesn't see anything. An animal then appears in front of her chair and jumps up onto her lap. She freezes not daring to move because she doesn't know if it is a friend or foe.

Lellan reads her reaction, 'It is ok – completely harmless. I call him Snoot. His kind, are actually called the Snootiabalare, but Snoot is easier so that is what I named him.'

'Hello…Snoot, nice to meet you.' She looks at him trying to decipher what he reminds her of. His face is similar to a child's teddy bear with rounded ears, similar nose which is not so long but squat, and little round black button eyes. His body and legs are like that of a small dog. The legs aren't overly long and are well proportioned with the rest of him. Finally he bizarrely has a tail that is long and fury like a ring-tailed lemur. He has a ruff fawn coat all over and is about the size of a fox.

'You… are… so… cute…' She smiles at Snoot. Lellan laughs.

Snoots little fluffy face comes very close to Gee's face. She sits and lets him investigate and his whiskers tickle her skin. His very hairy tail appears and wraps itself around her neck like an extravagant warm scarf and pulls her closer. She can hear his nose sniffing. Snoot sniffs every inch of her face, her eyebrows and when he reaches round to her ears she gets a face full of his fur. When he seems satisfied he jumps down off her lap and scampers off into the kitchen.

'He is adorable and very nosey…just like *somebody* else I know, but not so rough.' She chuckles and Lellan looks embarrassed, 'Is he a pet?'

'He *is* like my pet but he comes and goes as he pleases. I see more of him during winter when it is cold outside and also like today when it is hot. I always leave him out some water and scraps. I feel quite attached… to him. He only comes here, not to see anybody else. He is very loyal.'

'On Earth we have dogs but they are not free like your Snoot. But they are very loyal too and only want our love.'

Snoot returns after having a drink and jumps back on Gee's lap. He curls up with his tail wrapped around his body and enjoys a fuss and then has a nap. Lellan informs her that he won't sit on just anybody's lap because he can be a bit choosey.

Early last light soon looms and Gee is sad to be leaving Lellan. She has found him to be charming and great company to be around. Lellan is going to miss the earthling and wishes she doesn't have to leave. He walks her to the great cavern mouth opening while they wait for her father to escort her home. They both lean against the cave wall, both with the same thoughts. Lellan moves closer to close the obvious and uncomfortable gap between them.

'I have enjoyed today Gee.' He looks down at her

hoping she has too.

'So have I. Thank you Lellan.' She looks up shyly feeling emotions she has never felt before.

She thought butterflies in the stomach, were a myth, but now she knows they aren't.

'I will look forward to seeing you again. After all it is your punishment for sneaking out.' He laughs. 'I hope it was not too gruelling?'

'Oh I don't know.' She grins, 'Seriously though, I have had a brilliant day. If that was my punishment then I want more,' she giggles.

She looks into his eyes and he notices she is blushing, 'I have enjoyed being with *you* Lellan.'

'If you want more of me, I can certainly arrange that Gee. I have particularly relished in your company aswell. Now come here.' He pulls her into his arms and kisses her on the head over joyed that she has enjoyed herself too.

She stands leaning against him in his arms while waiting for her father, wishing she could stay.

Posall is on time and before she leaves, Lellan gives her another hug and an affectionate kiss on the top of her head. She catches a ride back and talks non-stop all the way home and Posall tells her to put it down in the journal except for her obvious liking of Lellan. When she gets home, she is very happy after the day she has had and joins Cam on the sofa.

'What is that bloody smell Gee?' Cam jumps up from his seat and holds his nose.

'Oh I had completely forgotten. It's Neapi repellent.' She grins.

'A Neapi repellent! Are you sure it isn't a Brother repellent?'

'Oh it isn't that bad once you are wearing it. It isn't noticeable and Lellan swears it works otherwise why would he wear it? I'm going to put it in the journal so it can be researched and you never know they might be able to find a way of making it smell better for the wearer and then we can ditch these horrible helmets.'

'She has a point Son,' Posall chips in. 'Maybe you should go and have a shower honey before your Mother returns.'

'Yeah she will freak out,' Cam reels, now standing on the other side of the room next to an open window. Gee hadn't quite realised how bad the smell was but undeterred by it all she does as her father suggests.

Chapter 11

Many days have gone by and it is now much later into the Nuvdeau. Due to her strange problem, Gee has been successfully checked over by the Spognoff medics from the Gladestine tribe under Mogues watchful eye. She will get the results in due course. Gee enters the house in high spirits with some good news after spending another day with Lellan. Posall had made it home early so Lellan had seen her back to the Isca Bridge safely. He only occasionally comes back to her house because he feels uncomfortable in the weak pre-fabricated material that protrudes from the ground, unlike his home hidden within a cave. Lellans first impression of where she lives was that the building looked uninviting, square and unnatural and it led to Gee trying to explain how comfortable it was inside and he understood it is what she is used to.

'I have to pack. Lellan asked if I wanted to go away for three days – back on the third. We are going to see his Uncle. I'm leaving at first light.'

The Goshles are all pleased because the summers seem to be extra long on Teeria. The seasons on Earth over time became merged with no clear indications of where they began or ended. The weather had become somewhat erratic.

'You will need a light weight coat honey,' says Posall, looking up from some paperwork at the dining table.

'Oh but it's so warm,' says Gee on the move.

'Trust me you will need it where he is taking you.'

'How do you know where he's taking me?'

'He told me when I saw him the other day.'

'Father...! Where is he taking me?'

'You will soon see honey. You will love it.'

With his last comment he shuts off from the conversation, deep in thought and back into his paperwork, before he is questioned further. He doesn't want to ruin the surprise. Gee can see her father is busy so doesn't press him further. Her excitement hasn't waned and she goes and packs. She rolls up the all important lightweight coat, still puzzled, and packs it into her cloth bag first. She is now convinced that the trip must have a good destination for her father to keep it quiet which adds to her excitement. She packs another change of clothes, consisting of a purple T-shirt and a pair of cream cropped trousers and the essentials, like socks. It doesn't take her long because she is always a person who travels light.

* * *

Gee is standing at the entrance of the Isca Bridge at first light full of contemplation. She cannot wait to find out where they are going. Lellan arrives on their ride of the four legged variety – Han. Han and Gee are pleased to see each other as always. Han bows his head so she can reach his favourite scratching spot behind his ear. She always gives into him and pays him special attention when they meet because she feels privileged to know him. Han only lowers slightly so that Lellan can reach Gees hand to pull her up. Gee sits in front of Lellan with her bag out of the way down by her right leg. Lellan has a worn leather bag attached to his waist on a long tie allowing it to hang down snugly behind his leg.

'Are you going to tell me where you are taking me Lellan Weebwra?'

'Not at all Gee Goshle. You will soon see,' says Lellan with a cheeky grin.

He hears an exasperated sigh. Lellan taunts, 'It is

making you, what is the word? Crazy...'

'Maybe a little, I'm not known for my patience.' Lellan takes her hand in his and gives it a warm and tender squeeze.

She leans back into his chest so that his chin is resting on her shoulder, both very much at ease with each other.

'You are a tease,' concludes Gee tamed by his close presence.

Lellan chuckles, 'Yes I am but you do think that I am "adorable" after all.'

'When did I say that?' puzzles Gee with a private smile.

'When you were comparing Snoot and I.'

They both burst out laughing. He wraps his arms around her body smirking because he knows the suspense is killing her. Before she can say another word he nudges Han who quickly goes from a slow walk to a fall blown gallop.

They ride up along the coast instead of going back through the open plains. It is more direct for Han and less treacherous. After half an hour of galloping at Han's full speed they turn right, away from the coastline. Gee is thrilled they have come this way because she hadn't ventured in this direction before. They travel through another area of open plains that covers most of the south coast and head for some trees that soon materialise. They enter the forested area which is flat and easy on foot for Han.

It isn't long before Gee realises where they are. It is the forest where they had met the Aterfly all those weeks ago. She wonders what could possibly be more exciting than seeing the Aterfly. It clicks for her - they *are* going to see her again. She gets Lellans attention by squeezing his arm that's wrapped around her waist and fills him in of her theory which makes him laugh. He also tells her she is only partly right. She is now miffed but happy for him to take the lead and enjoys her ride.

They dismount Han nearby the Aterflies clearing and approach her quietly. Han is following as per usual. This time when they have reached the edge of the clearing and see the Aterfly in all her glory, Lellan gives Han some treats and some small fish by way of saying 'thank you' then sends him on his way much to Gee's amazement.

'Are we staying here with her for a bit then walking somewhere?'

'Yes and then she is going to take us for a ride.' He points at the Aterfly looking very calm.

'You *are* joking?'

'No not at all. She will be our ride for the day.'

'Is she safe? I thought we were going to see your Uncle?'

'We are and she is extremely safe. Now we need to feed her and then she will be a very happy girl.'

They go and get some leaves and reintroduce themselves to the Aterfly. Gee had forgotten how adorable her face was. When the leaves have all been eaten Lellan gets out a flimsy looking leather harness from his bag. He then walks to her tail end leaving Gee watching from where they were stood. He pats her side, then miraculously her tail coils up and he then throws the harness up into the center of the coil. He climbs up very quickly hardly putting any of his weight on her. He disappears into the small space in the center made up by the coiled tail. There is enough room to comfortably sit up to four passengers, sitting side by side. He works quickly and threads the harness through and lays it out, then jumps down from the other side then runs back round with the long girth and fastens it in place.

Lellan calls Gee now that the Aterfly is ready for

flight and that they must not delay now the harness is on. Gee walks the length of the docile animal by taking big strides to measure the rough length. Even with the tail coiled up it is still a staggering thirteen metres. She joins Lellan holding his bag. He gives her strict instructions of how she must not pull the hair or grab the Aterfly when she climbs up because it will frighten her and due to her size she warrants the care.

Gee looks up at where they need to go and it is high. She wishes she has a ladder to hand because she cannot see any way of getting up without one. Lellan shows her how. The bulk of the harness is at the top where they are going. He dislodges a long strap with loops woven into it by using a thin branch. The strap looks flimsy to Gee that lies against the Aterflies soft side. Lellan takes one strap in his hand at shoulder level then places the ball of his foot into the bottom loop that is a foot off the ground. He then pulls himself up putting his feet in one loop at a time. He does it quickly and encourages Gee to follow. She tries not to think too hard about what she is about to do. She holds a loop at shoulder height and puts her foot in the first loop – so far so good she thinks to herself. Then she hoists herself up with her weak arms and is able to find another foot loop but then goes face first into the Aterflies side and sinks into the soft cushioning of the insect. She feels like she is being swallowed into an oversized cotton wool ball. She struggles to regain her balance, trying desperately hard not to flap about and then feels Lellan's grip. He grabs hold of her wrist and hand and pulls her out of the swamping hair. Before she knows it she is where she had been aiming for and sat on what is like a soft green fluffy rug. Lellan gives her a hopeless look and they both can't help but laugh knowing it was a long shot for her to be able to get up in one piece. She puts her coat on knowing it is going to keep out any drafts and keep her warm. Lellan checks the harness and then runs a strap around their waists connecting the pair of them together and to the Aterfly. Facing forward with Lellan sitting to her right Gee is now in the center of the Aterflies coiled up tail.

He points his spear to the front along the side of the Aterflies body and gives her a couple of gentle taps. Gee sees that Lellan is holding a loop of the harness on a length of strap and baring his weight against it so he can look around the curled up tail to see. He can see what their transport is doing. Gee does the same on her side because she doesn't want to miss anything and takes the strap provided and peers around her side. The Aterflies wings have fanned out either side and begin to move. Gee cannot help but hold her breath as the wings quicken with every beat. Then they start to lift straight upwards in a very smooth manner. Once they are above the canopy of the trees Lellan steers by tapping her right side to move right or her back for a movement to the left. Gee looks back through the green hairy tunnel and watches Lellan who has everything under control. As she turns back to the view beneath them she is in awe at how incredibly talented Lellan is. Lellan shouts through the windy tunnel as he has seen that she is in one of her thoughtful trances and asks if she is alright. This brings her back to the buffeting winds of reality. She smiles at him warmly satisfying his question. Lellan never pries into her thoughts and just lets her know he is there to listen if she needs to talk.

They fly over four hundred miles to the north east of their original grounded position. The Aterfly glides along with her green hair flattened making her more streamlined and gracefully quick. They fly over many savannahs, mountainous regions, forest's and even miles of desert. The Aterfly isn't accustomed to flying in a straight line. Instead she swoops up and down following the high and low currents. Sometimes when the Aterfly is flying low her movements are jerky because she is catching and eating insects in her path but the harness keeps the two passengers steady. She also takes them through clouds that are cold and wet and tiny beads of dew gather on Gees coat; who is very glad to be wearing it and whispers a 'thank you' to her father. Lellan is only wearing a shirt, his leggings and waist cloth as usual. The shirt looks wet but the water just runs off the buckskin leggings.

After enduring nearly two human hours of flying, Gee can see in the sky line ahead, a strange object and she looks at Lellan. He has a broad smile and says they are nearly there. Gee wonders where "there" is. The strange object gets closer and Gee makes it out to be some kind of vessel in amongst a cloud. As the Aterfly approaches she slows her speed down and then circles it the once. Gee is so overwhelmed that she has her mouth open in disbelief as she looks at the beautiful scene that unravels in front of her. It could be magical because the reality doesn't seem plausible. She pinches herself just to make sure she isn't asleep and having a wonderful dream. From above she sees what looks like an enormous white feather appearing to be the deck of some sort of ship. The vessel is the length and width of an old sailing ship with cream wings stretching out either side at the front and cream tail feathers fanned out at the rear. Gee looks hard through the great expanse of the cloud engulfing the ship to see that there is a wooden platform at each end and a long length of board above the deck feather connecting the two halves. As they get closer she can see, jutting out of the two platforms, poles that rise upwards with ropes and netting attached in all manner of different places and directions. They cannot see below the decking and feather because of the cloud coverage.

'We are here! My Uncle's cloud ship.'

'My god Lellan is there no end to your surprises. This has beaten everything else you have shown me.'

'Well not all I hope...' says Lellan suggestively with a smile.

'Is there more?'

'You will see tomorrow – I am saving the best for last. Now hold on because we are going to fly along side of the ship then hop off.'

They do exactly that and fly alongside the cloud ship. Lellan helps Gee off first onto a wooden platform and then he follows. He cleverly had positioned the Aterfly on the correct side so he can easily undo the buckle that kept the harness fastened up and removes it all together in one go.

'How on earth are we going to get back if you let her go?'

'We can leave when ever we need too. We are not returning by riding her we...' Just as he is about to explain he sees his uncle approaching.

Lellan's uncle is called Kwarn and is quite a bit younger than his brother Mogue. He greets them both with great welcome and eyes up Gee, then gives his nephew a big hug. Lellan makes the introductions and Kwarn shakes Gee's hand. Kwarn is even less dressed than Lellan and Gee ponders while they talk, on why he isn't shivering with the dampness of the surrounding clouds. She rationalises that he is hardened to this climate. Then Lellan takes off his wet shirt and ties it around his waist, to reveal his muscular torso and his back of silky black hair that's wet like an animal's coat which has just been caught out in a rain shower. The three of them are stood on the platform with the quill of the feather protruding out at the bow of the ship.

Kwarn takes them from the front platform across the board walk to the rear platform which is nestled in front of the tail feathers at the stern, where there are some people waiting. The board walk is precarious because it is only balanced across some thick black netting. Gee copes well most of the way but then she takes a look through the netting not concentrating on her footing and wobbles but Lellan steadies her. She sees what looks like the feather she had thought she had originally seen from above on their approach. It is the largest feather she has ever seen which is cream and shiny on closer inspection. She kneels down wanting to touch it below the netting. Kwarn kneels down beside her now aware of her curious nature. She touches it and it is firm and ridged and made up of millions of tiny feathers all knitted and interlinked together. Kwarn tells her the reason why they refrain from standing on it is in order to preserve and keep it close to its original condition.

Kwarn had found the tail feather many years ago washed up on one of the beaches and had used the idea of what it represents to build his unusual ship. The feather had come from a bird called the Morhi that is a ground dweller that never flies because of its size and very long individual tail feathers. Despite its size the bird looks elegant strutting around covered in ivory cream feathers with a long tail and a tufted crest on its head. He wanted to celebrate his find of the Morhi feather and so built a great and impressive air ship. He put the original feather he found along the center of the ship like a prized trophy and had gone out searching for other feathers that had fallen out of the birds to construct the two wings at the front of the ship and its tail. For him and his crew each flight is out of respect for the ground dwelling Morhi. Every so often they have to track a Morhi and gather some fallen feathers as replacements for the wings and tail on the great cloud ship.

Kwarn, Lellan and Gee reach the other platform which has a waist high, semi circular wooden carved railing, around it, giving it the look of a stern on a grand old ship. Gee instantly spots that she isn't the only human onboard which is an unexpected welcome comfort. This is not because she is worried about being the only human but because her ways and thoughts are similar to theirs which is relaxing. They all follow Kwarn down a hatch which is like a trap door that is fastened securely from the inside. Gee follows Lellan and takes it all in. The back end of the ship is made from hard wood and every floor, wall and ceiling is varnished to bring out the natural red and brown colours of auburn. She wonders what tree is responsible for producing such lovely coloured wood. They climb down three solid and robust ladders all within a short distance from each other. Gee sees small cabins off each of the walk ways and guesses that they are used for living quarters, meeting rooms or utilities.

Once they are on the bottom deck they walk along a narrow walkway and head in the direction towards the bow of the ship. They reach some double solid wooden doors after passing through a refreshment area like a private cosy den. Kwarn opens the double doors and reveals a large open space. The real treasure of the room however, isn't the size and vast space or even what it holds, but it having the presence of glass walls, floor and ceiling. The glass is not truly transparent in colour and has a hint of silver to it. When it was made the glass was melted down and mixed with a metal much like our titanium and then shaped to Kwarns specifications. The reinforced glass is light weight, weather resistant and incredibly strong. The silver colour is marginal and does not detract from the views. The hall is scattered with seating and tables randomly placed to each side of the room. At the far end is a very large table with charts sprawled across it and eight high backed chairs. It looks like a captains table.

Gee can understand why Lellan wanted to keep this as surprise because it is a magnificent ship and out of this world. It reminds her of an ornament ship made out of glass with intricate details that is for sale in a gift shop window with an expensive price tag daintily hanging on it. At the far end, under the front platform, Gee can see the mechanics and workings that are behind the beautiful ship. A small group of five is at the helm and in charge of the great beauty as she glides through the sky in amongst her chosen clouds. To the right looking through the glass is a window opened up by the clouds and the view is overwhelming. Gee walks to the nearly invisible window, crossing the glass floor, to look out over Teeria. To be a crew member on the ship with a dislike for heights would be impossible and would never work because the floor is forever changing from clouds or a bird's eye view of the sheer drop below.

Lellan goes with Kwarn as he has a letter to give to his uncle from his father, Mogue. Gee is happy to get accustomed with her surroundings and gets comfortable while Lellan takes care of business. Gee thought she had a spectacular perspective of things when she was riding on the Aterfly but nothing like this. She stands and enjoys every moment. She is joined by a female Spognoff named Huntelle. Gee hasn't had the pleasure of talking to a female Spognoff before. She finds her charming and notes she is very attractive with feminine features and long black hair with plaits purposely positioned around her face. Each plait has beads or a white or cream ribbon of soft leather running through it. She wears a short skirt and top which both just cover up the essentials but are highly decorated in beads and made from soft pliable cream leather. She has a friendly smile and offers Gee a refreshing and much needed cup of tea. While Huntelle goes and gets Gee her drink one of the human men comes over to talk to her.

Gee finds out the man is called Dion and was one of the Mission Star Finder crew members of the Exploration Light 259 vessel and, one of the few who were responsible for the find of Teeria. He was re-assigned to TRF once the treaty had been made because he was awarded a medal of commendation along with the others. Dion was granted his wish to stay on Teeria as he had shown great interest and enthusiasm for what Teeria was to become in the future. TRF had found out about the nomadic ways of the Spognoffs and wanted volunteers to travel with them and so Dion put his name forward. The nomads travelled in many forms, some by foot, some by sky ships and some by mammal. Dion had been chosen to travel with Kwarn on his sky ship for a limited time. Dion had enjoyed his experience and had become very involved and was seen as one of the crew by all and when it came to leaving he decided he didn't want to leave and so he stayed and had then become a nomad himself for the past four years. He still reports back to TRF head quarters once every nine days via the particle link up, with his exciting findings which prove to be invaluable and a show of his loyalty. He has travelled all over Teeria with Kwarn and his crew. They do not venture too close to the poles because it would be detrimental to the ship and its passengers.

Huntelle returns with Gees cup of tea and stands close to Dion and kisses him on the cheek.

'Thanks for getting our new guest a drink Hun.'

'Well of course. She is a friend of Lellans who is our special guest.'

'I have just been telling Gee how I become one of

the crew.' Dion winks at Huntelle.

'Yes he did not need much persuasion to stay on. We have seen many glorious sights together,' says Huntelle looking tenderly at Dion. 'However, sometimes we do not see anyone from one season to the next.'

Gee has already noticed how very close the pair is to one another. She finds herself interested in the two before her and wonders what their story is. It is clear to anyone how much they care for each other because they don't hide it. She then turns her thoughts to Lellan and herself, at how close they have become recently. She has to find out more as her curiosity is overwhelming.

'I'm sorry to speak out of place and you can tell me to mind my own business - but are you two... together?'

'Yes we are. We first met when I joined Kwarns crew. We were married two years later,' says Dion with a laugh and Huntelle with a chuckle as they are clearly in love with each other.

'Wow congratulations,' speaks Gee in a surprised tone which catches Huntelle's attention.

'Thank you. We had a combined ceremony from both of our beliefs and cultures. May I say you seemed a little surprised?'

'I'm...' stalls Gee, trying to find the right way forward with what she thought wrongly was a delicate subject, 'I was curious and a romantic at heart. I could see how close you both are and just had to ask. I didn't know we could... marry... each other. I'm sorry I sounded surprised I thought it was a... delicate topic. I have asked myself such questions because others alike are working together and I have contemplated what the outcome would be if our races lived together as couples – obvious really. The inevitable, given both our natural instincts,' Gee says with an almost hidden smile.

'Oh… you do not need to apologise you are new here – ask away. It is very far from delicate. It was agreed on by each treaty party at the beginning of our coexistence that if the foreseeable occurred it was to be embraced, but… the path was to be trodden carefully by all involved. I speak from experience and say that we have not had any difficulties. Sure our cultures and traditions are different but we get to embrace both.' Huntelle smiles at Dion. She continues, 'So you and Lellan are not together then?'

'No we are just good friends,' ponders Gee not wanting to say too much, but Huntelle is all too in tune with what she really wants to say.

'I see - your secret is safe with us,' winks Huntelle, tapping her nose and then coaxes Dion away as Lellan approaches from the other end of the room.

Gee is left standing and staring out into oblivion not daring to continue her thoughts of where the conversation had finished. Lellan appears after giving Kwarn the letter and tells Gee all about the news he had just found out. The letter was an invitation to the Ariak-deau annual festivities to celebrate the year that has past and to embrace the uncertainty of what was to follow with a fresh year ahead. It takes place around the stone circle and is an excuse for all family members to come together to eat, drink and dance. Lellan explains that even though it is early to be arranging such occasions they don't have a postal system as there is no real need for one. The letters are few and far between and get sent out by a rider should there be any urgency for a secured mailing.

Lellan and Gee stay in the grand glass hall and marvel over it and the views. They go and sit with Huntelle and Dion who are sat on one of the many comfortable sofas around the edge of the main floor. There is a thick maroon rug between the two cream sofas that face each other which helps to soothe Gee's giddiness from the strange sensation of seeing everything that goes by beneath them. Gee sits comfortably close to Lellan and rests her head on his shoulder while they talk and she relaxes into the dream like surroundings and slips into a light sleep.

By late sun the large tables are brought together in the middle of the room and set up in a long line ready for the Captain and his crew to eat. The food bought out looks more of an elaborate display than something that is eaten. There are hot and cold meats, vegetables, salads and fruits; with many dairy foods placed in the small gaps between the other dishes. Everyone is spoilt for choice. For the ship mates it's an everyday occurrence at late sun because of all the hard work they have done.

* * *

After the feast, which took up several hours, Lellan asks Gee to go with him up on deck. They go back up on deck the way they had come. It feels nice to draw the fresh air into their lungs. They go to the other platform by crossing the board walk. The fabricated wings are fully stretched out and the ship is riding high on the currents alongside the clouds. Lellan carried up two blankets with him. He lays one blanket down up against a solid wooden mast which looks like an uprooted tree trunk because it still has the smooth silvery bark of its predecessor, minus the branches. He sits down facing the direction that the ship is heading. He pats a spot next to him looking at Gee. She sits down with a shiver as it is starting to cool down as the sun lowers in front of them. Lellan puts the remaining blanket around their shoulders and they each have a corner of it to hold close and tight to their chests to keep out the draft. They lean back against the tree mast huddled together.

'I had completely forgotten. But how do we get down from here Lellan?' Gee starts to warm up beside the warmth of his body under the blanket.

'Ah that. We could parachute off.' He smirks.

'Parachute off here, over the edge, you are joking?'

'Not at all, I have one in my bag.'

'Oh… is it safe?'

'It is perfectly safe.'

'I've never parachuted, have thought about it before though.'

'Good…' He laughs, 'Because it is the only way down.' She jokingly thumps him on the arm but in truth she is not overly worried by the idea.

'You do not seem concerned about jumping.'

'Maybe a little surprised. It's something I would have liked to have done back on Earth but never got around to it. I like to take each day in its stride.'

'I *am* impressed.'

'I aim to please.' She laughs.

'I will have to remember that.' He chuckles, 'I will be glad to show you how to parachute safely. I have done it many times.'

'Thanks and it's a good thing I don't mind as we may have been stuck up here.' Gee looks up thinking it wouldn't be a bad spot to be stranded and then adds, 'However I am looking forward to the whole experience of jumping.'

'I could have been very persuasive if you were not open to the parachuting; in fact I am a little disappointed that you did not need any.' She shoves him.

He smiles and puts his arm around her waist and pulls her closer under the blanket then they sit in a comfortable silence looking at the scenery, each in their own thoughts.

All around them is a forest of clouds. Some are monumentally tall rising up like mountains which could never be climbed and the clouds that do not stand so tall are longer than the width of a small island. The ship and the cloud forest ride along, side by side, in unison. The surrounding forest is lit up in pastel pinks and purples as the sun is setting. The clouds that are immediately around the ship almost look like pink candyfloss with streaks of a deeper pink running through them where the sugar has caramelised making it look good enough to eat. Lellan points to a break in the clouds to the rivers below. The rivers look silvery, like liquid mercury, because of dusk falling upon them. They can see veins of silver running everywhere below. They even get to see a powerful waterfall that has the silvery looking element flowing over it in cascades. It is something that Gee will never forget.

'I hope you have enjoyed your day?' asks Lellan gently.

'This is breath-taking Lellan – thank you. Really wish I had bought my camera, I could have got some fantastic shots to show them back home. They'd have been jealous,' giggles Gee.

She looks up into his bright piecing magenta and cyan eyes and finds she is absorbed by the gorgeous colours.

'We can come again when my Uncle is back in the area if you like. I'm glad you are having a nice time.'

'Are you kidding? It has been more than nice. You have given me a brilliant day. Thank you for taking the time to show me all of these wonders.' She gestures at the pink forest around her.

'I have my reasons.' He smiles, 'I wanted to give you this.' He rummages in a pocket on his waist band.

He pulls out a small bag with a draw string across

the top and gives it to Gee.

'What is it Lellan?' The bag fits neatly into her hand.

She touches it gently and respectfully and appreciates the handcrafted bag in her palm. It feels soft because of the supple brown leather it has been made from, with some stiffness on one side because of a hand sewn pattern. The pattern itself is a gift alone which by Gees first impression looks like a perfect spider's web but made from many colourful threads and beads.

'The bag is stunning. Does the patterned web have a meaning?' She touches the intricate needlework again with her finger and feels every smooth stitch and tiny bead.

'Yes it does. We see a web as the threads of all life and most importantly, all are interconnected and rely on one another. We sew the web in many different colours to represent everything that is living around us.' He touches the web pattern himself out of admiration for its representation.

'Wow what an eye opening way to see everything. I will never see a spider's web in the same way again.'

'Open it.' He doesn't take his eyes off her even to blink.

She loosens the string with great care and peers inside to see it is stuffed with something. She tugs at it and out comes a matchbox sized tiny cushion made from a midnight blue velvet fabric. Wrapped around the little cushion is a silver chain with a pendant attached. Gee gasps at the gift.

'Oh… Lellan… it's gorgeous…' She kisses him on the cheek making a small blue impression on his skin, but she turns back to the necklace and doesn't notice.

She unwinds the chain and takes the exquisite pendant in her hand and looks at it very closely. It is the shape of a pear drop. Inside the droplet is a petite dark violet flower with a yellow pin prick of colour at the center. The pendant looks like glass with a wispy white pearly cloud behind the flower.

'It is one of nature's beauties because the droplet is made from a white resin. When the resin sets the white separates and sinks to where gravity pulls it within the drop and it gives the overall effect of glass.'

'But how did the flower get inside?'

'I would like to show you where I got the droplet from tomorrow. It came from a cave.'

'A cave?'

'Yes, a cave where these flowers grow in abundance. The resin seeps out from above in the cave and catches the colours below.'

'Wow I can't wait to see such a site...' She then pauses. 'A pretty gift from you to me,' she says and turns to look at her friend with questions in her eyes.

'You deserve this pretty necklace and more. I do not want to over step the mark and jeopardise our friendship...'

'Go on.' She looks at him intently and he looks at her with anguish in his eyes, 'Tell me Lellan... it's alright.'

'My feelings for you have grown. I give you this gift to seal our friendship, if nothing else... if nothing more can be between us. When I think of you now, my feelings are much more than what a friend should feel. I really miss you when you are not with me...'

'You care for me like I care for you. There is nothing wrong in that and I miss you when I'm not with you too.'

'I *do* care for you but I need you to understand it is more than that. The feelings I have for you are strong and run very deeply. It is more than caring or lust... Nia paur luow.' He pauses and exhales then translates

144

what he has just said, 'I … I love you Gee.'

'Look at me…' She puts a hand under his chin and lifts it up so they can look into each others eyes.

His eyes are full of emotion and hers are filled with elation making her eyes glazed with hidden tears. She smiles at him and so do her eyes.

'I have come to think of you as more than a friend too. I ignored the way I felt because… I thought you would only be interested in female Spognoff's - not me. I have learnt on this trip that it is entirely up to the individual and I was wrong to make such assumptions. I can imagine you with someone who is hardy, courageous and worthy of your affections. From my world you are royalty – a Prince, because of who your Father is.'

A low growl comes from Lellan which to Gee sounds like a grumble of frustration.

'You said yourself it is up to the individual – it is up to me. Look at Dion and Huntelle. We are here on Teeria and things are different – open to change. You are the most courageous woman I have ever known and far more worthy of my affections than any other I have met.'

'The true reason I haven't seen you as much as I would've liked is because I was trying to give you your own space and not get in the way of your future path. How can I ignore the fact that you *are* the Chief's Son?'

'My Father has seen us getting closer and he is happy about our friendship. He knows me and doesn't even have to ask how I feel – to him it is obvious.' He looks her square in the eyes, 'What does your heart say?'

'I don't like spending time apart from you either… I feel so silly for making assumptions and hiding from my feelings.' She pauses as a lump swells in her throat,

'I feel the same and have done for sometime. I love you too.' A tear rolls down her cheek.

Lellan wipes away the tear with his thumb and cups her small face in his large hands. He slowly and gently kisses her on the lips. He feels her soft warm lips against his; that he had admired from afar for so long. As a reality check in a brief second he runs his thumb along her bottom lip. She gently kisses him back savouring every moment. She moves onto his lap and passionately kisses him back, awakening her whole body and his. Lellan can hear she is breathing a little heavier than normal. He politely and very slightly pulls himself away and along with a very happy smile he asks, 'Can I help you put your necklace on?'

'Yes – then you will be with me all the time.' She grins and he kisses her lips once more. She produces the pendant that was safely tucked away in her clasped hand. He takes it and moves her hair to one side. He niftily fastens it and kisses her shoulder before moving her hair back in place. She turns back round to face him and they both look at the necklace now in its rightful place. He looks very satisfied with it hanging so perfectly against her tanned skin.

'This is a seal of our friendship and may I say now… our love?'

'Yes I like the sound of that and thank you Lellan, thank you for everything.' She looks down and smiles his favourite smile.

They cuddle up under the blanket and enjoy the last of the sun and their new found freedom. Eventually they retire for the evening. Gee is exhausted. They are each shown a room next door to one another. Lellan gives her a memorable kiss good night at her door and tells her to get him if she needs anything. Her room is like what you would expect to find on an old fashioned ship. It is very compact with a bed down one side, a bathroom to the left as you enter the room and a small chest of draws with a mirror hanging above it to the right. The room is so small there is barely room to walk between the bed and draws. The bathroom isn't much different which comprises of a shower, tiny sink and toilet. Gee feels so tired that she is not fussed or fazed by the small enclosed space and takes a shower to freshen up then settles down in bed. She lays on her front and looks out of the round port hole and can just about see the outline of the clouds under the moonlight of Ni and Caar. She takes a long last look at her glass droplet and smiles knowing what a comfort it has given her. She is no longer a fish out of water and feels she belongs to Teeria and to Lellan. She flicks the side lamp off and falls asleep quickly.

* * *

Lellan knocks gently on the door the following first light and a faint 'come in' is heard from the other side. He quietly opens the door and pops his head in. He sees that Gee is still in bed looking like he has just woke her up.

'Come in Lellan – I'm sorry I must have over slept.' He enters and closes the door behind him and stands at the end of the bed.

'Come over here. You don't need to stand on ceremony with me.' She wearily pats the bed.

He lay's on the bed beside her against the wall and she cuddles up into his arms. As he kisses her on the head she closes her eyes again, comforted by his presence.

'I'm sorry to have woken you it is still early. It has just gone first light.'

'Phew, I don't want to hold up our day,' she says sleepily still with her eyes closed.

'How did you sleep?'

'As soon as I turned off my lamp I fell asleep – I was exhausted – I guess it was all the fresh air.'

'Well we will have an easier day to day. When we get our feet back onto solid ground it is only a short walk to the place where I got your resin droplet.'

'Sounds good – I can't wait to see where you got this.' She looks at her necklace and smiles.

'You like it?'

'I love it. I feel like I belong somehow… to you…' she blushes, '…and to Teeria. It doesn't seem so alien anymore.'

'We belong to each other and Teeria is your home.'

'It is for now, but, once my Father's contract finishes we have to make a choice,' she saddens.

'A choice?' He detects her sad tone.

'Yes we can go back home – to Earth - or stay here. I want to be here with you. I also feel like I kind of fit here somehow and wish to do everything I can to help with our future settlement but I cannot speak for the rest of my family. I want to stay here so much but I do not want to lose my family either. It is still early days and there is a chance that my Brother may find a foot hold and want to have a future here too. Earth seems so injured compared to Teeria and to me there is no comparison.'

'I had not realised the full extent of your worries. Like you have said it *is* still early days and you will be strong enough and wiser to make such a decision when the time is right. I believe we will be together for an eternity.'

'How do you know?' She is very awake now.

'It is an unmistakeable feeling I have.'

'I will go with that,' she says contently.

They cuddle up again both in their own thoughts. They are so comfortable with each others company it is very refreshing for Gee. She hasn't had a serious partner for acouple of years because she has been too busy indulging in her own interests and studies. The relationships she did have were not as lovers, but platonic, and she had never wanted or was interested in indulging past the latter. Her feeling's are on a different par and a higher plain, both mentally and physically with Lellan. She can easily see herself being his lover because apart from being attracted to his personality, additionally her whole body is willingly being drawn to his. It is a welcome feeling of safety with Lellans warm arm's wrapped around her.

'We have time for breakfast and you can have as much time to wake properly. There is a small window of time to parachute off to where we wish to land, but not until just before mid sun.'

'I'm quite happy being here with you – I'm not one for lying in but I could make an exception.' Lellan laughs at Gees word's and kisses her and is more than happy to allow her to indulge a little longer.

Once Gee is ready to get up Lellan politely leaves letting her get dressed privately while he goes and gathers his own belongings. She gets dressed slowly relishing in a dream like state about Lellan. Gee feels easy around him because he has old fashioned morals and values. She doesn't have the need for worry, embarrassment or hasn't even experienced any uncomfortable moments while in his company. She knows in her heart that he wouldn't take advantage of her because she has seen he has a soft and kind heart after the long season she has known him. He is always one step ahead of her with only one thing in mind and that is to make her comfortable in his own presence, with no added and unnecessary pressures. She feels after last nights heart to heart that she could walk on water or fly like a bird from the euphoric feelings she has this morning. She is so happy to know that Lellan feels as she does and has always looked forward to each time spent with him, but even more so now, knowing that she can simply hold his hand or kiss him looking into his gorgeous eyes. With that thought she hurries.

Gee joins Lellan in the glass hall. She is wearing a pair of jeans and the top Lellan gave her all those weeks ago; when she had hurt herself and tore her own top. She wears it quite a lot when she is out and about with Lellan because it is comfortable and the fabric is so light weight. Lellan has told her already the colour and style suits her very well. Huntelle nudges Dion and rests her eyes on Lellan and Gee who are sat across the table opposite them. Dion's eyes widen and can instantly see they are sat very close together and completely caught up with each other. Dion picks up his glass of water as a gesture and mouths 'cheers' to Lellan and Gee. Gee looks over to see Huntelle truly happy for them both and looks down with a blush. Lellan is not so shy pulling Gee even closer, kissing her on the head with a chuckle amused by her venerability at unexpected times. They both eat a good hearty breakfast and afterwards spend some time with Kwarn and the others.

When the time comes for Lellan and Gee to leave, everyone gathers on the decked platform at the rear of the ship. Kwarn helps Lellan rig up the harness so it is ready to be worn. Gee had the option to go it alone with her own parachute but she preferred the alternative of being strapped into Lellan's harness. Lellan stands behind Gee while her feet and his feet are fed into the dual harness. She is tugged and pulled to make sure everything is tight and secure. They are both now snuggly strapped together, with Lellan having the all important back pack that contains the awaiting parachute.

Gee's nerves start to get the better of her with the thought of jumping off the platform into what seems like oblivion. Lellan assures her everything is going to be alright and he will take the lead and she should simply hold onto the shoulder braces and enjoy the ride. They back to the edge of the deck and say their goodbyes to his uncle and the others and tell them they will be back to see them when they are passing again. Lellan gives a reassuring quick squeeze then tells Gee they are going to jump on three. She has a firm hold of her brace straps and follows his backward steps and he counts, 'One... Two... Three.' Then they topple off the edge.

Gee chickens out and closes her eyes as they summersault backwards while falling, making it difficult for her to catch her breath. She only opens her eyes when she hears Lellan roaring from pleasure. She sees the ground far below but still approaching with the air rushing and buffeting past her with such a force it is hard to keep her eyes open. She struggles and turns to Lellan who is most definitely having an adrenaline rush and he has his arms spread out either side and appears to be hovering like a bird of prey. Gee copies as she wants to experience the full effect. They then bring their arms closer to their bodies which make them swoop forward. For the first time ever she can start to understand what it is like for a bird by soaring and gliding herself. With plenty of good time left Lellan releases the parachute which slows them down with a tremendous jolt. Lellan guides the parachute by the straps to a clearing he has been aiming for. They both simultaneously lift their legs into a seated position ready to land. He manages to bring them down in a gradual decline and they land and lightly bump along on their bums. Gee is sat on Lellans lap as they are so tightly bound together. She feels his hands smoothing her hair down and when she turns he cups her face. He makes sure she is alright and they both grin at each other because they have just had a mind blowing sky dive.

As they are so relieved to be down safely, they lay back in a heap wrapped up in the parachute and manage to have a satisfying kiss. They have landed in a small sloped clearing surrounded by brushwood with low lying thick undergrowth and young trees. When they have caught their breath they begin to unstrap which is as timely as when they were helped into it. Lellan bundles up the harness and as there is no real hurry only partly folds up the parachute with Gees help so they can both sit down on it. They automatically look up and search for the ship they have just left. Lellan points out Kwarn's ship now in the distance. It is hard to see because the bulk of it is glass helping it to be camouflaged against the clouds. Gee is impressed by Kwarn's invention and she cannot wait to see the cloud forests again. Gee is surprised by how quick the time has gone by as it is early late sun already. They have a bite to eat and drink, all of which was packed up by the kitchen mates of the ship.

Once they have done and packed the parachute away they head east. Gee is pleased that Lellan knows where he is going because it all looks the same to her. They head for a group of high rocks in the distance. As they get closer Gee can see they are actually mountains but nowhere near as big as the one Lellan calls home at Roudruom. Lellan is pleased with himself because he had steered the parachute quite close to their destination as he had promised Gee there would not be much walking today. Their journey is only about a mile away. After the short distance they get to the base of a small mountain standing centred and adjoined to other larger mountains that loom up from behind. To the right is a meandering path leading up the side of the rough rock face. They steadily amble along taking in the views as they gradually climb higher. The path leads them half way up and then through two closely enclosed monstrous walls of rock either side. A turn then takes them left and towards a tiny dark cave opening leading them back into the small mountain they have been climbing. The opening is small and jagged but large enough for a thin upright person to fit through. It leads into a tunnel with a dusty trodden path. On entering, the light is very dim and Gee holds onto Lellan's shirt so she doesn't walk into anything like a hard wall.

Gee is completely reliant on Lellan and his eyesight which is exceptional because the further they go along the tunnel the less she can see. After a long human five minutes light can be seen ahead. Gee picks up her pace with excitement wanting to see what is at the end of this damp, cold and gloomy tunnel. They enter into a large cavern at the end of the tunnel on the south side within the small mountain. The cave has an uneven damp rock floor but is bright because there is an opening over the far side high up where water has worn away the rock during wet weather.

Lellan takes Gees hand which is noticeably cold. He rubs her hand as they walk towards the sky opening in the cave's ceiling. As they approach the shaft of light, the cave floor dries out and dust takes its place because of the considerably sized opening. They follow a worn path across the uneven floor. Gee stops abruptly when they are about to enter the stream of daylight that is flooding in from above. On the floor she see's natural debris making up a thick layer of soil and on its surface, like a blanket, Gee can make out a large circular shape of the glass droplets. They are glistening in the sun's brightness, similar to a sequined fabric, and can be seen as far as the light touches in a three hundred and sixty degree arrangement. Lellan encourages her forward and they tread carefully along the forever narrowing path that a mouse could have worn down because it is so thin. Gee estimates the droplets are three to four metres deep from the edge of the brightest part of the light shaft to the shade of the darkness. The center has a scattering of boulders which are randomly placed, that had once been part of the cave ceiling. Over time the elements have rounded their edges and smoothed their surfaces. The floor has a thin layer of dust which has been blown in from above from the thirst deprived landscape due to the dry weather of the last season. It is apparent that the droplets have formed on the edge of safety making the unique ring, due to the weather that comes in through the gaping hole that bombards the middle.

They go over to one of the protruding boulders, put down their bags and lean up against it. Gee hasn't said a word since they had entered the room because she responded immediately to the quietness and how the slightest sound echoed from each scuffed step in the depths of the cavern. She respects the tranquillity and feels at peace in the room and hasn't felt the need to talk. She has been enjoying the sound of nothingness and loving the secluded retreat that Lellan had known about for years.

'You've excelled yourself this time Lellan and I thought this trip couldn't get any better when we went and saw your Uncle. It is so peaceful and pretty here.' She holds her own droplet ever so pleased to see where it has come from, 'Where are the little flowers?'

'Let us go and have a closer look,' says Lellan quietly.

They squat down by the edge of the huge resin drop

ring. Leaning in closer they see the tiny dark violet flowers with the light bouncing off the yellow centres like shooting stars. The droplets look like gems gleaming in the sunlight at close range. Lellan points out some flowers that are free from the resin which helps pave the way for the droplet carpet to live on. They see the white resin seeping through the cracks in the rock above and dripping against the walls and boulders onto the flowers below. Lellan informs her that nobody knows how long the resin will continue seeping and how long this marvel will survive.

'Would you like to stay here tonight and sleep under the stars?' he asks softly.

'Could we? It would be great to sleep in amongst my fellow droplets.' She smiles, and they stand for some time looking at the wonders of the room which will be theirs for one night.

Lellan breaks the silence before the light starts to fade, 'The cave acts as safety. We should not venture out after dark. If we keep a small fire going in here it will keep anything unpleasant away.'

'We'd best get to work then. It's already the middle of late sun.'

A busy and short late sun goes by. Lellan leaves Gee in charge of collecting some fire wood from the nearby brush at the foot of the main cave path while he goes and gets them a meal. Gee firstly piles up twigs and then drags huge fallen thick branches up to the entrance of the cave, and is left wondering if she has collected too much. She decides any left overs can be for others who need the cavern's shelter for a night. Lellan is pleased with her efforts and tells her that there is probably too much wood but it is a kind sentiment to leave it for others. He had returned with a limp carcass of a small hairy animal minus its head, lower limbs and insides. Gees natural response to seeing the dead animal is to put a hand over her mouth, before shortly returning to auto pilot and carrying on with the wood staking. Lellan knew that Gee wouldn't cope very well with seeing a small furry animal being dealt with in the respected and correct manner. It is still early days by his way of living and there is still much for her to learn. He does not want to force anything on her. Everything she wants to learn or do is her choice. She has coped so far and faired well by living with Teerian nature for the past couple of days and she has even compared it to her world. The thought of living out in the wilderness on Earth like they are doing is no longer appealing or at all viable. Lellan has always known that his world is a far cry from hers and different to what she is used to. Once the excitement of the newness has worn off he knows she has spirit and courage to fit right in and bring both knowledge and meaning back to the Spognoffs and humans. He wants her to follow her own path of curiosity and grow from it with him by her side.

Before the animal has been skinned and prepared for cooking they both go and collect some large leaves. Lellan gives Gee the job of placing the large leaves like rugs down on the ground to save dust getting in the food and blankets. While he attends to the meat she places the leaves around the edge of the built up fire and the sleeping area, up against some boulders, which Lellan had marked out on their arrival. She stands puzzled looking at the area not moving with her back to Lellan.

'Everything alright?' Lellan asks in the middle of lighting the fire.

'Of course... just wondering about sleeping arrangements.' She turns and looks at him.

'There in front of where you are standing – nice spot and the fire will keep our feet warm... unless... you would like me to sleep the other side of this fire.' He points at it with a thin lit stick then pokes it deep into the heart of the built up dry wood. It roars to life in an instant with a whoosh.

'No… no, I just didn't want to assume. It will be nice falling asleep under your watchful eye.'

'Who said we will be sleeping!' He smirks while erecting a spit frame for the skinned animal.

'Oh don't push your luck.' She steps closer to him and gives a gentle shove.

'Oh…' He imitates and stands the frame up, 'I meant talking.' He threads the animal on a thick sturdy branch and rests it over the fire while Gee is lying down and testing out the bed. It is made up with blankets and she has used her coat as a pillow. He catches her looking at him in an odd kind of way and realised she hadn't answered back and it didn't look like she was intending to either. He cleans up as he is sitting by the fire and then gives it a good stoke and adds another large bit of wood. He then turns his attention to Gee. He approaches her on all fours and then pounces on top of her. She backs up a little because of his approach which had taken her by surprise. He laughs and is careful not to put any weight on her fragile and delicate body.

'Did I make you jump?' He rests on his side and elbow and strokes her hair.

'Yes you moved very fast. I can't do that.'

'Can I kiss you?' He teases her with his eyes.

'You don't have to ask.'

'It is only polite when I took you by surprise.' He scoops her up in his arms and gives her the most passionate kiss of all.

They are entwined with Gee running her fingers over each muscle in his arm and then wrapping her fingers in his very long black hair. She has never felt as alive as she does right at this very moment and she wants him. He kisses her, with his hand touching the side of her face liking the softness of her skin against his. He moves from her lips to her neck and can hear that her breathing is getting deeper. She looks up to see blue fluttering on his face and arms, like her own adrenaline coursing through her veins which is bought on by the excitement of his touch. He continues kissing her mouth and neck but his hand moves down her body over her clothes. She feels drawn like a magnet to each touch of his hand making her body writhe up. He stops above the waist line of her belted jeans and returns moving his hands up again the way they had come feeling her soft body through the clothes. His hand returns to her glossy hair and then gives her another kiss.

'You are so beautiful. I fell in love with you that day when I saw you had hurt yourself. You looked so peaceful and were a vision of angelic beauty,' he strokes her hair while never leaving her eyes. 'I… want it to be right between us before we interlace together as one. I will be your first and I want you to be completely comfortable.'

Gee flushes, 'H… how did you know?'

Lellan smiles gently never looking away, 'I am not sure how to explain but I…know these things. I think it is what you would call instinct, there is no need to be embarrassed.'

'Oh no, I… I am… was thrown. I have been toying with the idea whether I should tell you soon or not. Will I be your first, when it is right for us?'

'Yes,' he smirks with a blue fluttering of his cheeks making Gee's heart leap. 'Yes, you will be my first, my sweet Gee. I could easily want more from you and you seem to want the same but we have all night and there is always a tomorrow.'

'You are too good to be true and thank you for your

beautiful words. I understand… but it is so hard to resist you.' She strokes his chest of soft hair.

'And I you.' He doesn't want to rush into anything but it is so hard for him not to take things further. He has to fight against his instinct and be in control. He has wanted to be as one with her for some time but hadn't dared to hope it would happen, and so wants to be patient which will help solidify the base of their relationship.

'I first saw you when I was with my family at the beach. I thought how handsome you looked. You are incredibly good looking and I want to savour you and every moment with you.'

'I feel the same and when we do join together, it will be a powerful and exhilarating union and shared by us both. I want to touch… caress… and please… you, all night long. Now however, I have to be very patient and I would not forgive myself if we rushed or had a brief encounter. You and I deserve more than that.'

'Lellan can I just say you have a lovely way with words. You are not only handsome on the outside but very wise on the inside.' She sees a faint flutter of blue touch his skin as she strokes his temple.

'Thank you. Now alas I must tend to our meat before it becomes too charred on one side.' He very reluctantly lets her go from his grasp and sits back by the fire and turns the meat.

She joins him by his side and helps.

* * *

The night is drawing in and Gee can see stars through the huge sky light. They have eaten and she hadn't known how hungry she was until she tried some of the roasted meat. It was delicious and they both thoroughly enjoyed their meal. Kwarn had also given them a few supplies such as bread, cheese and fruit for their journey. He wanted them to have a good day and could see how close they were. He knew Lellan was taking her to the cave of droplets and didn't want them to want for anything but each other. Gee had helped by stoking up the fire several times through the remainder of the late sun and last light because she felt it was the least she could do with everything Lellan had done for them both.

The fire has been built up higher, now that it isn't being used for cooking and they can now relax. They both lay on the cushioned blankets watching the flames and the dancing shadows on the cave walls. It is mesmerizing. The droplets seem to come alive with the dancing light of the fire. They are surrounded by a sparkly amber loop of light that never rests because of it. The loop of light is far enough away from the fire to not pose it any threat or damage. Despite the fire roaring at its full potential Gee shudders. She has enjoyed her day but is not used to sleeping under the stars. Lellan convinces her that she wouldn't miss anything if she got under the blanket. Before she gets under the blanket she decides to change into some thicker socks and puts on a jumper over her top. Lellan watches. The cold hasn't affected him yet, as he still only wears his thin loin cloth and three quarter length leggings. He took his shirt off hours ago and just recently his boots. Gee snuggles down into Lellan's arms. After a while of talking he joins her. They are both weary from their travels of the past couple of days and so, fall asleep cuddled up.

Chapter 12

Looking out of her mother and father's bedroom window Gee feels troubled. She tries to understand why, especially when she has one of her favourite days ahead of her with Lellan. She woke at her usual hour but had a bad feeling on waking.

In the year 12,327, education took a leap forward. Children were introduced to a newly taught class in school named 'Intuition'. This class encouraged children to embrace and pursue the newly proven sixth sense of perception, intuition, and to gain an insight of the human brain. Not every child or adult had the extra sense and a test was derived for young children to determine if they had it. The ones who did have the ability were automatically enrolled in the Intuition class. The class was not set up with any intention of isolating the pupils from others, but to encourage a gift like those who had the gift to learn a different language. Those who achieved well in the new strain of education where then classed as being fully utilised and their results were encouraging. Gee is prone to this ability and her schooling had helped her see it as a positive and not a negative.

To Gee it is like there is a dark cloud looming over her. She knows from experience that she cannot ignore the bad feeling and it is best to go along with it, but being careful at the same time. She looks out in the direction towards where the Gladestines settlement is and wonders what could be so bad or wrong. She shakes her head as a dismissal and decides to confide in her mum.

Ameel is all too aware of her daughter's sixth sense and helps where she can. Ameel reminds her daughter that just because they have left Earth, that doesn't stop her senses from working. The sense that Gee can feel may be heightened on Teeria and Ameel suggests she has an easy day in order not to aggravate anything or anyone and to stay close to Lellan's people. It is the first episode of her blind foresight since they have been on Teeria so there wouldn't be any harm in being cautious. They both conclude that now that she is more settled on Teeria her senses are back up and running at full steam. Ameel can see that it has unnerved Gee and makes a refreshing camomile tea for her to drink before she leaves with Posall to join Lellan.

Gee has also gained her results from her second check up after a long wait from the medical team of the Gladestine tribe. After collaborating with the TRF results and their own Spognoff medical team, it is agreed that the initial outcome is roughly correct and that Gee is sensitive to the marginally slight difference in the gravitational pull. The Spognoffs quite rightly pointed out the obvious. There is only one possible reason that she is experiencing the difference and that is because she has a known ability of foresight, like other humans on Teeria. However, her ability is more pronounced and accurate than the others. Gee is relieved that her known ability is at the heart of light footedness and thankful that the Spognoffs found the given reason. She understands why it is her who is left with a spring in her step and nobody else and doesn't complain. To add to it and have "a bad feeling" is like a welcome hug from a long lost friend and it all fits into place neatly.

When Gee joins Lellan she tells him of her senses and that she has the ability which doesn't surprise him in the least. He has learnt that some humans do have the gift but has never met one until now. He is glad that she has told him and intrigued by how it all works. He is amazed at how non plus she deals with it by simply taking it in her stride, without sugar coating the ability and using it like she would her little finger. She actually takes the advice of her mother and stays close to the cave while Lellan goes hunting during early sun. Gee goes to the grand hall where she had first met Mogue. She finds Mogue at the heart of a meeting. The meeting turns out to be more of a heated debate about another Spognoff tribe to the far west who are not to be trifled with because of their higher numbers. Mogue is the peace keeper and always manages to keep everyone happy but even this subject is a test for his skills.

The troublesome tribe are called the Moounkies. They had settled just like the Gladestines and are usually a peaceful tribe. The problem that caused the debate is that they want to temporarily shelter amongst the Gladestines to learn the ways of the humans first hand. Sadly the Gladestines do not have the space to house all of the Moounkies and extra hunting would be required and it would upset the balance around them. It has been a ridiculous suggestion and now the Gladestines have to come up with a solution to keep both tribes happy. In the end it was settled that only half a dozen could stay. As Gee is now a welcome face she suggested volunteering her services, as a human they can meet when the guests are visiting. She offered some of her free time; after all her kind was the reason the Gladestines were going to have company in thirty days time. It was inevitable that this would happen because as the humans start to live amongst the Spognoffs in months and years to come it is understandable that the Spognoff tribes of Teeria would want to know who they may bump into.

When the meeting comes to an end everyone disperses and Gee decides to stay knowing that Mogue will be back in due course to handle further matters that may need his attention. She goes and sits down on one of the large steps, which are covered in a thick fur hide. She guesses it had once belonged to a Leeaque as it is large and covers quite an area. She is deep in contemplation as to when Lellan would be back and hazards a guess to anytime now.

All of a sudden she feels a presence behind her and something up close against her back. Before she can turn around she feels a hard metal object thrust up against her throat.

She guesses it is a knife. She hardly dares to breathe and doesn't move or speak until she is spoken to.

'You have to leave us alone. The next time you are here your life will end,' says a male Spognoff.

Gee can feel the blade from a knife press harder against her skin. With one quick and accurate move he nicks her skin and makes her jump.

Not wanting to provoke the Spognoff she doesn't say a word. He then jumps down in front of her. She automatically holds her hand against the small cut which is wet to the touch as it is slowly seeping blood. Her hand is becoming a rusty red from the fresh blood. She has to put more pressure on the cut with the palm of her hand to slow the bleeding. She knows it was made on purpose as a scare tactic and not meant to cause damage. He grabs her shoulders still dangerously holding the knife.

Despite being threatened Gee isn't willing to back down so easily.

'Why should I leave my friends… Lellan?' She is looking at a young male Spognoff with defiance, who she guesses is nineteen human years old.

He has small facial features and random braids in his long shoulder length dark hair.

'All you need to know is that you are not welcome here. Take that cut to your throat as a warning,' he growls almost spitting at her with rage.

'Unhand her immediately!' booms Mogue.

He is accompanied by Lellan and another Spognoff Gee does not know. His name is Baaron and he is a close friend of Lellans.

'She has to leave here and not return!' shouts the young volatile Spognoff gripping Gee harder, clearly annoyed he hadn't fled sooner as planned before being caught.

'Tell me why or drop this now!' Mogue is very agitated and Lellan slips off while the young Spognoff's attention is turned.

'This human...' He shakes Gee roughly, 'is interfering with our future blood. She should not be allowed to carry on with your Son. There are others more suitable!'

'Like your sister - Azala?'

'We have only kissed,' squeaks Gee.

'Enough Gee. It is none of his business or ours. Now I will only ask you one more time to unhand her!'

Lellan pounces from behind and splits the pair up. Gee topples down a level and Lellan punches the Spognoff before he is able to get to his feet. Lellan then takes the Spognoff by the scruff of the neck and shoves him into the grip of his fellow Spognoff, Baaron.

'Not that it is your concern...' Lellan growls, 'but it is up to me who I spend my time with and it is not your sister. Azala and I are good friends and always will be as we have grown up together... She will be very upset when she hears about this.' He is soon at Gees side.

She hadn't moved with all of the commotion and was still laying on the step. With Lellan's help she sits up but is left shaken. By this time a crowd has gathered and one of the female Spognoffs is attending to Gee's wound with a clean bowl of water and cloth.

The troubled Spognoff is about to be led away to the center floor of the hall.

'Wait!' Gee shouts standing up shakily and walking towards the bound youth. Lellan rushes to her side surprised by her action. Everyone looks at the human with question. The youth looks at her still with anger in his eyes.

'What is your name?' Gee straightens up. The male Spognoff looks at Mogue for permission to speak. Mogue nods with a smirk and admiration for the young human woman.

'Grenant. Why?' he says sarcastically looking at Gee.

'Because Grenant...' Gee uses the same tone, 'I have asked the same questions myself and have even given Lellan the space so that he can follow his own path. I would appreciate it - if anyone has any concerns to come and talk to me, instead of *this*.' She points at her cleanly dressed neck with annoyance. Her attention is caught by Grenant's familiar appearance leaving her with an odd feeling, 'You look familiar. Do I know you?'

'No but we may have crossed paths out and about.' Grenant shifts uncomfortably on the spot. His sarcasm and anger has suddenly diminished which hasn't gone unnoticed.

'What are you up to Grenant?' asks Mogue.

'Nothing,' he says quickly to Mogue, wanting to carry on the conversation with Gee to cover the hidden truth, 'If you have asked such questions then why are you still here?' Lellan gives a low grumble of protest at his question and Gee has to hold him back behind her before he throws another punch. Grenant has already got a bleeding lip.

'I am still here because Lellan spelt out a few things and helped me understand how ridiculous I was being. This is inevitable in the future... for humans and Spognoffs. You should have spoken to Lellan or

166

anyone for that matter, and not go about it like an unthinkable idiot. I'm sorry it has upset you Grenant.'

'And… They both have my blessing,' adds Mogue, cementing the situation before it gets out of hand with others.

'I am… sorry… for hurting you. I should have spoken first.' Grenant gives Gee a strange look but she brushes it off assuming he is still somewhat thrown by his own behaviour.

'You are young and have much to learn. Now can we let him go?' Gee looks at Mogue satisfied she has rectified the situation.

'No, we have a policy and he has to go to council. We will take his apology into account and the fact that you want to be lenient with him, but we cannot ignore that he has threatened you. Take him,' Mogue orders and Grenant is led to council.

'What will happen to him?' asks Gee worried.

'My Father will tell a group of Spognoffs who represent all of us of what has happened. They will then ask Grenant questions and then will make a decision of punishment.'

'Punishment?' Gee abruptly shouts. 'But… once we spoke I could see that he understood that he had took the wrong approach.'

'Yes whether you like it or not… he harmed you which is unacceptable. We do not stand for such outrageous behaviour.'

'What will the punishment be?'

'They will take into account that it is his first misconduct. I would have thought they will agree to give him a severe verbal warning and isolate him away from his family and friends for eighteen to twenty seven passed suns. This will give him time to really think about what he has done and what the implications could have been if he had taken it further if we hadn't of shown up when we did.'

'Isolation sounds drastic.' Gee pouts feeling guilty.

'He hurt... *you,*' growls Lellan with frustration, 'You forget that he has cut you – our and my guest. It is our way and much is at stake for us to handle it properly. A full report will be sent to your Father to make sure he is happy with the outcome. Now we have to go and find Azala so she can be here when council begins...'

'Ok. I will be glad to help and explain. I guess that bad feeling I had was because of what has happened here.' They walk out of the hall to find Azala.

'It would make sense – pardon the pun,' he laughs along with Gee at the bad joke. 'The bad feeling you get – is it when you are in danger?'

'No not necessarily, it could be me or anyone, or anything I care about. Like in your case it could have been to do with Snoot getting injured or simply a thorn stuck in his paw. The stronger the feeling generally the worse it will be. I'm very intuitive. I haven't had any inclination since we moved. It surprised me this early sun as it was so strong.'

'It is good to know how it works but probably a worry for you to. You can relax now Gee.' He slips his arm around her waist while they walk.

'Yes I can, can't I,' she says smiling his favourite smile at him.

* * *

Gee is walked to the Isca Bridge by Lellan and Baaron as they need to go to the market and Posall is out in the field carrying out some extra work. Lellan is carrying a freshly caught Dirum carcass over his shoulder to trade which is very similar to our small roe deer. Baaron has a cloth satchel slung over his shoulder which he intends to fill up with the traded goods. Lellan never lets Gee walk home alone which is appreciated by her and her parents as it is quite a trek. Lellan watches as she crosses the Isca Bridge then goes about getting some goods from the market for the value of the Dirum. One Dirum fetches many staple food items and luxury goods. Lellan intends to give the staple food to his friend Jjaym the chef and get a book for Gee amongst other things.

Gee gets home and immediately heads to find the research journal to make a note of what happened with Grenant. She wants to make sure it is logged in her own words so nothing is left unsaid. She gets to the cubby hole where the journal is always placed, but it isn't there. She turns around and quickly scans the room. She sees some books are out of place on the side table next to her dad's chair.

A sickening feeling then comes over her as she realises there is somebody else present in the room and jumps. There is a silhouette of a figure sat by the front window looking incredibly laid back, reading the journal.

Gee musters to move a step forward to get a good look at the intruder who has broken into the Goshle house. Gee lets out a gasp of horror.

'How did you know where I live? Get out of here!' She shouts angrily from the pit of her stomach as she makes her way over to where Aidy Campion is sat. She isn't scared anymore.

'I have my sources… Oh, and it's nice to see you too Gee.' He doesn't elaborate on who his source was. He continues, 'you could show more appreciation, what with me coming so far to see you. It has been too long.' He stands and smiles wryly.

'Good and well I didn't ask you to come. I cannot forgive you for killing innocent people. All they wanted was to help those who wanted to leave Earth. What have you done and… become?' She hardly recognises him.

He has a harder exterior and the gawkiness that once shone has vanished. His whole appearance is bulkier and the thin stick of a person she remembers is gone.

'I didn't want you to leave. Why didn't you tell me you were leaving?'

'I couldn't, we weren't allowed to tell anyone.'

'I could have gotten you out of this and had papers drawn up.'

'I wanted to come don't you see? I was looking forward at seeing a new planet. I *am* sorry if you feel let down, but we were only ever mail pals. I don't understand what all the fuss is about,' she says calmly.

'I thought and think of you as far more than a mail pal…' he says grumpily. 'I told you in an email I would see you again once I had settled on EMMA. This…' he gestures at the room in disgust, 'is not for you!'

'I don't want you here. We are no longer friends after that stunt your group pulled. How could you? What has happened to you Aidy?' She is genuinely concerned for the man and cannot understand how different he is.

'I *am* here! I *am* taking you back with me! We are EMMA's future and you *will* be by my side.'

'No, do you hear you stupid man? Have you had a brain transplant or something? I do not recognise you anymore Aidy. The answer is no! Your people are murderers!' She is so cross at his presumptions and the thought of it rocked her as she spoke. He seems to think she will obey his every command.

'You don't have a choice!'

'What are you going to do kidnap me?' She laughs out of hysteria.

'Yes if I need to or you can come along willingly.'

'Never!' she shouts and the colour drains from her cheeks.

Aidy throws the family journal and it clatters to the floor at his feet. He destroys it further by stamping on it with his boot.

He walks around Gee in a large circle, 'You *are* coming with me. Nobody will know where you have gone. They will think are staying out for the night. When they realise, it will be too late. I snuck in here without anybody knowing so we will leave the same way. We are leaving now.' He steps closer to her. Gee tries to evade his advances to the door but he grabs her arm. She twists round to fight him off and he slaps her using the back of his hand. It knocks her off her feet and she ends up on the floor next to the broken journal. She reaches for it and as she does he grabs her by the hair and pulls her to her feet. She screams out in pain, but she still lashes out at him. He holds her tightly but struggles to keep a good hold as she is fighting so hard against him.

He decides on a different tactic and lets her go. She runs straight for the door. Gee can't believe she managed to fight free and then hears, 'I wouldn't if I was you!' Aidy says in a sure low tone.

Gee swivels around to see that he is pointing a small weapon at her.

'You're going to shoot me now Aidy?' She stands up straight not taking her eye off the gun.

'Yes, if I have to. A shot doesn't have to kill you, just maim! Now get away from the door.' Gee turns white in colour but does as she is told. 'You are not staying here or having anyfurther relationship with that ape man – Lellan.'

'He is a Spognoff and not… an ape man.' She is stood in front of him and the gun; and surprised he had the time to read so much of the journal.

'Well it certainly isn't safe for you here, look at your neck.' He rips off the dressing and touches it which makes Gee wince away; but not because of any pain but because of him.

He is annoyed by her reaction and by her being harmed. He grabs her arm and glares at her.

As if reading his thoughts she quickly defends Lellan.

'Lellan didn't do this. It was a misunderstanding and it is all sorted out now. It is just a nick of the skin and the dressing made it out to be worse than it is.'

'That's my girl, always being supportive and loyal. Now get some stuff together we are going.' He shoves her in the direction of the other rooms and stands on the spot watching, and then follows as she goes upstairs.

Gee is shaken up and her mind is racing, wondering how she can get word to someone. Keeping her head down she gathers her essentials quickly, not wanting to irritate him further. She cannot bear to look at him. They go back down and she heads into the kitchen. He is in close pursuit but then stops at the doorway and keeps a lookout through the front room windows. This is an opportunity and she grabs it by digging out a pen from her bag. She quickly scribbles on the card board lid of the camomile tea box while pretending to get some tea, "The bad feeling is true. HELP. Aidy here and kidnapping me. Taking me to EMMA."

'What's taking you so long Gee?' Aidy shouts as he enters the kitchen after being satisfied that all is well out the front.

'Tea bags…' Gee holds them up shakily then stuffs them into her bag.

She hopes and prays that her mother will be predictable in a crisis and have a cup of camomile tea.

'Come on, stop stalling,' he snaps.

Aidy is very composed and confident and unaware

of the scribbled note. He hurries her out of the front door. She has her bag over her shoulder with Aidy's arm around her waist. His other hand is concealed resting inside his jacket whilst holding the gun pointed at her. They leave her home and head the way he came, towards the Isca Bridge.

The walk is quiet with the odd straggler because it is last light and the end of the day for everyone. Each person has a job or purpose so most of them are busy finishing off their days work.

Aidy tightens his grip, pressing the gun against her side and whispers in her ear that if she so much as picks up the walking pace, he will not be responsible for who he shoots. Gee just does as she is told, all the time aware that a dangerous gun is pressed against her ribs.

They walk side by side all the way out of Isca. They even walk past the school where her mother Ameel teaches. Gee takes a quick glance to see if she can see her mum, but there is no sign of her in the playground, playtime was over long ago.

This was her last hope at this time of day of somebody she knew seeing her. Her mother would have recognised Aidy and questioned it. Her father and brother are out in the field and Lellan will probably be on his way back home by now.

She cries inside not daring to draw attention to herself and put anyone in danger. Her walking is on autopilot as she is not willing her feet to move.

Once they are across Isca Bridge they are faced with a crowd of people. Humans and Spognoffs are all going about their trading. Aidy squeezes Gee even closer. Gee daren't move her head, so with her eyes she searches the crowd and spots a familiar stance.

It is Baaron. He turns just at the right time and sees Gee with the stranger. He can also see she looks petrified and quickly hurries to the next stall where

Lellan is doing a deal on the final part of the Dirum leg.

She feels like she is going to get caught out any second and her heart is racing quickly. She closes her eyes for a brief second and takes in a deep quiet breath to calm down. All the time Aidy is oblivious to Gees quiet find.

Baaron points out Gee and the unfamiliar man to Lellan. Lellan has spent long enough in her presence to know she is with him under protest.

Gees eyes widen when she sees Lellan about to march towards their direction which makes her jump because of the gun threat but luckily Baaron holds him back. Aidy feels her jump and pushes them both on harder through the crowd.

Lellan and Baaron are no longer in her eye line and she cannot see what is going on. They head east along the coast towards the TRF head quarters premises.

* * *

Lellan and Baaron are both panicked by what they have just seen. They knew by how wide Gee's eyes were and how pale she was with fright to know something was seriously wrong. They think quickly on the spot not moving from the hustle and bustle of the crowd. Lellan gives the remaining goods to Baaron to put in the bag and then tells him roughly where her family live. Baaron was to leave immediately so the scent of Gee and the stranger would be fresh and easier for him to find her home. He was to find out any clues and wait for a family member. Lellan is to follow Gee and the kidnapper because he is exceptionally good at hunting.

Lellan and Baaron go their separate ways. Lellan soon picks up Gees very familiar scent. He runs and swiftly catches them up. He hangs back a little not wanting to get Gee hurt or to spook the stranger. While watching Gee he remembers what kind of day she has had and the bad feeling she had woken up with and how it had worried her. They were both wrong about Grenant being the one to blame. Her feeling was strong which they had both taken lightly and he now knows that caution is the key to this unexplained problem. He creeps along and sees that they walk around the back of the TRF head quarters. He doesn't understand where the stranger is taking her or why.

By now they are out the back of TRF's head quarters by half a mile. Lellan has to duck and take cover in the long grass and lay low as Gee and the unknown man have stopped. The man presses a button on his wrist band. With one touch of the button a small space vessel is uncloaked. He shoves Gee along as a ramp lowers on their approach. Lellan hurries forward not wanting her to leave. Once they have reached the ramp Lellan is almost upon them but still hidden. When they have disappeared inside, Lellan creeps up the ramp and enters into the ship, slowly.

'Watch Out!' shouts Gee.

'Ge...e...e...' Aidy hits him over the head with the gun before he can ask her if she is alright and he slumps to the ground unconscious.

'Well what do we have here?' says Aidy straightening up his clothing.

'Don't hurt him, please,' begs Gee.

Aidy chains Lellan up because he has read about the Spognoff's strength. He feels very sure of himself after bagging himself a Spognoff. Just as he is about to set the ship into motion, by giving his personal agent Bryne the orders and closing up the ramp, Grenant appears. Gee looks at him and frowns. She is confused to see that Grenant is not in council and that he seems to know Aidy.

'I have done what you wanted; now give me what I

175

asked for in return,' says Grenant with an irritated tone.

Gee is sitting next to Lellan, who is still unconscious, with her mouth open disbelieving what her ears are hearing.

'How the hell do you two know each other?' she asks.

'Keep out of it Gee,' Aidy silences her. 'You shouldn't have come,' Aidy says while closing the hatch.

'We had a deal! Where are my goods?' repeats Grenant.

'There were never any goods. You better get going on your way Grenant before we take off,' says Aidy.

'I am not leaving without my goods we had agreed on. I would not have done it otherwise and Lellan was not part of the deal.' Grenant feels angry and misled, clenching his fists ready to strike Aidy.

Aidy is one step ahead and is very much unfazed by being caught and pulls out the unseen gun which was tucked away under his jacket. He doesn't want to waste time arguing with Grenant and decides to take him instead too. Aidy orders Grenant to sit down and he chains him up not wanting another untamed Spognoff on the loose. Now he has his Gee and two Spognoffs aswell for his efforts so all in all it has been a successful trip.

'How did you get out of the council? You have responsibilities and you cut me.' Gee gets up as she is unchained.

Her hands are tied but she knows that won't stop her kicking him. Aidy happily keeps her restrained by holding her around the waist.

'I am quick and the councillors are slow and old. I soon became invisible in the caves. I was trying to make you see sense back there – to scare you off Teeria but you just had to ruin it and talk to me didn't you. I

176

would have left before Mogue had found me and you would have done what I had asked. I would have been heavily guarded if you hadn't of been so insistent to help my plea. Look,' he shakes his chains desperately trying to get loose, 'this is your doing!' He growls and it makes Gee try to shake Aidy loose but he has a firm grasp.

'This is not my fault; I'm not holding you captive. Let him go Aidy. Let us all go!'

'It's too late, once my mind is made up that's it.' Aidy says in a matter of fact manner.

'Why would you want to scare me off Teeria?' says Gee referring back to the conversation with Grenant without letting it drop.

She looks at Grenant confused. Her expression turns blank. It all suddenly makes sense to her that Grenant and Aidy were in on it together and that is how they know each other. She had seen Grenant close to her family home many days ago but didn't know him and just assumed he was running errands. Earlier she had took pity on him for being young and acting first instead of thinking, but he had been instructed to do what he had done, it was all a ploy.

'It was you Grenant! I saw you on Isca. You set me up – you bloody fool – you trusted an outsider? Let go of me!' she shouts and stamps hard on Aidy's foot to get free.

She is so angry by her revelation she turns on Aidy. She launches herself at him, kicking him twice before Bryne can get a firm hold on her.

'You are feisty Gee. You and I are going to get along just fine. Now sit down and behave…' says Aidy. He makes sure her hands are still tied tightly so he has some control of her, 'Oh, I can confirm Grenant has helped me, but look where it has gotten him.' He looks at Grenant and speaks, 'You shouldn't have marked my

Gee. You and Lellan will come in very useful back on EMMA.'

Chapter 13

Lellan opens his eyes disorientated. He is suffering from a throbbing headache having been hit over the back of the head. He can feel something tight around his wrists, restraining them behind his back and something across his mouth. The last thing he can remember is watching Gee board the unknown vessel and not being too far behind her.

'Thank God Lellan. It's me – Gee. Are you alright?' whispers Gee.

She is tied up next to the slouched Spognoff on the deck floor of the cargo hold of the small vessel. She strains to get as close to him as possible and rests her head on his shoulder.

'What…happened?' His voice is barely audible and unclear because of the gag in his mouth.

'We have been kidnapped. You followed me onto the ship and then Aidy hit you on the head.'

'Kidnapped?' he growls through his gag. 'Who is…Aidy?' He sits up a little with difficulty because of his restraints which makes him groan from the discomfort.

'The man is delusional. Our family met him years ago back on Earth during one of our holidays and we stayed in touch. I was too polite to tell him I wasn't interested in staying in contact and then he told me he had joined the EMMA group.'

'EMMA?'

'Yes I only stayed in touch to find out what I could. EMMA is an over sized space sphere. They created it so that when Earth gradually gets harder to live on people can be evacuated there but then NASA made the discovery you and I both know about. To my family there isn't a comparison of living in a tin can or living on a planet.'

'So he has abducted you to take you back to EMMA for good?'

'Yes! And that's not all. Look…' She points over to where Grenant is sitting motionless over the far side. 'He was in on this the whole time. He had an arrangement with Aidy for trading purposes!' she almost shrieks.

'This just gets better – it does make sense now. It was so unlike Grenant back there. It has not done him any favours. I will deal with him later – if I could get hold of him now he would get hurt,' rumbles Lellan flushing red.

'What are we going to do? Aidy was waiting in the house for me. I managed to write a brief note on my Mum's tea box lid.'

'That is good. I had sent Baaron back to yours to pick up clues as to what was going on and he is good. He is good at puzzles.'

'This isn't a puzzle,' Gee nearly shouts. 'He means business. When we had only just departed Earth Aidy had had a Teerian shuttle blown up. It was following us and was second to take off, we were lucky to survive. He then had a gun pointed at me in the house and on the walk to this ship. Then he managed to kidnap three of us in total. We have been flying for, I'm guessing, a couple of Earth hours now – what the hell are we going to do?' She looks panicked.

'We need to stay calm and go with it, we do not have much choice and we haven't a clue where we are. He did not gag you so he does not see you as a threat. He probably wanted you to talk some sense into me after waking so I did not try and get out of my restraints and break the hull which would cause an accident. I do not have the strength to get out of them or we could take command of this vessel.' He leans forward so Gee can see what he is bound with.

'It looks like they are shackles and made out of some sort of strong metal – no wonder you are stuck, you are also chained to the wall.' He leans back against Gee and they both close their eyes hoping everything will be alright.

'I thought I heard voices.' Aidy is stood in front of them with a sly grin plastered across his face, arms folded across his chest.

'What do you want with us?' Lellan growls through his gag with every muscle tensed in his body.

'Gee is mine. You and Grenant will be used for research. Your species are of great interest to us, with your strength and pigmentation.' Gee gets up in an uncontrollable rage and slams into him then kicks him and Lellan is helpless as he watches her.

'I will never be yours – never!' she shouts in a rage like the wild cat Lellan had once already seen.

Aidy grabs her by the arm and pushes her to the other side of the cargo hold. He chains her up this time to the opposite wall of Lellan. He moves over to Lellan and kicks him in the leg like a dog.

'This is your punishment Gee for kicking me. Your actions have consequences.' Lellan doesn't flinch but his skin starts to faintly flutter in waves of red. Lellan soon gets control of it in seconds and it goes unnoticed. Aidy walks off and Gee is in floods of tears. Lellan doesn't look fazed by the pathetic kick from the kidnapper and he doesn't want to give him the satisfaction or to worry Gee.

* * *

Ameel enters her home after a difficult and trying day. She puts her bag and paperwork down on a table in the hallway before heading into the kitchen. She walks past the living room door and shrieks. In her living room is a male Spognoff who she doesn't know. He turns and looks at her directly.

'Take what you want then please leave,' she shrieks again now rooted to the floor.

'Please do not be afraid. Lellan sent me, I'm Baaron,' he says simply trying not to elevate the situation.

'You say Lellan sent you?' she says sounding calmer after hearing his name.

'Yes. Please sit down Mrs Goshle. We have a situation.'

'I don't like the sound of that.' She sits with her hands clasped nervously in her lap, 'What situation? Is Gee ok?'

Baaron fills her in on what exactly has happened so Ameel can make her own judgement. Before they go anyfurther she contacts Posall who cuts his extra long working day short and makes his way home as soon as he can. When he reaches TRF head quarters he goes directly to see General Carter. He fills him in on everything that his wife has told him which isn't much help but enough for General Carter to authorise TRF to head a search party with volunteers. While Baaron and Ameel are waiting for Posall's arrival they go through each room seeing what has been disturbed because they have already seen the smashed up journal on the floor in the sitting room and various items that have been moved. They both enter Gee's room for clues and see that she had left in a hurry because her draws had been pulled out and not returned back into place. Ameel knows that it is unlike her daughter to leave her room in a mess.

Baaron growls on his return to the sitting room, as he did when he had entered the property, because he can smell a strong unknown scent.

With certainty he says, 'The intruder has been all around the house with your Daughter, but it is strongest in here.'

Ameel is shaken by his revelation and sits down once again. She is beside herself with worry and hasn't a clue who would kidnap her daughter. She is visibly shaken and is starting to get stressed and frustrated with the situation and annoyed that her husband hasn't returned yet. Baaron goes to the middle of the floor and gets down on one knee to look at the carpet. He has found some long black hair.

'This must be Gee's hair because the man she was with only had short brown hair. She must have fought him to lose this amount of hair,' says Baaron.

He holds it up so it is easily seen and takes it to Ameel whose eyes are wide and brimming with tears of dread and anger. Just then they hear the front door open and Baaron is immediately on the defensive because it is clear to him a serious struggle had taken place in this house and he wasn't about to let anything else happen to this poor woman who has had her daughter taken with no explanation. There was no need for Baaron to worry as it is Posall returning home along with Cam. Posall had picked Cam up on his way home and had told him what was going on.

Posall is immediately concerned about his wife as soon as he sets eyes on her. He sits on the edge of her chair and comforts her and tells Baaron to start from the beginning. Once Posall and Cam are up to date Ameel feels even more frustrated because time is still passing by and nothing has been achieved. Posall tells Cam to make a drink for them all and a camomile tea for his mother. Posall gets in touch with the search party. They hadn't found Gee or Lellan but did find marks in the long grass behind the head quarters building thanks to some volunteer Spognoffs' tracking abilities. TRF rightfully think that the marks are from the flat footed landing gear of a small ship. Posall finishes the conversation by agreeing that security should check the surveillance footage and check for any unknown aircraft entering in or leaving the Teerian atmosphere throughout the day.

'Son of a bitch!' Cam angrily shouts from the kitchen.

Everyone turns around towards the direction of the outburst to see Cam coming back into the room looking very angry, 'I found this…it's in Gee's hand writing.' Cam is holding the box of camomile tea. He shows it to everyone and reads the written message out aloud, "The bad feeling is true. HELP. Aidy here and kidnapping me. Taking me to EMMA."

'That bastard has come here and taken our Gee. Who does he think he is?! She hadn't been in touch with him for a long time or at least since she found out we were leaving because she didn't want to compromise your work.' Cam glares at everyone fit for bursting.

'Aidy has taken her?' Ameel cannot comprehend what she has heard.

'It's here in black and white Mum.'

'It makes you wonder how she managed to get this past Aidy,' says Posall taking the tea box from Cam and re-reading it again.

'She was bloody lucky and quick on her feet if you ask me! He has hurt her Dad, just look at the hair he has pulled out that Mum is still holding. What are we going to do?'

'Well we now know where she is going thankfully because of the risky chance she took. Thank God you love camomile tea Ameel or we wouldn't be anyfurther forward and still waiting for TRF's findings.'

'Happy to help,' Ameel says dryly.

'That is why Gee did it because she knows what Mother is like in a crisis.'

'We will contact General Carter, and Baaron, you really need to get back and tell Mogue what has happened. You must tell him that Lellan has possibly been kidnapped too unless TRF have found him. Have him call me directly then we will go and get them both back if that's the case. Cam, go with him and take him back using a shuttle – it's quicker. Get back as soon as. You are coming with me.'

'Hold on one minute,' says Ameel. 'I'm not being left here alone while you two go off gaily vaunting about.'

'Good point love.'

'Maybe you should go back with Baaron…no…no. Stay here. Cam on your way back, go and get Tiarla and Ven so your Mother has company.' Ameel couldn't argue with what Posall had proposed and knew it was the best thing to do, as she didn't want to slow them up.

Ameel cannot understand what would possess Aidy to carry out such an act. All she hopes for is that her daughter is returned unharmed.

'I should have been more understanding,' says Ameel guiltily.

'Why love?'

'It's the bad feeling she wrote about – she had told me this morning. If I hadn't of let her out of my sight none of this would have happened.'

'This Aidy sounds like a determined man. You could have got hurt in his path,' says Baaron logically.

Baaron then tells them all about Gee's day and the attack from Grenant. He told them how she had misconstrued that to have been the problem she was to face during her day otherwise she wouldn't have been left alone. There was no reason to believe she was going to come to any harm in her own home. This helps ease Ameel's guilt but she feels sick to the pit of her stomach and anguished by what her daughter is going through.

* * *

Lellan and Gee look at each other helplessly knowing that Aidy is in full control. Gee has worked out roughly that the journey will take about three days to get to EMMA. It will not take as long as it did in the NASA ship because it is a smaller, lighter vessel. They both cringe at the thought of being cooped up in the cargo bay for so long on the hard floor. They can only just make out Grenant in the dull light and both agree an animal would be treated with more respect. Aidy appears and roots out some blankets to try and make Gee more comfortable. She kicks them away not interested in his efforts of kindness.

'If you play nicely Gee I will untie you – but I'm not willing to take any risks when we are flying through space. It is up to you?' He waits for her to mull over what he has just said.

Gee looks in Lellans direction. He nods at her and with his eyes, wills her to behave, for her sake at least.

'If I agree... will you lay off Lellan? You mustn't hurt him or I will not rest until you pay for what you are doing.' Gee says calmly.

'You are not in a position to bargain for his life...,' but he can see she means what she has said, '...but for the research purpose he can be alive so I will spare his life if you cooperate. I cannot be any fairer.'

Once again Gee looks at Lellan just wishing this ridiculous nightmare would end. She cannot believe she is bartering for his life. Lellan nods again and winks with a twinkle. She takes the sign as a positive move and agrees reluctantly with Aidy.

Aidy removes her chains at once and takes her into the cabin at the front of the ship. Aidy purposely leaves the doors ajar so Lellan can see that he isn't invited to the party. Gee sits down in a comfortable seat and has a drink. While she sips her drink she feels guilt with every drop that goes down her throat. Aidy takes some water to the Spognoffs.

'She has just bought you your life so I suggest you behave - Spognoff!' Aidy hisses and removes Lellan's gag and rearranges his chain so he is able to drink and feed.

Lellan accepts the water but says nothing keeping his thoughts to himself. Aidy closes the door to the cargo bay so no more interaction can take place between "his" Gee and the Spognoff.

The journey seems endless and far from comfortable for Lellan and Grenant who are still shackled; and for Gee who feels awkward about keeping up her end of the bargain. She despises Aidy for what he has done and for what he is now doing. All she wants is to go home but instead she is curled up in a chair looking very upset. She knows with her agreement she has bought them both a little time before her father and TRF can make a rescue attempt, with all hope resting on a small cardboard box which holds the key to where she is. She doesn't know how long she can keep up being civilised with Aidy. "Calm" she reminds herself of Lellan's words. She thinks back to the twinkle he had in his eye and wonders if it is perhaps because she *had* bought them both a little more time which suited him. Lellan is a clever being and a quick thinker. She knows he won't settle until he is at a point of content where everyone is safe.

During the journey Aidy keeps to his word and treats Lellan with the respect Gee has asked for. She is only in the cockpit cabin because Lellan had wanted her to be there. She isn't allowed to go and talk to him or allowed to look in his direction. Each time they are both fed and watered, she manages to see Lellan, and then the door is closed. She is then reprimanded by either Aidy or Bryne. She is constantly being closely watched by them. They remind her of the deal she had made and drum it into her so should she go back on her word and cause trouble, "the Spognoffs" could be just as useful dead. But Gee lives for the tiny glimpses, it is the only comfort she can look forward to, while being kept under lock and key by the two men she doesn't know. When the door is open she can see Lellan has the same idea to catch a glimpse of her. She is alarmed that when Lellan looks up to see her, Aidy boots him in the side as a reminder that she is no longer his.

Aidy has a cabin bed set aside for Gee but she doesn't want to be far from Lellan – her Lellan. She knows he is just the other side of the door but isn't sure if she will ever see him again. She just wants to untie him and sit in his arms. She misses him and it has made her feel ill because he looks so vulnerable and separated in the dim light of the cargo bay. Gee looks incredible pale by the stress and ordeal and has only picked at the food put in front of her. When it is time to sleep she doesn't know if she has slept or is awake because of the shock and trauma. She has never seen anyone she loves hurt in such a ruthless manner or been faced with knowing that she may not ever see them again. It is heart wrenching and has taken its toll on her. The vibrant and feisty character of Gee is diminishing as each day passes due to the grip of responsibility and torment of keeping Lellan and Grenant alive. She knows she has to behave but to what end? And what will happen to her friends? She is trapped with no way out of Aidy's ever enclosing grasp.

Chapter 14

EMMA looms in the distance like a dangerous alien planet. It is a perfectly engineered metal sphere with the habitants living within. It looks very big from the outside, the size of a small planet. The blank metal does not give anything away of what is hidden inside apart from the lighting suggesting the saying, "the light is on but is anyone home?" Aidy has noticed how quiet Gee has been throughout the journey and hopes he can break her out of her sombre mood. He is extremely pleased as they approach EMMA. He cannot wait to get more space between the Spognoffs and his Gee. For Gee the reverse has taken a hold of her and she is very troubled. The lack of sleep and food has changed her outgoing personality considerably and she has hardly moved off the chair Aidy had first sat her down on.

The docking station to EMMA is immense. To each side of the long dock are bays leading off to different areas of the sphere. Aidy's ship travels through the dock and past countless numbers of docking bays. It heads closer to the center of the grand honeycombed lump of metal. From the outside to the center of the core of EMMA it takes an hour and thirty minutes at high speed. While travelling, Aidy contacts a security guard party so they can be in place on their arrival. When the ship finally comes to rest in a bay on the left, Aidy immediately tells Bryne to keep Gee contained while he goes and 'deals' with the other passengers. Bryne has his hand on Gee's shoulder to keep her in place in her chair, knowing she may not be so well behaved when she sees Lellan being carted away.

Gee sees Aidy disappear off into the gloom of the cargo bay and then light floods in because of the lowering of the ramp. Six guards approach the ship.

They are wearing black uniforms. Each one has an ear piece for communication and an electronic immobiliser stick, should the captives not cooperate.

The guards enter the ship, three stop at Grenant and three others approach Lellan. Gee can hear a growl and knows it is from Lellan. One of the guards gently touches him with the immobiliser stick in the ribs, as a warning, giving Lellan a small shock. Gee tries to stand up, but she feels weak and forgets Bryne has a hand on her shoulder. She feels helpless as she watches Lellan being hauled up and unchained from the ships hull. Lellan looks at her as long as he is allowed. He can see she is in a fragile state and winks at her to raise her spirits. Gee does the same in return with the tears that are already brimming, running down her cheeks. She cannot bear it and without thinking she makes a desperate attempt to get free. She bites Brynes hand and manages to wriggle free from his continuous grasps and runs straight to Lellan.

Lellan leans forward unable to hold her because of his shackled hands. Gee wraps her arms around his waist tightly. He knows it can only last for seconds and whispers in her ear, 'Grenant and I can look after ourselves. Do what you have to do. Trust me when I say ignore his blackmail attempts – no matter what the consequences are.' He looks into her eyes, 'I love you Gee.'

'I love you too Lellan.' She touches his face making it flutter blue. Suddenly, Lellans sturdy stance is weakened and he is stunned from a blow to his ribs by an immobiliser on a stronger setting. Gee is dragged away from Lellan by Bryne who finally has a firm hold on her. Lellan uses all of his strength and lashes out at the three guards and knocks two clean off their feet and into the side of the ship. Two men who are attending Grenant come over to help. Grenant is being held by one guard at arms length with an immobiliser stick turned up to full strength. The other two approach Lellan with caution even though he is still shackled but he is not secured by any guard. One guard walks straight towards Lellan with his arm out stretched gaining his attention. The other two sneak either side and then all three use the immobilisers to take control of him.

Gee is frantically trying to get free and Bryne has a hell of a job to keep hold of her. Aidy has to come and give him a hand. They both have hold of her while she watches Lellan being dragged away. He is barely able to walk after such a nasty assault. Gee's body goes limp after the effort to get to Lellan and she feels weak again, now that the adrenaline has waned. She collapses in her kidnappers arms after fainting from exhaustion.

* * *

Gee wakes up to the sound of voices close by, 'Is she alright?' Aidy asks quietly.

'She is exhausted Sir.' Gee hears another man speak and keeps her eyes closed.

She instantly remembers what happened and doesn't wish to see where she is.

Aware of Aidy's silence the Dr continues, 'Give her time. She is a very healthy young woman. It shouldn't be much longer.' Gee wonders how long she'd been asleep.

'Ok thank you,' says Aidy sounding disappointed. The other man leaves.

Gee feels the bed move when someone sits on the side of it. Someone takes her hand and cups it in theirs. She automatically snatches it away opening her eyes to see it is Aidy. Aidy takes back her hand and holds it with both of his as he is so relieved to see she is awakening. Her eyes are open at last.

'Glad to see you are back with us Gee.' He smiles.

Gee looks around still feeling groggy. She sees a square room with a door off to the right. The room is plainly decorated. She is immediately aware that there are no windows, just walls with a painting on each. She is in a bed made up with white cotton fabric. All she is wearing is a pink striped night shirt under the covers and her hair is splayed across the pillows.

'Who undressed me?' she says groggily with a scowl.

'The good doctor. Dr Wainwright. He has been looking after you in my absence. You have been out of it for nearly twenty four hours my dear.'

'And Lellan?' Gee desperately wants to leave this mess behind but until then she needs to know that he is alright.

Aidy decides whether to answer but knows it is best to keep her happy, for now at least.

'He is fine and in good hands. It was a damn shame he had to fight us when we landed – sorry you had to see that.' Tears appear in Gee's eyes as it is still all too fresh in her thoughts. Aidy adds, 'When you are on your feet you can see him – if that will put your mind to rest.'

'I want to see him now.' Gee tries to sit up but feels peculiar and weak making her lay back down.

'Give yourself time to recover Gee. You must eat something.' He can see she doesn't look convinced and so gently persuades her, 'It will help make you strong again. I promise.' She knows she doesn't have much of a choice at the moment.

'Ok,' she says with a grudge.

'Good. That's a nice necklace you have. Can I?'

'No.'

'Come, come Gee, there is no need to be like that.'

192

He ignores her and reaches out to take the necklace in his hand. 'It is exquisite. Where did you get it?' He lays it back against her skin.

'My parents gave it to me as a gift.' She doesn't want to tell him the truth because it is the only part of Lellan she has close at the moment and knows of the risk in losing it if she had told him the truth.

'They have a good eye. It suits you.'

He exits the room with a sly smirk; everything went very well and he is pleasantly surprised by how civil she had been. He intends to use her good behaviour to show her the sites on EMMA. He makes a call from the other room and orders some food for his guest. Gee lies in the double bed like an invalid. All she wants to do is to go and find Lellan. She decides once she has eaten she'll get dressed then see what can be found out. She groans knowing it will not be as easy as that and Aidy will take some persuading, but she is determined to try – she has to. Every limb and muscle is too weak for her to fight Aidy at the moment, but she isn't intending to give in so easily.

* * *

On their arrival Lellan and Grenant were led deep into the southern abyss of EMMA. After many corridors and lifts they were pushed into a holding room. When the guard left, each was still shackled like an animal.

The room is built up on three sides with an extremely hard quartz stone work. The flint based quartz is a dark blackish-grey. The fourth wall, which Lellan has hit and kicked with the intention of breaking it, has a sheet of reinforced glass from floor to ceiling. They are treated like lab rats locked up in a cage. The glass is for viewing purposes for the scientists. The cage chamber has been built against one of the walls inside a science lab.

'What have I done? Azala is going to be mad at me. I would rather face the isolation back home,' says Grenant with his head hung low.

'Yes, Azala can have a sharp tongue. But she will also know you do not have the number of suns to aid your decisions like us.'

'Still, this *is* all my fault. I am truly sorry for getting you and Gee caught up in this. I did not mean what I said to Gee about the whole messing with "blood lines"; even though… it would have been great having you as a kind of father figure, would settle for your friendship right now though,' says Grenant looking at his enclosed surroundings.

'I will always be your friend; and no, your sister and I just do not see each other that way. We are more like Brother and Sister. I was so mad at you back home and even my Father could not make sense of it all, but now it does. Let us get through this together as true friends and watch each other's backs.' Lellan gives him a friendly shove.

'Sounds good and thanks Lellan. Others would not be as understanding as you are. Maybe you could have a word with Azala when we return?' Grenant says with a grin.

Now that Lellan and Grenant have made amends and cleared the air of what had happened back on Teeria they can now try to think about escaping. After all they have known each other many years. Grenant can see he was naive to trust an outsider who hadn't been vetted by TRF. He is frightened and paces the small ten foot room backwards and forwards like a bored and restless zoo animal. Grenant is not only younger in years but younger in the ways of living. Grenant doesn't know much about other worlds outside of Teeria unlike Lellan who is well versed about the dying planet of Earth. Lellan persuades Grenant to sit beside him on the wooden bench provided and then they wait.

After an uncomfortable nights sleep, the guard gave them both some water to drink. Neither of them had had a drink since they were on the ship. A short time after, two guards escort Grenant out of the room leaving Lellan on his own. He is taken into the adjacent room and told to lie down on a table under the threat of the immobiliser. Lellan cannot hear what they are saying to Grenant through the thick glass and he stands still watching intently.

Grenant is tied down to the table with wide leather straps. The guard strapped his wrists, ankles, chest, hips and neck so tight that Grenant cannot move hardly an inch. Once he is securely in place, three scientists, a man and two women, enter the room from the far side. They are all dressed in white surgical coats with aprons securely tied.

Lellan sees that each one has a job to do. One goes and gets a metal trolley and wheels it to the side of Grenants table. The second retrieves some surgical gloves, suction pipes, including a pump; the third gathers some lethal looking surgical equipment, needles and swathing. The surgical equipment consists of scalpels, surgery scissors, bone cutters and clamps. Each horrendous item is laid out on the metal trolley in a neat row.

The surgical scissors are used to cut away Grenant's clothing by each scientist and then they are bagged up. Lellan stares at them all in disbelief with growl upon growl filling his room in a continuous echo. He is powerless and all he can do is protest the only way he knows how. He knows that Grenant is in real trouble and in grave danger.

The growling from Lellan is so loud that the

scientists and Grenant can hear from the room enveloping the cage chamber. Grenant cannot see what they are doing because he is strapped down and can only see the light above shining down on him. Grenant tries to strain against the straps with all of his strength, making them creak, but it is of no use.

The two women scientists begin with routine blood samples by taking tube upon tube for analysis. The next interest is in the skin pigmentation and flushing. They want to know the full extent of pain Grenant can endure until he flushes a strong red colour all over.

The head scientist takes a scalpel to Grenant's arm. He presses the scalpel to the skin of the arm then makes a shallow incision, sliding it along leaving a small cut line. The blood slowly seeps to the surface. Grenant doesn't make a sound because to him it is like an animal scratch but the scientists notice there was a brief and very faint fluttering of red around the cut.

Next the man makes a much longer incision on the inside of Grenant's arm which produces a longer period of red flushing. But still Grenant does not cry out.

The scientists then all look at each other and not saying a word, they all nod. Again the man takes the lead and takes the bone cutter scissors off the metal trolley and lines up a finger in between its blades. They note again there is a faint red flushing all over Grenants body which isn't because of the pain but because of the threat. The handles of the scissors are then squeezed shut, like a pair of sharp secateurs cutting through a tough stem of a shrub, slicing through the finger and taking it clean off. Grenant growls and tries to thrash about. His whole body is continually flushing red for a long time.

His amputated finger is put in a tub of ice and shut in a fridge. The scientists bandage up the stub where the finger used to be attached only because of the high volume of blood loss. They don't want him dead yet. They now know that a Spognoff's pain threshold is extremely high.

A mouth piece is then fitted into Grenant's mouth so anyfurther sound is muted. The man uses the scalpel again. It cuts Grenant deep this time in a straight line from chest to pelvis. Grenant screams out despite the mouth piece and Lellan can see tears running down his cheeks leaving a puddle on the table.

Lellan no longer watches what they are doing and keeps his focus on Grenant's face. With all the straining and thrashing Grenant's head has moved slightly and Lellan is in view. Their eyes lock and Lellan touches the glass reaching out to his young friend. Grenant then closes his eyes and loses consciousness.

Lellan is beside himself with rage and continues to bash his hands like a club against the window. He is wild, powerful and strong, fuelled by his anger and resentment. Each bash on the glass makes a tremendous racket in the adjacent room and the head scientist sends the guards to, 'shut the other prisoner up'.

Two guards enter Lellan's room with immobilisers at the ready. Lellan quickly crouches with both hands on the floor for balance, unperturbed by his shackles, then swings his leg around from behind. His leg slams into both of the guards lower legs and unbalances them. Lellan then pounces on one and throws a punch and knocks him unconscious. He gets back up and struggles to get hold of the other guard who has pressed an emergency buzzer.

Five other guards then enter the room and in a structured manner walk towards him. Lellan is backed into a corner. In one attempt the guards demobilise Lellan and leave him stunned and unconscious on the floor.

Lellan looks down at his hands after waking up. They are covered in blood from the repetitive beating of the glass and wall. He does not know how long he has been passed out on the floor where the guards had left him. He struggles to his feet, still feeling weak after the immobiliser assault. He looks through the glass which is smeared with his blood. On the table is the dead body of Grenant. Lellan turns away from the horror that has been left on the table for anyone to see. Lellan doesn't care if he is stunned again and growls and roars for Grenant's death. Lellan kicks the glass and hits the stone walls with his shackles out of retaliation. He desperately wants to get out and go to Grenant to give him the dignity he deserves. Lellan can see that his body has been emptied of its organs. He assumes they were put on ice for research purposes like the cut off finger. It haunts him the way Grenant was butchered in such a horrific way with no sedation.

Lellan knows eventually he will be next on the table to be butchered. Gee had managed to buy him some time but he doesn't know for how long. He doesn't know if he will ever see her again. He sits down on the floor, his head in his hands, knowing that he needs to get out of this room somehow. The women scientists return to the room and collect the blood samples from Grenant for analysis. Lellan can hear the muffled voices of the two women. He takes the sound for granted for a split second and then it dawns on him the frame must be broken or become loose. For him to hear them in the adjacent room it must be dislodged. He looks at the window and knows it is too strong to break. The frame on the left hand side catches his eye. It doesn't look flush like the other side. After the women have left he pulls at it with his finger and it lifts away slightly. The frame *has* loosened from all of the bashing and thumping earlier. He is relieved with the thought he may be in with a fighting chance to loosen it further. He scans the rest of his chamber and in the far corner he can see something on the floor. He walks over to the corner and picks up a shard of flint. It is very hard with a sharp edge and is just the right size to be hidden in his hand. He instantly conceals it by tucking the shard of flint in his waist band. Lellan then takes a seat on the floor and leans up in the corner between the window frame and the wall and devises a plan.

A guard enters the adjacent room followed by Aidy. Aidy looks at the room in disgust because the dead body has been left out and pools of blood are everywhere.

'This needs cleaning up now!' he bellows. He turns and looks in the direction of where Lellan is being held and continues, 'He'd better be cleaned up too. He will be having a visitor in a couple of days and there is to be no sign of what went on here. I don't care what happens to him after. Sedate him if you have to but clean up this bloody mess.'

'Yes Sir, right away.' Aidy walks over to Lellan and peers through the glass and he shakes his head.

'Get me Dr Simmons who was in-charge! Now!' he shouts at a guard.

He looks at the state of the glass all covered in blood and looks through at Lellan and can see he has hurt himself. Lellan's hands are covered in blood from all the thrashing about. As Lellan can now hear what they are saying it gratifies him. The head scientist enters making Lellan stand up and growl with hate for the man.

'Dr Simmons, he… was not to be harmed. Look at the state of him. You personally, are going to go in there and patch him up. This mess…' He turns to the rest of the room, '…is very unprofessional and be assured that after he is cleaned up you are out of a job!'

'I'm not going in there. Absolutely not!' says Dr Simmons.

'Guard!' Aidy signals for their presence just in case he needs a little persuasion.

Dr Simmons collects all that will be needed to clean up Lellan. Another group enter the room and start to clean up. A guard unlocks Lellan's door. Aidy enters without showing any fear and such confidence that Dr Simmons who has to clean up Lellan is astonished. Aidy squats down in front of Lellan who is quietly growling as he watches his friend being bagged up like an animal carcass.

'I am so sorry you have been put through such an ordeal. Please let us clean you up. I don't want to have to sedate you.' He leans in closer, 'Do what you like with Dr Simmons… who has murdered your friend.' Lellan just nods not wanting to have anything to do with any of them. He knows Aidy is playing games and trying to keep everything sweet for Gee.

Dr Simmons gingerly puts down a bowl of water in front of Lellan so he can wash his hands. With shaking hands Dr Simmons looks at Lellans hands while under the scrutiny of Aidy and the guard. Lellan has cuts and scraps to his knuckles, outside of his hands and to his wrists where the shackles have dug in. Dr Simmons removes the shackles in order to stop anyfurther abrasion. Dr Simmons can barely bandage properly because he is shaking so much as Lellan has so much hate in his eyes. Lellan doesn't know how much longer he can keep himself from losing control.

'Why didn't you sedate Grenant?' says Lellan with a low rumble behind each word.

'His name was Grenant?' says Dr Simmons in a

quiet voice surprised he had a name.

'Yes, you didn't bother to find out. Answer the question!' Lellan would rather rant at him in his mother tongue but knows it would be a waist of his time.

He wants Dr Simmons to know exactly what he is saying.

'I cannot answer.' Again Dr Simmons answers quietly.

Lellan stands up. Dr Simmons staggers back with Lellan towering over him. Lellan grabs Dr Simmons around the neck and pushes him up against the wall so his eyes are at the same level as his own. Dr Simmons is no longer touching the floor.

'Answer the question...' repeats Lellan still growling.

'I... We...' Dr Simmons looks at Aidy who is somewhat closer than before showing an interest in the way the conversation has turned out, 'I had my orders to follow and they were clear not to waist time and use sedation. Also the tests would not have had an accurate result with the use of sedation; it would have interfered with them.'

'We are an intelligent race and some say, more superior to Earthlings.' Lellan turns and looks at Aidy impressing his point, 'An animal would have been treated with more respect than me or my friend. Pain caused on any life, no matter if animal or not, is inexcusable.' Lellan hisses.

Lellan plants Dr Simmons' feet on the floor still with his hand firmly gripped around his neck. With the other hand he easily gains control and gets hold of Dr Simmons' hand. Lellan turns it so the palm is facing him in a splayed position. With one quick movement Lellan presses firmly on the middle finger and snaps it backwards breaking it. Dr Simmons body is writhing in pain unable to move because of Lellan's grip. All Dr

Simmons can do is paw at Lellan's arm to be freed. Lellan proceeds to snap the other three fingers and thumb in the same way. Dr Simmons is crying out in pain unable to bear it in the same manner as Grenant had done.

'Each finger broken is for the harm and cut you made to my friend. You should be ashamed of your own behaviour and arrogance, regardless of orders. To follow such cruel orders show you do not have any intelligence or a conscience with respect to others. Otherwise if you had you would undoubtedly have disagreed with what Aidy had wanted you to do. Now you know what it is like to be in pain without sedation!' Lellan launches Dr Simmons towards the door, where he lands at the feet of the guard, before he kills him out of rage.

'You should have killed him,' says Aidy with surprise.

'I wanted to teach him a lesson. I respect the living. This organisation and its occupants have no regard for life. Their minds are bought by you and they are not free.' Lellan then goes and sits on the bench to supress his anger once more.

Chapter 15

Gee wakes and stretches out her arms, legs and arches her back and it feels good. She is unaware of what has happened to Grenant and Lellan.

A pile of her clothes are folded neatly on a chair in the corner of the room. They have been washed and pressed and are awaiting her presence. Gee slips into her clothes as quickly and quietly as she dare, not wanting anyone to enter the room while she is changing. Her clothes give her comfort. The top she is now wearing is the top Lellan had given her. She has long mastered the fastenings and takes pleasure from doing them up again. The skirt was also a gift which Lellan had given her to go with her favourite top. The skirt sits just above the knee. The fabrics are so soft between her fingers it is like being wrapped in a comfort blanket.

Now that Gee is up and about she wants to know what is in the room next to hers. She hasn't seen much of Aidy as he told her he had errands to run. She was hoping she wouldn't have to see him anymore but knows it is an unrealistic thought. As quietly as possible she opens the door ajar and peers through. The bland décor follows into the next room which is surprisingly much bigger than her small square box room. From what she can see in the large room there is nobody present and so she opens the door a little further and slips through not making a sound. She doesn't walk too far away from the door for reassurance. The room in front of her is laid out in an open plan style as a sitting room with soft seating, low tables and rugs; with a large desk in the distant corner for paperwork purposes.

'Good morning Gee,' says Aidy in high spirits.

Gee swivels round to the left and sees Aidy sitting up at a dining table eating his breakfast. She can't speak and is noticeably gutted to see Aidy looking so bloody happy to see her. It does not deter him, 'Come and sit down and join me for breakfast. You are looking so much better.' Gee walks to a chair and plonks herself down like a naughty school girl with the pout to match.

He points to her clothes, 'They aren't your usual attire.'

'No they were a gift from Lellan and *I* really like them.' She cannot be bothered to hold back anymore.

'Well I better get you some fresh clothes, can't have you being constantly reminded of Teeria.'

'How long do you intend to keep up this elaborate façade? You kidnaped Lellan, Grenant and me and the people back home *will* find us!' Gee says sternly.

'Of course they won't. They will assume you and Lellan will have gone off on your travels on Teeria and remember Grenant has gone into hiding and will not be found and classed as a fugitive. Nobody will know you are here Gee – get used to it. I want you and need you with me, it is all I have thought about and the Spognoffs are merely a bonus. Now, you better eat because now that you are up and feeling better I want to show you EMMA.' Aidy takes a big bite of toast which is spread lavishly with strawberry jam and smiles very happily after his logical explanation.

Gee thinks back to the little note she has wrote and certainly knows that her own family will assume otherwise. She wishes she could slap the smug smile off Aidy's face and then replace it with the truth, but that would be dangerous and he would more than likely move all three of them off EMMA. Her happy spirit has soon dispersed but she still takes a little bit of comfort from the hidden knowledge of her written note and the wearing of her own clothes. She certainly has no intention of taking them off again.

With the thought of being weakened again if she doesn't eat Gee tucks into some breakfast. Aidy can't get over how hungry she is but is satisfied to see she is trying, unaware of her motivation. After having her fill of food and coffee Gee is led by Aidy around his apartment. Gee had been asleep for a couple of days in a spare room and his master room was at the other end off a long hall. The hall gives way to a grand kitchen, games room and several more bedrooms and bathrooms. After seeing the rest of his apartment she gets the impression the small box room she had been sleeping in had been changed to suit his needs so he could keep a close eye on her. Each room hasn't got any windows but instead an extensive range of lighting.

'Pretty big aye. What do you think?' His smug smile returns.

'I miss the open space and seeing the sky,' says Gee who ambles along beside Aidy not at all interested in what he is showing her.

She is there in body but her mind is back on Teeria.

'I can solve that.' He smiles.

'Are you taking me, Lellan and Grenant back home then?' Gee's eyes brighten.

'Don't be silly, you will never go back there. You are staying with me.' Gee looks straight ahead and doesn't pass comment feeling kind of numb from his last remark. He changes the subject, 'Now this sphere holds some very impressive technology and I will give you the sky you want, follow me.' Gee does not reply and walks in silence.

Corridor upon corridor and lifts come and go taking them out of EMMA's core heading north. The fabricated walls, lifts and walk ways are all spotlessly clean from any form of wear and tear making it all look brand new. On her travels Gee takes in everything and observes many guards appointed to certain areas and people in white coats. She wonders what is being hidden behind the doors that are heavily guarded. She is well aware that Lellan could be in one of the many rooms lining both sides of the corridors.

Gee does not hear a word Aidy is saying with her mind being elsewhere. Lellan is at the forefront of all her thoughts. The thought of him being held prisoner fills her with anger. It also makes her feel ashamed for being human as it is not the way to treat any intelligent life let alone Lellan or Grenant. She needs to know he is well and decides she needs to play a different tactic with Aidy. Instead of dragging her heals she decides it is best to show some interest in what Aidy wants to show her in order to get back on his good side so she can see Lellan as soon as possible. Aidy notices the change in her attitude and smiles quietly, assuming she is starting to appreciate EMMA and his company. Aidy shows her what the occupants of Earth would see if they decide to live on EMMA.

Curiosity gets the better of Gee and she starts to ask questions about its capacity and learns that EMMA is actually the size of Mars, measuring roughly half the size of Earth. Aidy quite rightly points out that because, like Mars, EMMA is half the size of Earth there is the same amount of room to inhabit if not more because Earth is actually covered by seventy percent of water and other inhospitable areas like deserts and mountains.

Due to her sudden shown interest he no longer wants to appease her by showing her the simulation technology but decides to take her by lift to the very top of EMMA. Aidy is excited to show her the cherry on the cake. They finally step out of the lift which they had to ride for half an hour with people entering and exiting all the time. Aidy and Gee enter out into a domed concreted area covered in glass. The dome covers an eighth of the top of EMMA like a glass cap to a northern Hemisphere. The dome cap goes as far as the eye can see. The ground is very smoothly surfaced by concrete for easy mobility of small shuttles.

'Wow... I can see why you like it here.' She actually laughs completely blown away by the views and the mammoth dome.

Space is really something else. To see it so up close through a window really puts everything into perspective. It makes our existence look fragile somehow and a complex miracle. Gee walks to one of the benches provided which are near the lift's entrance and sits down. The lift stands alone protruding out of the ground in the barren and dull expanse and it is the only given clue that it is attached to something bigger below. It is incredibly dark with light only coming from the Earth and its moon.

'I admit it is one of the advantages, and our guests seem to approve.' Aidy smiles and for the first time Gee can see the man she once knew as a friend. 'Because we are positioned just outside our solar system to the north of our Earth we can get a good view. If we stand in just the right spot, at just the right time up here with the aid of a super telescope we can see the four terrestrial planets, Venus, Earth, Mars and Jupiter quite clearly. The astronomers are one of our regular visitors. The view of our Earth is of course exceptional at all times.'

'You have done your homework.'

'I have learnt a thing or two, it is hard not to in such exceptional surroundings. Any significant and particular viewing points are marked out by a touch pad. It is built into the concrete giving the viewer instant and relevant information of what can be seen from that location. Maybe we can come back when we are not so pushed for time?' Gee stares at him blankly for a brief moment, hoping she won't be on EMMA much longer.

Should the circumstances be different and not held against her will, she knows she couldn't be kept away from the dome cap.

'I like the sound of that,' she says with as much enthusiasm as she can muster.

'Good to hear. Do you still want to see some good old fashioned sky?'

'I *am* a sentimentalist.'

Aidy leads her back the way they came covering most of the distance by the use of the lift which accommodates all of the levels on EMMA. Gee is getting more accustomed with the layout of EMMA and feels certain the excursion with her captive has been worthwhile. They stop close to Aidy's apartment at yet another set of double white doors. Aidy takes his time with the touch pad beside the door entering in some information. He opens the door which isn't locked and lets Gee enter first.

Gee stands with her mouth open because in front of her she is faced with a realistic looking meadow with a meandering river running through it with trees to the distant left and a clear blue sky above. She eagerly steps into the simulated landscape. She lowers her hands and feels the grasses touch and brush past them.

'Thank you,' is all Gee can manage to say.

'Glad you like it.' He is stood close by taking in the marvellous simulation he had created for her. 'We can create any illusion of a perfect world obviously based on a snippet of any landscape from Earth. We can go for a walk and you can enjoy it until your heart's content?'

'If you wouldn't mind, could I have some time to myself?' She is desperate to go and find a nice spot in the grasses by the river and lie down and gaze at the purest of blue skies.

'Of course…,' this pleases Aidy, 'have as much time as you would like. When you are done exit the room which is clearly marked and a guard will show you back to the apartment. We can then have lunch and then may I suggest we go and see your friend Lellan?'

'Oh yes that sounds great – tha… thanks - Aidy.' She is over the moon to hear that she will get to see Lellan and the fact that Aidy had suggested it without her asking shows that Lellan *is* alright. Aidy leaves her to it knowing he has made her happy.

Gee walks further into the meadow for half a mile. She then stands and does a three hundred and sixty degree turn. She catches a distant glimpse of the exit sign showing her the way out, and the sight of it saddens her making her sigh out aloud knowing that reality is on the other side of the door. The meadow remarkably goes as far as her eye can see making Gee acknowledge that the science and technology behind the simulation is an astounding feat. To pull this off she knows there have to be some very, very clever people responsible for this who have worked hard. It occurs to her that those people would not have done it without being won over somehow to aid EMMA and she guesses that money most likely changed hands. She shakes the thoughts out of her head about dirty money and bribery, trying to relax and make the most of her time alone.

The grass has been flattened enough by her feet so she can sit down comfortably. She lies back with her hands behind her head, gazing up at the sky with the sound of the river flowing past her. As remarkable as it is the meadow isn't real and nor is the perfect blue sky. She thinks back to the Teerian sky which is clean and so pretty and overwhelmingly beautiful at night. The night sky is beyond the imagination and filled with many colours and stars because it is at the heart of the immense star cluster of the R136 in the Tarantula nebula which envelopes them all. She had felt back on Teeria to have been very lucky to have experienced such a natural wonder and even more so now that she is away from it. With the little time she has had to think she truly misses Teeria in its entirety and of course she misses her family and Lellan, so much so it causes a knot to form in her throat.

Gee rolls over onto her front and focuses on a strand of seeded grass, to keep the sadness away, knowing that to get through this she has to be strong and clear minded. As she stares at the grass she can see that it isn't made up of tiny grass cells but of synthetic strands. By snapping a bit off she is amazed that before her very own eyes the snapped off piece that is still left rooted in the ground regrows by self replicating Nanos. Nano technology was solved and a long awaited breakthrough was achieved in the year 9,949. It no longer only belonged to science fiction, but was now an actual part of our reality and very much understood. The Nano technology had opened up many gateways of possibilities and was utilised rapidly. Gee has seen other Nano simulators during her travels and it never ceases to surprise her or to become old. As Nano technology has been around for many years it is old in comparison to today's technology. But as Wardelf Shooper knew, old tech was cheaper and if used in the right way, can be just as effective.

The Nano technology reforms the complex structure of the fresh blade of grass again. Gee has a really close look at the blade of grass in her hand, fascinated by its make up and realises as soon as it is taken out of its given simulated environment, it will vanish. It is only surviving as a synthetic structure which was put in place by the first class technology of amplified Nanos. This thought brings her back to Aidy who would give her anything and everything she wants, but not a true reality and *not* Lellan, just synthetics. She feels like a prisoner despite all of Aidy's attempts to make her comfortable.

This spurs her on, for hers, Lellan's and Grenant's freedom. She now feels ready for the next instalment of Aidy. It will get her closer to her mission of seeing Lellan then she hopes a combined escape. Taking her droplet pendant in her hand she remembers the evening when Lellan had given it to her and misses him terribly. With the droplet as a reminder to be strong, like its creator, she heads back to the exit.

On her return to Aidy's apartment, after being escorted closely by a guard, lunch is laid out on the table where they had had breakfast. There are assorted sandwiches and fruit. Gee has forgotten what it is like to eat traditional fruit freely which she had once been accustomed to and savours the flavours knowing by some miracle it is the last meal she will be having with Aidy. While crunching into a juicy pear she starts to make a plan of escape which includes taking a systematic mental note of the route when they visit Lellan.

* * *

After having plenty of time to think Lellan decides not to be too hasty with his escape and exit. He had overheard Aidy say that he will be visited by Gee soon and that was the deciding factor for him to bide his time. He has decided to break out of the prison room once Aidy and Gee have visited and then follow Gee's scent. He of course wanted to break out sooner and then follow Aidy's scent but it isn't aswell known to him as

Gee's. If he went about it alone and up against the guards without the help of Gee it could be far more risky. Lellan is sat in his corner next to the broken frame which nobody has noticed. With people coming and going he has kept a watchful eye and has only seen one guard posted outside the door to the adjacent room. As there is not a guard closely watching him it has allowed him time to loosen the frame further by hand and as extra leverage to help, he uses the strong shard of flint to tease away the material holding the glass in place. As he doesn't plan to escape yet he cannot create too much noise as it would alert the guard outside, making his work a painfully slow process in order to keep quiet. He doesn't want to giveaway his secret until it is absolutely necessary when he is on the edge of escaping.

Lellan misses Gee, he cannot wait to see her beautiful face and smell her scent again. He hates that he has not seen Gee for so long. He hopes if nothing else she has been treated properly and fed because the last image he remembers was when she had looked so fragile on Aidy's ship. He rests back against the corner wall and closes his eyes thinking back to the gorgeous human he has fallen in love with. He smiles to himself with the memories of her curiosity getting the better of her and getting her into trouble. She had taken a big chance and it had taken a lot of courage to simply see a Spognoff in the flesh and it was this and her beauty that had caught his attention. He hopes she is still wearing the droplet which bound them together on their special evening on Kwarn's ship. His memories are the only thing that is keeping him sane and the thought of seeing her soon is the first bit of real hope he has had for days. He knows he will see her very soon because he has overheard the cleaners talk who have repeatedly cleaned the room. He has seen Aidy check the room several times with a critical eye for detail because he doesn't want one trace left of the harrowing truth of Grenant's demise to come to light. Lellan hopes he will be able to speak to Gee but is aware there are no certainties when Aidy is involved because he does not value the heart beat and the emotions of the living. Lellan accepts that if he is not allowed to speak to her then he will have to wait to talk to her after their escape. He is certain they will escape and accepts nothing less. He uses the waiting as an incentive and sets his mind to focus on the matter at hand and not let his emotions get the better of him which could jeopardise his judgement.

Lellans train of thought is interrupted making him look up because he hears the mechanism to the guarded door being unlocked. He takes position and stares at the floor as if he cannot hear anything. He doesn't look up until he sees a familiar pair of shoes stood at the window. Gee is motionless looking at him with very sad eyes. She holds her pendant for strength. She sees Lellan in a subdued state and his once vibrant brown skin looks pasty. Lellan's face doesn't show any emotion from behind the glass but deep inside he is glad to see she is looking healthy again.

'Can I talk to him?' asks Gee who notices Aidy clearly revelling from the enjoyment of being in control.

'I guess it won't hurt.' He walks to the side door of the prison chamber and asks a guard to unlock it. Aidy enters first and has a brief and quiet word with Lellan, 'Do not mention what has happened here or my exemplary behaviour towards you will vanish!'

Aidy steps out of the chamber giving Gee some room after the warning. Gee is impatient with the unknown hold up and frowns at Aidy.

Lellan stands with his arms outstretched

understanding that his time with her is limited and precious. Gee crashes into Lellan with such genuine enthusiasm and affection it makes Aidy turn away with jealousy. Gee notices that Lellan isn't standing with his normally strong posture that she is used too and looks into his eyes. His eyes are full of pain and sorrow.

'Listen to me,' Lellan whispers quietly.

'Are you ok Lellan? You look dreadful.' She smooth's his hair and then touches his face with one hand which he leans against.

She sees one tear roll down his cheek making her more than determined to put an end to all of this.

'We can talk about it later…' He leans in closely to her ear and sniffs his favourite scent then whispers, 'When you leave I will break out, I have a plan to follow your scent.'

'Good – be careful. I will meet you here or somewhere in between as I finally know the way here. It may take me a bit of time to break free from him,' Gee whispers between kissing his cheek.

'What are you two whispering about?' asks a jealous Aidy.

'I am making sure he is alright he looks pale, have you been feeding him?' Gee turns the conversation around to throw Aidy's suspicions.

'Yes of course, what do you take us for?' snaps Aidy.

Gee looks into Lellan's eyes and they tell a different story. 'It is time to leave,' says Aidy abruptly standing right behind Gee.

Gee winks with a whisper almost without a sound, 'I love you. Bide your time and eat.'

'I miss you and love you all the more Gee.' He feels something being pushed into his hand. He doesn't look at what it is but hides it in his clothing.

Gee is then yanked out and pushed back around to

the front of the glass. She puts her hands on the glass and Lellan puts his hands on hers from his side. She looks into his pained eyes and he looks into her anguished eyes which can see his unspoken pain. He smiles weakly and then sees a glimpse of fire in her eyes which is as good as any tonic or medicine for strength. Aidy enters his room while the guard keeps an eye on Gee.

'She will never be yours, she *is* mine!' spits out Aidy with contempt.

'She doesn't belong to either of us at the moment but I do know she will never be yours!' Lellan growls with a tone of unmistakable certainty in his voice which unnerves Aidy.

Aidy exits the chamber and it is locked again.

Aidy tells the guard to take Gee outside. Gee struggles against the strength of the uniformed man not wanting to leave Lellan alone again despite their plans. The guard holds her securely in the corridor the other side of the door while Aidy makes an in-house phone call.

'Yeah he is now ready and be quick about it, I want this over. And please, we are not animals here so sedate him first will you!'

Lellan has heard every word Aidy had said during the call and knows he hasn't much time left. When Aidy leaves after the call Lellan looks at what he has stuffed in his clothing. Gee had smuggled him a wrapped up and very squashed meaty sandwich and a small apple. He doesn't care that he doesn't recognise the meat in the sandwich, which is ham, because he feels utterly famished. To him the fact that Gee has given it to him means it is safe for him to eat. The sight of the squashed sandwich makes him smile and then he tucks into it with vengeance.

* * *

Aidy has to physically drag Gee back with the help and aid of the guard. Aidy knew it was an error on his part to please Gee. He is annoyed that he had been foolish and weak and let the visit take place. He had seen her in the familiar way he was used to earlier on in the day and now that had vanished. He is uncomfortable with the bombardment of questions she has started asking since seeing Lellan. Everything he had put into place had changed and he wasn't about to let her slip through his fingers again. The sooner he gets her back to his apartment under lock and key the better.

'What about Grenant? Where is he?' Gee desperately asks.

'He is in a different room,' says Aidy.

'Can I see him too?'

'No you have seen enough.' Aidy's patience is at breaking point.

'Well, when can I see Lellan again?'

'That was your last time. You will never be allowed to see him again. You are mine and when I get you back I will make sure of it.'

Chapter 16

Gee is pushed by Aidy into his apartment when they get back. She can sense what he has got planned and doesn't know how to get out of it. Aidy instructs the guard to tell the Command Centre that he does not want to be disturbed unless it is an absolute emergency.

Aidy is full of anger which is laced by jealousy because of what Lellan and Gee have. He intends to break Gee's will and then she will be finally his. Gee backs away from him as he enters the room because of his startling anger.

'You are mine, please come here,' Aidy says firmly.

'I don't understand why you think we were ever together. It is all in your head. We used to be friends. Can't we talk about this Aidy?' pleads Gee.

'No I am keeping my word now come with me!'

'No,' says Gee backing up even further.

Aidy strides over towards her, she tries to evade him but he is too quick and he strikes her with the back of his hand. She holds her cheek that is stinging from his blow. He then takes hold of her roughly around the back of the neck and marches her to his bedroom up the far end of the hallway corridor. He pushes her into his room with force and shuts the door.

'Now strip off those Teerian clothes.'

'Please Aidy please don't do this. What was this morning all about? I was actually intrigued by what you had shown me and now you plan to kill Lellan because he isn't human. This *is* all a façade, what with all your shiny toys, you should be ashamed.'

'Shut... up... Gee; you don't know what you are talking about. Lellan will be used for research purposes simply because he wants you!'

'You are jealous.' Gee laughs at the ridiculous

reason.

Aidy steps forward and strikes her harder than before and this time, she falls back onto the bed. Before she can get up he jumps on top of and astride her so she cannot move her body and then he fights and gets a grasp of her throat with one hand. Gee cannot move under his firm grip and with his heavy weight resting on her.

Aidy looks down at Gee who is now firmly and literally within his grasp and who will soon, after the long wait, be his. His eye is drawn to her pendant. He looks at the pendant and then into her eyes which finally gives her away. He snatches it from her neck breaking the chain and throws it on the floor near the door in a rage.

'Lellan gave that to you didn't he? Not your Mother!'

'Yes and it is none of your bloody business. Who do you think you are?'

Aidy just looks up but doesn't give her the satisfaction of answering. She doesn't care about what he knows anymore because he wants to take her for himself without consent. She will cling onto what little is left of her and what she cares about most even when he is done. He cannot take her heart and she vows it will never be his as long as she still has breath.

He strokes her hair with the other hand and touches her face and bends down and kisses her on the lips. She tries to squirm but all she can do is keep her lips tight and scream from within. He kisses the bottom of her neck and then removing the hand from around her throat he takes both hands and rips open her top.

Gee hears the fabric tear and cries out, 'I will not do this willingly. I will never be yours – never!' chokes Gee in tears.

Aidy ignores her now and proceeds by touching and

kissing her quite roughly. He moves his legs between hers. She tries to move away but he holds her down again by the throat. As he is unbuckling his belt a repetitive beeping occurs from his pocket.

'Damn it.' He fishes out the beeping instrument and stares at it then switches the noise off and launches it across the bed deciding to ignore it.

'It may be important,' she squeaks barely able to breathe from the hand wrapped tightly around her neck.

He strikes her again with the back of his hand not in the mood for any conversation. He carries on loosening his belt and trousers and tries to move her legs into the right place but Gee fights with every ounce of strength for her life and dignity.

He overpowers her and tries to rip away her under garment with Gee hitting him and fighting against him all the time and then the beeper sounds again. Aidy shouts out of frustration and leans over to shut the beeper up while holding Gee down into position.

Aidy is so close to having what he has always wanted, but he has his business responsibilities and there is obviously a problem otherwise he would not be interrupted. He looks down at Gee pinned against the bed ready for him and decides she can wait a moment longer while he returns the call to find out what is so important and then he can get back to putting it all right again.

Gee can feel his grip loosen as he listens to the person on the other end. She wriggles to get away from the grasp and when Aidy turns around to see what she is doing she pretends she is making herself more comfortable giving him a false sense of trust and hope.

Her attention is caught by the one sided conversation when she hears him say, 'Turn it around or destroy the vessels. No traitor is welcome here.'

Aidy is so engrossed with the call that he hasn't

noticed Gee drawing her leg up to retrieve her flat healed shoe.

Gee counts quietly, 'One, two, three...' She then hits Aidy on the side of the head with the thick heal of her shoe. He collapses in a heap on the bed still with the phone in use. She struggles to shove him off her.

She gets off the bed in one swift move and hops along removing the other shoe and discards them. While heading to the door she sees in the doorway her pendant. While picking it up she glances back at Aidy who is slumped on the bed.

On a drawer unit by the right side of the door there is a small hard looking vase which she quickly grabs deciding it would serve as a better weapon than a shoe. Moving quickly and very decisively she runs to the door and opens it with such force it startles the guard giving her the edge she had hoped. She hits him on the head with the vase. He drops to the ground. Gee grabs his immobiliser and runs faster than she has ever done before because of the adrenaline that has now taken over.

* * *

Cam and Baaron are both sat opposite each other on the TRF vessel in silence. Cam eyes up the enormity of Baaron. He hasn't had the opportunity to really get to know many Spognoffs because he has been studying hard and looking forward to finishing his final degree of Ocean Science. Cam notes Baaron has a blank expression and is seemingly waiting like himself.

'Thank you for all of your help,' says Cam.

'I am pleased I can help,' says Baaron in an even tone.

'I'm glad we have you as muscle along for the ride. It may get heavy,' says Cam with a tone of excitement.

'Heavy?' questions Baaron, not ever hearing such a term used before.

'Yes "heavy". They may put up a bit of a fight as we will be unwanted visitors.' Baaron just nods. Cam continues, 'Can I ask a question?'

'Yes.'

'Are you and others alike all as strong as what is rumoured?'

'Yes,' says Baaron with a more seemingly interested expression.

'Could I interest you in an arm wrestle? We can measure each other's strength. I'm interested in how strong you are. I…' Cam is about to continue and explain that he keeps fit by running each day when Baaron interrupts him with a deep throaty laugh.

Baaron sits on the edge of his chair and says, 'I *will* beat you, but I am willing to confirm that the rumours of our strength are correct.'

By the time the arm wrestle was agreed it had drawn the interest of the other members onboard assigned by General Carter. It was light relief from a boring flight. Cam and Baaron are both in place sat on opposite sides of a table. Cam does an uncomfortable gulp because Baaron looks even bigger now that he is sat at closer quarters. Cam places his hand against Baaron's and gets a firm grasp. Cam is quick to notice that Baaron's arm is twice the thickness of his own. The arm wrestle begins with Cam putting all of his strength behind his arm but he cannot move it. It is like trying to knock over a wall and Baaron does not appear to be trying. Baaron takes pity on Cam and ends his torment and the arm wrestle is over in seconds much to Cam's disappointment.

'You have your answer,' says Baaron chirpily, getting up and patting Cam on the shoulder as a good will gesture for him even trying.

Cam sits down beside Baaron after recovering from the quick defeat. Cam is not one for brooding. They have both found a new respect for each other and a new friendship from the journey.

Not far in the distance is EMMA, like a planet that has gone off course. EMMA is lit up and covered in florescent bands that are thickly spaced apart in parallel rows acting as a homing beckon for ships traveling in space. Aidy had been alerted about three unknown ships approaching. The lead ship has Posall and Cam onboard along with Mogue and Baaron, and ten TRF security personnel including a negotiator. The other two ships are manned by the DOD (Department of Defence) from the US who is representing NASA's interests. The DOD ships had joined the TRF space shuttle out of range of EMMA's long distance radar. There are more DOD ships waiting out of range of EMMA's radar at a safe distance for backup purposes.

Out of EMMA's central docking port, four fighter ships depart and approach the three ships like angry wasps with a sting in their tail. The two DOD ships gage the threatening behaviour of the four fighter ships and move in front of the TRF ship for protection. The DOD ships feel threatened by the cavalier approach of EMMA's fighters and are not willing to take any chances after the fighter's past bad reputation so they contact the backup ships who move quickly within radar detection. EMMA's fighter vessels move closer with only attack in mind and then they slow right down at near enough a stand still as they are now faced with a whole fleet of DOD ships all ready to take fire. The fighter vessels are ordered to move out of the way by the Command Centre and let the three vessels through. The DOD can see that they are now allowed to continue with their mission and gain support from two more DOD ships, totalling five.

'Where the hell is Gee going to be? EMMA is bloody massive,' says Cam.

'We have backup Son – the DOD holds the warrant papers and a lot of fire power if we need it. I'm sure Aidy will not want EMMA to have a gaping hole in its side, plus there are civilians involved.'

'I suggest we follow suit and let the authorities handle it. They are trained to handle such difficult matters as this - to find Lellan and Gee.' Mogue points out.

The security personnel of TRF and Baaron let the others speculate as they are the muscles along for the ride to assist in any way they can. As they get very close and dwarfed by EMMA's presence, nobody says a word as they go behind enemy lines. The TRF ship is positioned in the middle of the DOD ships with two at point and two at six. One of the DOD vessels stands guard at the entrance of EMMA while the others enter the docking port. The vessel left at the entrance is keeping watch and communication going between the vessels inside and the fleet waiting outside.

* * *

After eating his squashed food offerings in just three or four bites Lellan feels more refreshed and is ready to leave. He is certain time is not on his side and while the guard and staff numbers are low in the immediate area he must not delay his escape any longer.

He goes to the left hand corner of the dislodged frame and with both hands easily yanks it off. It makes a hell of a noise and Lellan hurries in case the guard heard; who is posted on the other side of the lab room door. The seconds really do count. He then bounds to the other end of the glass.

With his back to the glass, with only a slight pause,

he runs with big strides towards the wall, jumps and places his feet half way up it and turns in mid air and launches himself in one movement toward the broken frame. Both feet crash onto the broken frame with his whole weight behind them.

The noise from the collision and breaking of the frame is tremendous. He knows he can only get away with another quick couple of tries to furthermore fracture the frame to create a gap wide enough to squeeze through. He moves fast and repeats his run up and launches a second and a third time very quickly with each blow loosening the frame further.

He pushes his shoulder up against the destroyed frame on his side and shoves it hard. It gives way without much fight. Lellan effortlessly slides through past the splintered frame that is still holding the glass.

Lellan looks back at what he has accomplished aware that not many beings could have pulled off such an unrealistic stunt. His strength is his weapon and they could not take that away from him.

Lellan hears the door being unlocked and then a guard enters wondering what all the noise is about. The guard sees Lellan standing in front of him with a stance ready for a fight. Lellan has his flint shard in his hand which balances the odds against the immobiliser stick the guard holds out.

The door then flies open which crashes against the wall causing Lellan and the guard to jump. They see Gee tumble into the room in a hurry and breathless. She had wondered where the guard was and thought she was too late to save Lellan.

She is as surprised, as the guard was, to see Lellan out of the prison chamber. Lellan is quick and as the guard looks around to Gee, he throws a punch and the guard falls to the floor.

Aidy then appears holding the side of his head

looking disorientated. He is shadowed by more security guards.

Before Gee can make it over to Lellan, Aidy grabs her. Lellan doesn't get the chance to pick up the immobiliser and quickly assesses the situation. Gee is made to drop her immobiliser, leaving her defenceless and now extremely worried.

Gee is looking panicked knowing that they are in serious danger because they have been caught.

'Do you know what has happened to Grenant?' Lellan asks Gee raising his eyebrows to get her attention and then looking down at the ground hoping she notices his hand to the side.

Gee stares at Lellan completely confused by his question and action. She looks at the ground where he appears to be looking and then looks at his feet and then she sees his hand moving oddly. She looks at the left hand puzzled then it starts to move oddly again. She sees his hand splayed out and then it clench's tight and then it flex's out again.

'Shut up Lellan,' commands Aidy.

'I have nothing to lose,' retorts Lellan.

Lellan is still repeating the hand signal under Aidy's nose without him knowing because he is caught up in what Lellan is threatening to say.

Lellan continues, 'Gee, they have butchered Grenant before my very own eyes!' growls Lellan.

He then looks down again to impress the signal on her.

Gee looks at the hand movement and then looks into Lellan's eyes suddenly with understanding what he is trying to communicate to her and what she has just heard.

'Oh…' Gee blurts out, putting everyone on edge, as she has realised that Lellan is using one of the many Spognoff hand signals; telling her to switch off the lights.

It is an old form of signalling for hunting or tracking and she has just been reading about it back home on Teeria. She had been reading out of interest not thinking she would need to know it. Lellan had remembered she had been learning about it and luckily for him she eventually recognised what he was doing. The splayed or flexed hand means the sun is at its brightest and when that is followed by a tight clench of the hand, the sun is going to be shut out by cloud cover or, darkness is eminent due to night time. She is also alarmed by the sad loss of Grenant.

Only seconds have passed, 'You lied to me. I asked if I could see him aswell and you lied! You are such a lying, vindictive bastard, you deserve everything you get,' she shouts full of rage and cohesion and kicks back into his leg.

The sudden kick from Gee makes Aidy lose his grip. Gee quickly moves to the other side of him and hits the switch for the lights. They are all in darkness.

Gee freezes unable to see anything but remembers that Lellan has brilliant eyesight in the dark. She then hears a commotion beside her and then the lights are turned back on.

Lellan is now stood beside her with one of his arms wrapped around both of Aidy's arms so he cannot move and the flint shard is held against his throat for leverage.

'Drop your weapons and any form of key and communicator,' Lellan orders.

The guards do not respond, shocked by the turn of events. Lellan pushes the flint deeper against Aidy's neck and they see a drop of blood escape.

Lellan notices the frame is still left ajar with a gap big enough for them to get through. Lellan repeats his order again, 'Drop your weapons now!' he flushes red with sheer anger. 'Go and enter the prison through the gap!' Lellan instinctively roars to persuade them further not realising how intimidating he can actually be.

His roar echoes, bouncing off all four walls making Gee jump.

Aidy carefully nods feeling under the mercy of the flint shard. The guards all drop their immobiliser sticks and ear pieces to one side and then one at a time enter the chamber as instructed once Gee has patted them down. Gee cannot believe what she is doing and it makes her hands shake with each search as she has only seen it done on television before. She finds two hidden keys and keeps hold of them.

Lellan walks with Aidy still holding him securely. Lellan then swivels him around to face him with a glare. Gee is now by Lellan's side and slaps Aidy again on the same side she had already hit him making him wince.

'You deserve more than a slap Aidy Campion, with the stunt you just tried to pull with me. I hate you!' she says shaking with anger from the ebbing adrenaline.

Lellan looks at her and frowns, 'Your clothes are torn? Did he do this,' he touches her top.

Gee hurriedly says, 'I will tell you later, please Lellan we need to go.' She doesn't know how Lellan will react to Aidy nearly raping her and she can't bear the thought of more blood shed no matter whose it is.

She concludes not wishing to speak or be near Aidy any longer, 'I will be happy to tell the authorities about everything that has happened, and about your "research" facilities then you will be locked up for a long, long time.' She turns away from Aidy disgusted.

Lellan takes him by the throat and picks him up off the floor and brings him close, 'You are lucky I do not kill you for what you have done to Grenant and us,' growls Lellan with such force Aidy can feel his warm breath exhale over his skin.

Lellan steps forward while still holding Aidy like a rag doll and then opens up the glass frame a little further. Lellan pushes Aidy with all of his strength at full force into the room. Aidy hits the far wall and crumples to the floor. A guard rushes to his aid.

Lellan pushes the glass back into place. Lellan instructs Gee to hold the immobiliser stick with it being on the highest setting and use it should anyone try to leave. Lellan then gets the metal table and hauls a heavy clinical wall unit to the glass chamber and wedges it tightly against the broken frame to close it shut with Aidy and the guards imprisoned within.

Gee is stood watching Lellan work quickly. She is shocked by the revelation he had told her about Grenant and concerned by what Lellan has actually seen.

'We need to go,' says Lellan with urgency and takes her hand.

'What about Grenant?' She doesn't want to leave him behind.

'It is too late; we can retrieve his body when we let TRF know what has happened. Now we must leave.'

Lellan and Gee run out of the door. Both of them are armed with an immobiliser stick for defence. Gee has difficulty keeping up with Lellan because he has large strides making him so much faster. She finds it is easier running without her abandoned shoes which helps a little. She remembers part of the way and they navigate through the corridors together. The familiarity of the corridors soon wears off and Gee does not recognise where they are anymore. She had thought she had sussed out the general layout of EMMA, but because she is running and not thinking as clearly, due to her heightened emotions, it all looks the same to her.

They pass lab technicians, plain clothed staff and individual guards in the corridors. When they are faced with a guard both Lellan and Gee extend their immobilisers out in front making the majority of them back down. The odd guard tries his luck to recapture the fugitives but Lellan is too quick for them when he is evenly matched leaving them either stunned or bruised.

'How do you know which way to go?' Gee pants.

'I am following the fresh air intake which should lead us to the bay and then we can get ourselves a ship and get out of here.' In a quiet corner he stops and looks down at her and sees her energy levels are flagging. He hasn't the strength to carry her.

It had taken a great deal of his own energy to leave the prison chamber and to move the heavy furniture to secure his captives. By securing them it has given them both a head start.

He takes her head in his hands and gives her a long and awaited kiss and she responds back in the same way. It gives them both the will power to carry on.

After several left and right turns they start to see signs for directions to the large docking station. They follow the signs and point their immobilisers at anyone who gets in their way. The guard numbers are higher now and instead of running at full speed they take the time to avoid them if possible as they would be out numbered.

They enter and exit lifts and then finally exit out onto the docking platform. The docking platform is at least fifteen metres wide with ships docked on both sides, to their far left and right.

* * *

The four ships have docked less than a mile in, not far from EMMA's entrance. Posall, Cam Goshle and Mogue Weebwra are heavily guarded and surrounded by their TRF security. The TRF negotiator and the

DOD are taking the lead in the search for Gee and Lellan, and start to question EMMA's guard. They spread out in an organised sweep of the docking bay so nobody can enter or exit unless they are aware of it. The DOD are not taking any chances and take the kidnapping of two people that have been abducted away from Teeria very seriously, Spognoff or otherwise.

Mogue is overwhelmed and feels out of his depth with the situation by standing on foreign ground. He has never flown through space before let alone ever stand in a giant globe of an alien vessel and be surrounded by hundreds of humans. Posall can see his friend feels somewhat alone surrounded by humans so he points to the highly engineered interior they are consumed within to take his mind off it. Mogue senses that Posall is nervous about the situation too so they both keep each other occupied to cushion the worry, each is naturally having about their grown up children. Posall and Mogue are engrossed into a conversation, despite the reason for their visit and given concerns, and both marvel at EMMA's build and learn a few ideas.

Cam is stood at the heart of the TRF group under the securities watchful protection. He sees the leading DOD colonel taking papers to one of EMMA's guards in order to speak to their superior. While the colonel waits Cam scans the dock both sides as far as the eye can see. To him it is like looking for a needle in a hay stack and it could take the DOD some time and more man power to make a clean sweep of EMMA.

Cam and Baaron each have the same idea and continuously scan every inch of what they can see. In the far, far distance on the side they are standing Cam can see two figures looking out of place. He really has to narrow his eyes to try and get a better look and then taps for Baaron's attention whose eyesight is much better than his own. Baaron nods to Cam and they both smile with relief.

'They are over there. Follow us,' alerts Cam just before he and Baaron run out of the group on foot. Everyone else instantly stops talking and half of the TRF personnel are quick to act and follow Cam and Baaron on foot.

As Cam gets closer he can see that Lellan is propping up Gee, just as much as she is propping up him and they both look ready to collapse. Cam can see they are both weakly poised ready for any trouble and holding some sort of weapon each.

'Gee... Lellan...' bellows Cam as he gets closer but they do not hear and head towards an unknown small space ship. Cam is desperate to get to them before they leave. He doesn't want to lose them now he is so close to letting them know their families are there for them.

'Gee... Lellan...' bellows Cam again, so loud his voice cracks with the TRF personnel close at his heals. He sees Lellan stop and Gee follow suit. Lellan turns and so does Gee copying him, wondering why he has stopped. Cam waves both hands at them making it very hard for them to miss him. Lellan looks over to where he thought he had heard his name called hoping it is not more of Aidy's men. His eyes then come to rest on Cam running at full speed towards them. It takes a brief second for Lellan to recognise Gee's brother. Cam sees Lellan point him out to Gee and she follows his line of sight. Now that Cam and Baaron are closer they can see the relief showing on their faces.

Lellan and Gee do not move and appear rooted to the ground, both overcome by exhaustion and the overwhelming emotions of being found. Lellan and Gee can now see the rest of the search party following Cam and Baaron. As Cam shortens the distance between them he can see they both look traumatised. He sees that his sister has no shoes on; a ripped topped which she is clutching together for dignity and Lellan who is looking drawn and thin. It has seemed like minutes to Cam and Baaron getting to them both but it has only taken seconds running along the lengthy dock. Nobody from EMMA's guard had a chance or had even dared to get in Cam or Baarons way with the on pursuit of the TRF Security and one unit of the DOD who finally caught on to what was happening.

Cam is so shocked by his sister's appearance because on closer inspection he sees she has bruised cheek bones and neck. He gives her a big comforting hug and the same for Lellan who looks like he needs it. Baaron is so pleased to see his friend that he gives him a strong tough hug because when he was last with him they were simply at the trading market back on Teeria.

'Hi Sis. I am so… glad we found you.'

'So are we.' Gee smiles wryly and looks up at Lellan. Cam can now see their eyes are both filled with pain and sorrow.

'What are you both doing out here? You looked lost.' He says gently.

'We were just about to steal that ship to escape,' she says pointing at the small ship they were about to take.

'It looks like we got here at the right moment then. Hello Son,' says Mogue appearing from behind Baaron and Cam.

Posall rushes over to his daughter and hugs and squeezes her and takes his jacket off after noticing her torn clothing and covers her up. Gee appreciates the jacket and doesn't feel so self conscious. Mogue walks over to his son and looks him squarely in the eyes and can see that he is very troubled.

'Hello Father,' Lellan manages to whisper.

He then falls to his knees at his father's feet. Gee

falls down beside Lellan feeling just as defeated, but also concerned for him because of what he has seen. Mogue kneels down in front of them.

'Let's get you two on the ship,' says Mogue helping his son up.

They get up slowly wishing they didn't have to journey anyfurther. Baaron supports Lellan and Posall wraps his arm around Gee's shoulders for added protection. Mogue and Cam lead the way back slowly to the TRF ship. When they are onboard Lellan and Gee sit down next to each other in a comfortable seated departure room. The DOD proceeds in separate small units, searching for the kidnapper while the TRF security guard the ship.

'I do not want to press you two too much but we need to know roughly what has happened here,' says Mogue.

Lellan looks up and nods but Gee can't bear the thought of reliving her near miss with Aidy.

Cam interjects, 'Cant we just get them out of here, why wait? Look at them they need to go home. We have found them; the others can find Aidy and arrest him.' Cam can see neither of them want to talk about what has happened yet, and they both look mentally and physically exhausted.

'We cannot leave yet.' Lellan looks at his father, 'Grenant is here and we must take him back!'

'Did you say Grenant?' asks Mogue.

'Yes. It is a long story. He got caught up by Aidy's promises and then kidnapped at the same time as us. We were research to Aidy, Father – research. Grenant is dead!' Mogue puts an arm around his son. Lellan continues, 'I watched them torture and murder Grenant before my very own eyes and I could not do anything to help. We must take his body home and give him the dignity he deserves.' Lellan silences again fighting back the emotions with his head down.

The only comfort he has is Gee next to him and her hand in his and his father now close by.

'Oh my dearest Son. What a horrific set of events you have witnessed. Poor dear Grenant... You are right he was too young to die. Aidy *will* pay for his crimes. I cannot even imagine what you have seen. I will help you – I promise,' says Mogue saddened. He then turns to Gee, 'Now you do not have to talk about it to me... perhaps your Father? But it looks like Aidy Campion has hurt you too Gee.'

Posall is close and he puts an arm around his daughter to encourage her to speak out and not harbour any harmful events. Gee bursts into tears not even wanting to say the word because it was an absolute miracle she had escaped him.

'Aidy... er... he tried... to...' Gee breaks down with the words.

Lellan squeezes her hand to will her on.

She fights back the tears and continues, 'He... nearly... r... r... raped me.' Then after a pause she shakily says, 'I only escaped because he had a phone call and I hit him over the head with my shoe. I can't believe I had to hit him, I said "no" but he wouldn't listen. I had to fight and hit others to... to escape.' Gee takes a very shaky breath in, relieved to have told her father of her horrifying experience.

'If I see him I will do more than that,' responds Posall.

'I should have killed him when I had the chance!' growls Lellan flushing red with rage.

Mogue and Posall have all the information they need for now and relay the facts to the leading officer. It is imperative that Aidy was found. Lellan and Gee are left alone to relax the best they can after what they have just announced to the others. They both go and freshen up and put some clean clothes on. When Lellan returns he is just wearing his full length leggings and sits beside Gee and kisses her softly.

'I am sorry I could not help you Gee, so, so sorry,' Lellan says sadly.

'I only wish I could have gotten you out sooner but I didn't know the way. I may aswell have been locked up as you were, the way I was guarded and treated. I can't wait to get back to Teeria.' She leans against his shoulder for comfort while they drink and eat.

Gee doesn't really feel like eating much but makes an effort. Lellan tucks in because he is clearly hungry after not eating properly for several days.

A figure wearing black clothing appears in the doorway of Lellan and Gees room on the ship. Out of the corner of their eye they assume it is one of the TRF security team because they wear black.

'I told you Lellan, that she will never be yours!'

Gee nearly chokes on her bit of bread and Lellan roars and stands up instantly recognising the voice.

'How did you get in here? I should have killed you after what you have done to Grenant and Gee. How dare you come near us again,' growls Lellan with his skin turning violently red.

He steps forward and puts Gee behind him out of harm's way. She can see the ridge of hair on his back standing up because of the threat.

'The so called DOD and TRF security is little to be desired. Come here Gee. I want you to tell these good people the truth and do not make anything up!' Aidy is so sure of himself it infuriates Lellan.

'She is not moving; you are!' Lellan steps forward to push Aidy back off the ship and then a gunshot rings out.

Cam and Baaron are first at the scene within seconds and are faced with Lellan passed out on the floor. Gee is by his side trying to revive him by gently shaking his shoulders and patting and kissing him. She can hardly see through the tears. They then see Aidy holding a gun and pointing it at Lellan.

Before giving Aidy anymore time to fire again, Cam and Baaron both barge into him and then simultaneously punch him, knocking him into the wall.

Gee looks at where Lellan has been shot. Lellan groans as she frantically puts pressure on the gun shot wound with a clean cloth to stem the blood flow.

'Lellan can you hear me? You are going to be alright. It hit your left shoulder. You were bloody lucky do you hear me! Please Lellan can you hear me?' Gees hands are shaking with panic and exhaustion and then she sees his eyes open and a faint smile appears.

She is so relieved to see he has regained consciousness; she gently kisses him on the lips and then watches his skin flutter a very faint and tired blue.

Gee leaves Lellan momentarily and walks right up to Aidy while he is restrained by her brother and Baaron.

'You're a disgrace! You failed the moment you showed up back on Teeria uninvited! I left a note and knew I only had to bide my time until we were rescued,' she snaps, absolutely seething.

'I'm very disappointed in you Gee,' says Aidy.

Gee slaps him so hard across the cheek it makes her hand sting and he recoils back.

'Your disappointment is not my concern! You have never meant anything to me and never will!'

She desperately wants some sort of immediate resolve by wiping away his smug and unrepentant look and she has succeeded. His head is hung low and his hair is out of place. Aidy is then dragged away and thrown into the custody of the DOD.

Gee returns to Lellan. With the help of Cam and

Baaron, she lifts him onto the bed for the TRF doctor to attend his wound. The doctor finishes up quickly and suggests Lellan has complete bed rest for as long as he needs to regain his strength.

'Come with me love,' suggests Posall. 'Let him get his rest.'

'I'm not leaving him Father. We cannot be apart not after what has happened, now that we have found each other again. I love him so much.' She bursts into tears and walks over to Lellan and lies down beside him. She wraps her arm around his waist and closes her eyes. Posall covers them both with blankets and leaves them in peace.

'I love you too my sweet Gee,' whispers Lellan with his eyes shut. 'Now let us sleep.'

Chapter 17

Gee had much to think about when she had arrived home. Ameel doted on her daughter and stayed close to her not wanting to let her out of her sight. Ameel saw that she needed to get her physical and mental strength back even though she didn't want to be far from Lellan. Gee tried to see him each day because she missed him and hated the living distance between them. Lellan is now safe in his own home recuperating with the help of Gee, Mogue and all his neighbouring friends after the ordeal he had been through. He wasn't in any fit state to travel to see Gee which tormented him further but knew the more he fed and built himself up the sooner his recovery would be. Gee wasn't allowed out alone by Lellan or her parents. Every time she wanted to see him she was escorted by her father, Baaron or Jjaym. She thought it was ridiculous being escorted everywhere because she thought it was an unnecessary fuss but she kept everyone happy and went along with it. In time Gee knew everything would be relaxed again the way she liked it.

Posall and Ameel had considered sending their offspring, Cam and Gee back to their Earth home to keep them away from any backlash that may have arisen between human and Spognoff. Even though their concern wasn't warranted they had asked each to consider leaving Teeria. Cam who wasn't keen to travel to another planet had surprised his parents. He said he was happy to stay on Teeria because he is excited about a promising career that was on the cards once he completed his Engineering and Ocean Science studies.

Gee thought long and hard before giving an answer to her parents. There was no question that Lellan was never far from her thoughts while making the decision.

When she had the choice to make she had gone and seen Lellan and confessed to him. Some may have taken her slow decision making the wrong way but not Lellan. He was glad that she was looking at each side in a sensible manner. He knew she would never leave Teeria because of everything they had missed when they were forcibly taken away and everything they have and had before. He had hoped that he hadn't got it wrong as he desperately didn't want her to leave. He didn't want to interfere with what she chose as it was her choice to make. He also knew she was being hard on herself because of what had happened and felt guilty. He could see, and rightly pointed out that two matters were bothering her, the guilt, and going back to Earth. She had to come to terms with the unfounded guilt and make a choice of where she wanted to live. It was easier making the decision of where she wanted to live than coming to terms with the guilt.

Obviously she didn't want to leave her new found relationship with Lellan but she needed to consider if there *was* a place for herself and a future on Teeria. She wanted to decide before her relationship turned serious with Lellan. Despite Earth soon having inhospitable living conditions, she misses its familiar ways but the thought of leaving Teeria all over again by her own choosing was heart wrenching. Gee knew it was still early days on Teeria but she can see for somebody like herself, who is naturally inquisitive, there is much to learn and gain. Teeria has a way of making her feel free and liberated. She is aware that her body is sensitive for whatever real reason there is on Teeria and she wishes to embrace it and let it run its natural course. Her choice was made and she wants to be one of the first humans in her generation to have their own future unravel on Teeria like her brother Cam.

Gee's guilt comes from the harm of Lellan and

death of Grenant and for not getting to them sooner. Gee is annoyed at herself for not foreseeing any problems when first meeting Aidy. If she hadn't of known Aidy Campion many years ago none of it would have happened. It is easy for her to see with hindsight what she should have done. She has wished every day since the kidnapping that she hadn't been email pals with him and wished she had told him the truth that she didn't want to stay in touch. Grenant and Lellan did not deserve the treatment they had received. The Spognoffs have only ever been a welcoming and peaceful race. The action's of Aidy have brought shame down on the humans, but because the Spognoffs are logical and an understanding race, they do not hold anyone responsible except for the kidnapper.

By having time away from studying under Ameel's watchful eye, it is now apparent to Gee that some humans would fear living on an alien planet such as Teeria but in her mind, we should be worried about our own safety from our own race. She is adamant that the humans who are currently living on Teeria need the help of the Gladestines to eventually right any wrongs that may occur. She *is* disappointed and embarrassed with whom she knew which is the root of her troubles. Lellan has told her time and time again she is being too hard with her thinking, but knows in time she will be alright. It will take sometime for it to be only a faded memory for them both with what happened on EMMA.

* * *

Twelve Teerian days have passed. Gee and her family follow the Gladestine tribe around to the right of the cave entrance at last light. Mogue, Lellan and Azala are at the front of the procession. Behind them are four Spognoffs carrying a wooden stretcher with Grenant's returned body. The stretcher is beautifully made from a sturdy and robust wooden carved frame. Grenant looks peaceful, laid out on a bed of giant leaves and flowers. Lellan is grateful to see him at rest again after the last haunting memories he has of him. The Spognoffs have laid Grenant out with his dignity intact by restoring his body and in turn returning his peace and youth.

Gee and her family feel like they needed and wanted to attend after what has happened. Ameel holds Gee's hand, glad that her daughter hadn't come back the same way as the unfortunate young Spognoff they are sending off today. The procession leads them through the trees and around to a clearing off to the side of the mountain. The clearing is an elevated sizeable ledge that juts out from the side of the mountain. It looks over a valley below and the horizon in the far distance. Not far from the edge of the ledge is a tidy stacked up pile of wood densely packed into a rectangular tower. The stack of wood is traditionally decorated with an assortment of pretty flowers in many soft colours with a white moss draping down amongst them. Azala, Mogue and Lellan stand in a line to one side of the wooden structure. Grenant is then placed carefully on top of it. Everyone else from the procession fans out some distance away from Grenant's resting place and watch quietly. Gee, her family, General Carter and two TRF personnel stand back to one side not wanting to intrude upon the proceedings. They are the only humans attending and are vastly out numbered by the Gladestines.

Azala has a quiet moment with her brother. She is traditionally dressed wearing a cream dress which is beaded with feathers daintily swaying from the arm and breast seams with plain cream moccasins. She is a picture of beauty and too young to lose her only brother and the last of her kin. Azala kisses Grenant's hand, his cheek and forehead then whispers something into his ear. She is then given a lit torch to begin the fire to send Grenant's spirit on its way. She can only look at Grenant and cannot bring herself to light the wood with the eager flame. A hand takes hold of the torch with hers, making her look up to see it is Lellan. She just nods at him in agreement and together they both light the wood. With the first touch of the flame everyone else kneels down out of respect and belief that it will help his spirit move on. Gee and the others copy exactly what the Gladestines do without hesitation.

After the ceremony, Lellan stays and comforts Azala along with Mogue. Gee and her family along with General Carter and his TRF personnel go home and leave the Gladestines to their traditions feeling out of place even though they were more than welcome to stay. Before Gee had left, Lellan had made arrangements with her to meet up in front of the cave entrance in four days. Gee couldn't help but worry why she couldn't see him sooner. She guessed because he was back on his feet and strong again, it was now his chance to have sometime alone, without everyone fussing.

Chapter 18

Four days have passed and it has driven Gee to the edge of distraction with wanting to see Lellan. She has a hand on the door handle and is about to leave when her father appears.

'You will need this bag for your travels love,' says Posall with a smirk.

'Not again Dad.' Gee beams already two steps ahead. 'Where is Lellan taking me this time? No in fact, I know the answer, "it's a surprise",' she says with excited frustration.

'You got that right. You both have a good time. Your Mother and I know what he has planned, so don't worry about staying out tonight.' Gee gives him a kiss on the cheek and takes the bag her mother had clearly packed because when she has a quick rummage she finds underwear and toiletries.

'I will be seeing you tomorrow then Father – thank you.' Posall watches his daughter, happy to see that her spirit is returning.

* * *

Gee waits patiently by the cave entrance for Lellan to appear. She doesn't have to wait long. She sees Lellan approaching on Han, coming through the brush via a narrow path into the clearing. Han is followed closely by a white Leeaque who Gee hasn't seen before. All three come to a stop close to the edge of the clearing. Lellan jumps down from Han without any effort as he is now fully recovered after being shot. He gives Han a treat and then the same to the white Leeaque. Gee walks over excited to see them all. She hasn't seen Han for a long time since before the kidnapping and is

243

intrigued by the white Leeaque's presence. She smiles Lellans favourite smile when they greet each other. After they have welcomed each other with a kiss Lellan stands with his arm around Gee as they both watch the black and white Leeaques who have begun to graze.

'I have missed you Gee,' says Lellan sounding relieved to see her again.

'I missed you too. I couldn't wait to see you today,' says Gee as she watches Han nuzzle the white Leeaque.

'I wanted to see you sooner.'

'I hope you had a good break? You deserved it... some time alone,' she asks looking up searching his expression for some sort of answer.

'It was more of a search actually. I wanted to give you a valuable gift.' He looks towards the Leeaques. 'I watched Han for a couple of days from a distance to see who he liked spending his time with and the white female was always with him. I have tamed her for you – thought you would appreciate having your own ride, if of course...' He smirks, 'I... was not nearby to assist. She is here for you.'

'Oh... Lellan...' She is so happy she jumps up and wraps her legs around his waist. She gives him an electrifying kiss then pulls away slightly and points out, 'There is only one problem; I don't know how to ride on my own.'

'I will teach you everything you need to know. As long as you have a treat for her, and treat her with kindness she will be your friend for as long as she is alive.' Gee jumps down eager to get started.

'Ok... I want to keep her happy while I learn. She *is* a stunning looking animal - beautiful. She may like my apples - Han loves them.'

'Yes and so will she. First you need to name her.'

'That's a challenge.' Lellan can see Gee is thinking which has made her quiet. While she eyes up the white

Leeaque deciding what would suit her, Lellan strokes them both. Gee then starts thinking out aloud, 'Well Han is short for handsome isn't it?'

'Yes,' Lellan nods in agreement and is amused by her way of thinking.

'And… she reminds me of the snow, so pristine and pure; I just want to touch it, like her…' She pauses. 'That's it,' grin's Gee. 'Snow. I will name her Snow. She is as beautiful as the snow that covers the ground like a white blanket during an Earth's winter.'

'Sn-o-w…,' he sounds the name. 'I like it. Now you better say "hello" and let her get used to her name. Get an apple; I know you have one or two in your bag, you always do. That is why Han is always trying to take a bite out of it,' Lellan smirks.

'There was me thinking he was just being friendly,' laughs Gee. She opens her bag and finds the culprit apple.

Lellan slices up the apple in the palm of his hand using a knife. He keeps some pieces so he can keep Han amused while Gee gets acquainted with Snow. Gee walks slowly over to stand in front of the giant white Leeaque who is looking at her with concern because of the strangers approach. Gee can see she is nervous which is just how she feels.

'Hello. I have named you Snow, I hope that is alright by you?' says Gee gently so Snow can get used to her voice.

Gee is fully aware that a Leeaque cannot speak but notices Snow seems to be staring intently at her and wonders if she did understand and looks up to see Lellan chuckling as he is finding it all very comical. Gee smiles sheepishly and returns to the matter in-hand.

Snow is a lot more slender and slight unlike Han who has a heavier build but she is just as tall if not taller in the leg and towers over Gee which she finds unnerving. She had gotten used to Hans big nostrils sniffing her hair up like two suction pipes, but knew he had been Lellan's friend for years and that this is different and there is a long way to go with Snow. Gee holds out a cube of apple and sensibly avoids eye contact with the Leeaque which could alarm her. Snow hesitates and sniffs the scent of the apple in the air. She then moves one, then two large hooves forward and stretches out her neck very slowly. Gee watches Snows big soft muzzle come closer to her hand and then feels her soft hairs against it when she gently takes the apple. Gee is filled with elation.

'This time when she takes another bit, have your other hand close so she can see it. It will not surprise her then when you stroke her nose. They soon get over their nervousness when they learn that they actually like it when they are stroked,' says Lellan softly while contending with Han's big nose routing after his share of fruit. Gee nods at him and does as he says without question.

Gee holds out the second piece of apple with her other hand beside it. As Snow stretches her neck and reaches out for more bits of apple Gee strokes the side of her nose successfully and feels how velvety it is. Gee repeats the pattern, all the time with Snow stretching out her neck. By the fifth time Snow takes a step closer to Gee. Snow is so close now her head is bent down against Gees chest. Gee is so relieved she had taken the step of trust. Without thinking and a flinch from Snow she gives her a hug around her great big head and scratches between her huge ears with the aid of the apple pieces. Gee plucks up the courage and slowly moves closer to Snow's side so that she can run her hands along her neck as far as she can reach up and across her side.

'Can I ride her?' Snow nudges her for more apples.

'Yes. You will be her first,' Lellan says calmly.

'You *are* joking; I don't know the first thing about sitting on an untrained Leeaque.'

'When have I ever joked,' says Lellan with a grin. 'Do not worry Gee, you are obviously a natural.' He directs her look to Han trying to sneak away some of Snows apple from her hand. Snow pushes him out of the way with her giant nose and slightly lowers her ears as a warning.

Lellan now has to instruct Gee to get Snow to lower down. He firstly feeds Snow some dried up fish scraps as a change to keep her interested and then tells Gee what to do. With Lellan's instructions she goes and finds a thin stick, two feet in length. She then has to run it down the side of one of Snow's legs so she gets used to being touched in a different place. Gee does this acouple of times and naturally strokes her aswell, then Lellan tells her to tap Snow gently just below the knee. Gee does as she is told and doesn't expect anything to happen but Snow bends her knee and then Lellan tells Gee to rest the stick upon it. By doing this Snow lowers herself.

'Good girl Snow.' Gee gives her a bit of apple.

'Now… you have to get on and hold her hair to steady yourself just in case she is unsure, oh and grip with your legs – very important.'

'Don't like the sound of that,' she says a little alarmed knowing all too well it could turnout disastrously. She has always just hopped up on Han with no given thought but wary to do the same with Snow as she has never been ridden before.

'I am sure she is alright, she has done everything you have asked so far. Better to try now – she is ready,' Lellan encourages.

Gee looks at him and he wills her on by nodding,

but it doesn't extinguish her apprehension.

Gee looks at Snow who is patiently waiting for her. She knows Lellan is right; she has to try *now* – its all or nothing. Gee gets closely behind Snow's front leg and makes an attempt to hop her right leg over the broad back. Gee isn't tall or strong enough and gets her leg caught which makes Snow flinch. Gee pats Snow for reassurance and is disappointed by her failed attempt and embarrassed because Lellan makes it look so easy. Gee stands and looks to Lellan for guidance who is still standing up front and then they both see Snow turn and look at Gee. Snow then lifts her head up and down and moves her knee out from underneath herself and touches the top of her own leg with her muzzle. Lellan can see exactly what Snow wants Gee to do.

'I have never seen this before. She wants to help you. Remarkable.' Lellan is starting to sense there is something more to Gee, something even Gee isn't aware of.

'What a clever girl you are,' says Gee oblivious of Lellans thinking.

'You have to use her knee.'

'Are you sure?' says Gee concerned not wanting to hurt her.

'Try, you will see.'

Gee takes hold of some of Snow's thick white hair and gingerly puts her small foot onto Snow's thick leg then bounces her other leg over. Snow doesn't flinch at all but steadily and immediately stands up with her new passenger onboard as if she is now glad to be off the ground. Gee is smiling from ear to ear and is so pleased that Snow had trusted her and wanted to help her mount.

'You are a good girl. Thank you Snow,' says Gee stroking her affectionately.

Lellan mounts up by tapping Han's leg as he is well

versed with what to do. Lellan doesn't want to push his luck and tells Gee that she should just walk today so the two of them can get acquainted. Gee is happy with the suggestion. Lellan squeezes his legs and guides Han while telling Gee how to get Snow moving where she wants. Snow follows Han out of the clearing, tail to nose. Lellan smirks as he leads in front because he can hear Gee chatting to Snow who moves her ears and head in response. All the time while they stroll along Gee twiddles Snows hair between her fingers and pat's her lower neck with a bit of a reach forward.

When they come to a wider path Han and Snow walk side by side making teeth chatter and neighing noises to each other like they are having a conversation. Gee finds Han and Snows communication amazing. She likes the fact that Han now has company while enjoying the ride. Lellan leans towards Gee and reaches over for a kiss and she reciprocates.

'Would you like to stay with me... tonight?' he asks nervously.

'Yes, I'd like that. I've missed your company so much. Where will we stay?'

'At... mine. The weather is getting too changeable outside now.'

'I will look forward to it, oh and Lellan thank you, I needed this.'

'Me to... I need and want to spend some quality time with you my sweet Gee.' He takes her hand in his.

'I couldn't agree with you more.' She kisses his hand and holds it against her cheek enjoying his warmth as the temperatures are getting cooler.

'We will ride Han and Snow for a little while longer. You have done very well. I do think having Han present helped Snow's temperament. The Leeaque is a very clever animal as you saw for yourself today. Each time we come out with Han and Snow we can ride a bit longer so she gets fully used to you. For first impressions, I think you two have hit it off well. Next year when you are experienced we can go travelling for a few nights and they can come with us if you like?' Lellan laughs because Han and Snow both nod their heads.

'I would like that and so it seems would Snow.' They both laugh by the Leeaque's reaction.

* * *

After a pleasant day of being out with their rides and happily back in the Teerian wilderness, Lellan and Gee return to the cave before the darkness draws in. The Spognoffs do not venture out during the darkness as they do not want to make themselves easy targets because the wildlife can be unpredictable and dangerous. Lellan informs Gee that a lot of the Spognoff's best academic work is done in the Ark-deau. He likes to hunt during first light and read during the dark awake hours. Gee is pleased to be back at Lellans after a physically tiring day. While Lellan makes arrangements for some food to eat, she finds comfort when she sees Snoot walk towards her chair. He is a regular visitor when the daylight draws in. She hasn't seen Snoot for a while, like Han, and makes a big fuss of him. She giggles when he wraps his tail around her neck and sniffs her face, not used to the unusual greeting, but then everything is unusual to Gee on Teeria and that is what she likes.

Lellan feels a little nervous about Gee staying with him for the night. He hasn't had her stay the night since she had hurt herself, which seems so long ago. When Lellan and Gee had eaten and freshened up he decides they should play a game to help them both relax and not give into nerves. Lellan teaches her a Spognoff game which involves a board, tiny twigs and small collected leaves. The game is very rustic but traditional which pleases Gee who surprises Lellan by being very good. There is a lot of skill involved in the game because there isn't one twig that is perfectly straight or smooth.

The basis of the game is they have to take alternative turns to lay down sticks in a shape of a square. After a square has been formed the next player has to place a leaf on top of a chosen twig. The next person then starts another row by adding another twig which is better placed diagonally across the corner of the previous square and nipping the leaf in place. The first one to dislodge or allow any leaf to fall is the loser. Lellan and Gee manage to construct a tall tower before its height and fragility get the better of them. A leaf about half way down loosens and falls inwards; floating down to the bottom on Gees turn declaring her the loser. They play several games while relaxing, chatting and enjoying each others company. There is an unmistakable closeness between them seen by family and close friends, but also by each other, which Lellan cannot ignore any longer.

'Would you spend the night with me Gee… in … my room? I have missed feeling you close.' Lellan looks so sincere that Gee can feel her eyes starting to glaze.

'I'd really like that, I feel safe in your arms.'

'Only if you are sure after what you went through. I can sleep out here if you would rather.' He wants her to be certain and doesn't intend to rush her.

'Oh… no… I'm fine really. It is very kind of you to think about my feelings though, but I assure you I *am* fine. These last four days have dragged on so slowly and now I am here I would like to freeze time – it goes too quickly when I am with you. I want to make the most of you and your delightful company,' she says smiling.

'Come here.' He cannot resist her beauty. She leans closer to him and he runs his fingers through her long untamed hair and kisses her on her lips to see if she is telling the truth. He can sense if she is hiding the truth now through a kiss because it is like reading a personal diary. He happily senses she indeed doesn't mind because Gee returns his kiss back with such enthusiasm he has difficulty controlling himself and whispers, 'Let me show you my room. I think you will like it.'

'Ok. What do you have in there apart from a bed?'

'It is my very own personal sanctuary where I go if I want some peace or to simply sleep. I do not get disturbed in there unlike out here,' he says pointing at the easily accessible hanging animal hide door. 'It is very private and secluded.' He smirks with a double meaning in his eyes.

'What are we waiting for?' says Gee with clear interest and understanding of what he is insinuating. Lellan leads her by her hand to his room.

Lellan's room is out to the back of his cave in another hollowed out room not far from the bathroom facilities. His room has a grand appearance with fabric and furs hanging like drapes covering some of the walls. The hard cold floor is covered in more furs and thicker fabrics for comfort under foot. Gee stands just inside the entrance and gasps at how cosy the room is. Predominantly the room has books, nick knacks and in the centre is a small table accompanied by two tall backed chairs like in his main living area. The room is like Aladdin's cave for someone who is interested in books and memorabilia. Gee can see this room belongs to the true Lellan and it surrounds him with everything he is passionate about. It is all his, which nobody can see unless they are invited, unlike the rest of his home which is open to everyone. Gee wishes she had her own space like this where she is in charge of its visitors, if any.

A collection of spears are horizontally hung up on one of the walls. Lellan explains that they have been past down through his family over many years. He is very proud to have his collection and is now in charge of looking after them on behalf of his father and uncle, Mogue and Kwarn. Gee walks over and looks closely at them but doesn't touch because of their age and she doesn't wish to leave any finger marks on the ancient wood because they are all immaculately cared for. Lellan tells her the history of the oldest spear. It dates back hundreds of Teerian years through a long list of his great ancestors. The shaft is charcoal black with an extremely worn carving ingrained along it; with the spear head embedded into the end without a covering sheath.

'This one belongs to my other Uncle - Uncle Capler.'

'Your Mother's Brother?'

'No my Father's eldest Brother,' says Lellan sounding sad.

'Oh I'm sorry has he gone too?'

'We do not know. He went off some years ago to investigate the Deep and never returned.'

'So your Uncle Capler is possibly still alive?'

'We searched for many years with the aid of Kwarn looking from above but to no avail. My Father had to sadly call off the search.'

'May I suggest I tell Cam of your sad loss and maybe when he is in his rightful place, researching the Teerian oceans, he may find a clue to what has happened?'

'That is very kind of you; it would be nice to know how Capler came to his end.'

'You think he is dead?'

'Yes or he would have come back,' Lellan says convinced.

'Your family hasn't had much luck. I'm so sorry and thank you.' She smiles up at him concerned.

'What for?'

'For trusting me, showing and sharing with me your family and ancestors history. It is a fascinating history and I find it very interesting. I like it when you talk about yours and Teerian history; it somehow helps me understand you and your customs.'

'I have plenty to show you, I didn't want to bore you before.'

'Don't be daft. These are apart of you,' she says and gestures at his collection. 'Apart of *who* you are.' Gee is so happy that Lellan feels that he can show her his treasures of ancestral importance.

'You have a knack at pointing out the obvious when it is not so easily seen, thank you. Now then, I have something to return back to you. Come with me,' he says with a wink.

Gee follows Lellan towards the right corner of his room. An elaborate alcove is very cleverly hidden away. Gee did not see it when she was looking around Lellan's room and it didn't even occur to her where the obvious was, his bed. The alcove is carved into the rock with a rounded ceiling and a comfortable, inviting bed beneath. Around the bed is a wide ledge that has been carved out of the dark rock on three sides with candles burning bright on each. Some one had taken the time to round off the edges of the ledge and corners to the interior walls.

Gee watches Lellan disappear into the alcove after taking off his moccasins. He crawls along the bed and rummages at the far end behind a long length of cushioning which acts as a pillow. His hand is in a

254

hidden recess and he finds what he is looking for. He comes back along the bed and sits on the end and pats it for Gee to join him. He has her droplet pendant in the palm of his hand.

'I got the chain mended for you. Can I put it back on, in its rightful place?'

'Oooow yes please.' Gee is so pleased to see it again.

It has been so long since she has worn it after it had been torn from her neck. She turns her back to Lellan and lifts up her long hair so he can fasten it with ease around her neck.

Once Lellan has fastened her droplet he strokes her shoulders and neck and sees her skin react with tiny little goose bumps which pleases him. Gee can feel Lellan's eyes on her back and lowers her hair. He wraps his arms around her waist and rests his head on her shoulder. Gee turns and kisses him passionately, at last with some time alone. After the long seductive kiss Lellan scoops her up into his arms and moves her further up the bed where they are surrounded by the flickering candles.

'This reminds me of the droplet cave.' Gee loves the alcove and it takes her back to their last time truly alone.

'Yes, it is why I carved it out before we were rudely taken. The candles remind me of the ring of droplets which were caught by the light of the fire. It was a good time. I shall look forward to more to come.' He has an unmistakable tone and means what he has said with a double meaning.

'Me too.' Gee smiles and understands his train of thought and says no more, wanting their anticipated moment to arrive.

Gee relaxes back into the softness of the blanket laid out on the bed watching Lellan take off his shirt revealing his muscled torso and then he removes his leggings and cloth. Gee's eyes widen and she likes what she sees and blushes. She has waited and even imagined what Lellan was like naked for so long and she is certainly not disappointed. Lellan is by far the most gorgeous male being she has ever seen with every muscle athletically toned.

Gee sits up and begs him to come over to have him close with the urge to touch him. She climbs onto his naked lap within the safety of his arms and runs her fingers across his firm chest. He kisses her gently and then unbuttons her top and removes it and then her skirt. Her skin feels so irresistibly soft when he touches her it urges him on. He is relieved he doesn't have to fight against his yearning for her anymore. Suddenly Gee is neither shy nor embarrassed but caught up in the overwhelming feeling of desire for Lellan. She can feel his warmth radiating against her skin as he touches her. Lellan holds her cradled in his arms and Gee relaxes and leans against his shoulder and warm body. He kisses her cheek, her neck and runs his fingers down the length of her naked back making her shudder. He can no longer resist her naked beauty.

Lellan lifts her chin and looks into her eyes and she looks up into his, instantly caught up in them and unable to resist his lure. He moves her hair which is draped either side of her neck to reveal her pure untouched body. Words are no longer needed and Lellan lays her down and rests against her side. He starts with a kiss on her inviting parted lips and feels her hands in his hair pulling him closer, wanting more. He strokes and smoothes her hair away from her face and whispers how much he loves her and she responds by reaching up to steal another kiss. His hand then works its way down to her breasts by pausing and caressing, then her abdomen while he watches her body move as she writhes with every touch from him. His touch drives her, sending floods of enjoyment, leaving her wanting more.

Lellan cannot believe how lucky he is to have such a beauty at his mercy. All the time he indulges in the softness of her flawlessly pale silky skin. He moves his hands and his attentions down to her thighs and fluently moves and rests between her legs. His attention turns back to the gorgeous being lying in front of him and he can see the look of the untamed in her eyes. He interlinks his fingers with her left hand holding it down gently and teases again with a kiss, she then gasps as he enters her and they unite as one.

They enjoy each other, caress each other and tame each other. The candles cast their intertwined silhouettes on the cave walls making them come alive by their passion, spirit and love for each other.

Lellan whispers, 'Nia paur luow.'

'Nia paur luow… too,' says Gee.

'I think we need to work on your dialect,' chuckles Lellan.

A timeline of historic events.

Year	Events
1,000	**Thousand**
	1,969 The first foot step on the moon by Neil Armstrong.
2,000	**2,010** Hubble space telescope/Kepler Satelite Exoplanets.
	3,284 Mandatory Health Screening.
5,000	**5,157-69** NASA and Dr. Haffnel solved space travel.
	6,693 Glacial Ice Age
	9,949 Nano technology breakthrough.
10,000	
	12,327 Education took a leap forward.
	13,774 Mercury destroyed.
	13,882 Influenza Outbreak.
	13,883 Viral Waves.
15,000	
	16,678 S.S.Stepping 01 completed.
	17,014 Exploration Light 259 crew embarked on search.
	17,017 Teeria discovered.
	17,020 Completion of EMMA.
	17,023 = Present Day.
20,000	
	31,035 = New and Proved End of Earth's Life.
50,000	
70,000	
100,000	
500,000	
1,000,000	**Million**
500,000,000	**Half Billion** **500,000,000** Old prediction of the end of Earth's life!
1,000,000,000	**Billion**
2,000,000,000	
3,000,000,000	
4,000,000,000	
5,000,000,000	**Billion** **5,000,000,000** End of the Sun's lifetime!